Dirk van den Boom

Stormy Heavens

DIRK VAN DEN BOOM

THE EMPEROR'S MEN

STORMY
HEAVENS

Copyright © 2021 by Atlantis Verlag Guido Latz,
Bergstraße 34, 52222 Stolberg (Germany)

ISBN 978-3-86402-797-0

Cover © Timo Kümmel
Editor: Rob Bignell

www.atlantis-verlag.de

1

Aritomo's right hand trembled. It was sticky with blood and stank. He had to make an effort not to drop the knife. The man in front of him gurgled. The blood poured out of the cut carotid artery with force, the metallic smell was numbing. The man winced again, his legs hit the ground, his heels scraped the dusty floor, then he lay still.

Aritomo dropped his right hand. Once again, a conscious decision was necessary not to let the knife's slippery handle fall out of your hand. The dead man in front of him had a contorted expression that relaxed slowly.

Steps from the outside. Then another man stood in the doorway. He did not attack, did not assault sleepers in the dark of the night, did not try to kill him with a murder instrument reminiscent of a garotte. One of the guards. One of the good guys. Aritomo felt the relief as it flowed through his body and finally washed the knife from his hand. It fell to the ground, and both men's eyes were on the corpse for a moment.

"My lord Aritomo Hara!"

"Here," said the latter in a weak voice and took a step back toward the place from where he'd just been brutally woken. He wasn't feeling well. Not good at all.

"Are you unharmed?"

The Japanese involuntarily grabbed his neck and touched the thin graze. He was hurt, but it would heal. His quick reaction had saved him from worse. Death had to wait, at least tonight. His demise had come very, very close to him, however, and his cold breath made him shiver all over despite the warm night.

"I'm okay. Are there more?"

"He was the only one."

The Mayan warrior stood waiting in the room, looked down at the dead man again, whose outline could be seen well in the glow of the torch that the guard was holding in the air.

"I know this man. He is a servant of Xicoc, a man who belongs to the court. The King must know about it!"

A statement uttered without any significant emotion. As if he hadn't expected anything else. Aritomo looked at his right hand, drying red, and moved his fingers as if he had to find out whether they could still be moved despite the sticky covering.

"Yes," said Aritomo softly. "But he should be taken away."

"I will take care of that. My lord ..."

"What?"

Aritomo's response was more rash than expected, but the warrior didn't seem to take it badly.

"The security guard in front of the house ... your companion ... he's dead."

Aritomo took a deep breath. He had feared it. There was no other explanation for this incident. He didn't want to look at the victim, but he had to.

"Show me."

The warrior lead the way. Aritomo climbed over the body, felt his bare feet get wet with the blood, and followed outside. The house had been made available to the time travelers so that they could finally escape the tightness of the boat. They had organized security themselves, but apparently had not expected to be attacked on friendly ground just a week after their move.

Hubris was the right word for this. And as always, hubris was quickly punished.

Aritomo finally faced the dead man, and conflicting feelings tortured him. Of course, he knew the man by name, a sailor named Kato, a simple, an obedient soldier. His neck showed deep wounds where the garotte had overpowered him, his tongue hung out of his mouth, and his eyes were wide open. Aritomo leaned down and closed his eyelids. They were so few, so terribly few. Every dead crew member was an irreplaceable loss.

Aritomo also felt unfairly treated. An absurd, almost silly emotion, but yes – here in Mutal they were the honored guests who had saved the city from its enemies and who would increase it's might to an unprecedented level. And here an assassin sneaked in, just to kill him, Aritomo, in a very targeted manner. The man who continually tried to balance Captain Inugami, the man who perceived the Mayans as primitive savages, not as a civilization with which they had to come to terms, a man who did not want them to perish in the maelstrom of history.

Aritomo was the good one. He would not have been surprised to see an attack on Inugami.

But he. Why he? It was definitely not fair.

It also showed him that there was a significant difference in the way he saw himself and how he was seen from the outside. For this assassin here, he was just one of the messengers of the gods who unbalanced everything and questioned the traditional order and tradition – a dangerous course of action, since they would inevitably bring down the wrath of the gods on them, gods to whom these messengers did not seem to pray at all.

Aritomo hadn't noticed. He hadn't suspected anything. He had been carefree, stupid, naive, blinded, and thus of dangerous negligence, unworthy behavior for an officer in the Imperial Japanese fleet.

There must have been a change of mood, somewhere beneath the surface of submissive kindness, constant respect, the rush to fulfill the wishes of the visitors. It must have become too much for someone. Aritomo knew that this was the case with the King of Mutal, the young Chitam. But would he provoke someone, of all people, to kill him, the first officer of the strange boat – and with him the voice of reason that had so far been able to prevent decisions that were to the detriment of the Maya?

No, that made absolutely no sense. Someone else must have taken the initiative, a traditionalist who saw Chitam for no more than the puppet Inugami actually intended to make him. Someone who did not differentiate, but saw the threat equally manifest in all messengers. It had to be that way.

Other crew members of the boat were now awake, came outside, rubbed their eyes, asked questions loudly, then fell silent when they saw the body of their comrade and the first officer as he leaned over and stared into the void. The Mayan warriors also had gathered, somewhat apart, in their own group, and they looked guilty. However the assassin had managed to get so close to the messengers' quarters, it was quite likely that he had received help.

Probably with the involvement of one of the guards.

Aritomo looked up, glanced at the Mayan warriors, and felt suspicion and fear spread through him. He knew which way he would follow if he gave these feelings too much room. It was the path that would lead him firmly to Inugami's side, not just driven by fantasies of omnipotence and delusions of grandeur but by constant fear, the need for security, and the false assumption that more and more power would fulfill that desire.

It was an illusion, Aritomo was sure of that. Here, at this time, in all its apparent superiority, this fact had just been effectively demonstrated.

"Lord, we have sent a messenger to the King," one of the Maya said to him.

Aritomo nodded. "That's good," he said softly. He waved two more of his sailors, pointing to the dead body in front of them. "Take him with you. Clean his body and prepare him for a funeral. I'll conduct the ceremony myself."

Aritomo didn't even know if he could keep that promise. That was another point that they had never thought about before. The wealthy Maya, men and women of nobility and high priests, gained renown from elaborate tombs to entire temple buildings for the kings. Simple Maya had to be content with simple burials, not for eternity but forgotten and lost as soon as their next of kin also found death.

But what precautions should one take for dead time travelers?

Aritomo would now have to deal with this question. He assumed that they would bury their own people the way they were used to at home. Everything else seemed absurd to him at the moment. A difficult topic, but one that was suddenly on the agenda.

And much earlier than he would have liked.

8

"We need to tighten security," said a voice next to him he knew well. It was the Briton Lengsley who had now appeared, looking at the men who were removing the soldier's body, and then lurking around, as if he was afraid of another attack at any moment.

"We could get back on the boat and nobody will attack us."

Aritomo said it but didn't believe it.

"That's true. But nobody can stand it anymore either. The men were overjoyed when they were finally allowed to move outside. We just shouldn't have accepted this house without dealing with all security issues ourselves. It worries me that Inugami is right, but we should move our camp to the training ground for his army. As soon as they are back, they offer us good protection, at least better than if we were targeted in the midst of the city proper."

"The slaves could kill us. After that they would be free," Aritomo said quietly.

Lengsley smiled cheerlessly.

"Inugami has them well under control. If they kill us, they are still slaves to Mutal. I'm not sure that would improve the situation for most of them."

Aritomo said nothing, but silently agreed with the man. Inugami had led his Janissaries' army on a campaign, and they hadn't heard anything about the outcome of the attack – they didn't even know if the captain himself was still alive. Aritomo knew that Inugami would not shy away from personal risk to gain respect beyond fear of the boat's few guns, pistols and cannon.

A boat that was still completely immobile on the top of Chitam's father's tomb, a tomb he couldn't even use, because the boat had to be removed from there first. Whenever that would be possible. If anytime at all. It didn't look like it.

Aritomo watched the situation slowly calm. Some of his comrades returned to their rooms, their faces concerned, while others spoke quietly. Sleep was out of the question for him, as the excitement still dominated thinking and breathing. He had to clean himself, change clothes, eat something. A mug of chi would do him good now that the boat's saké supplies had run out. Aritomo knew that Sarukazaki was experimenting with a still, and nobody was stopping him from spending his free time on this project. So far, however, it has been heard that the results have been of a rather unacceptable quality.

Now, at this minute, Aritomo wouldn't have said no to the worst from the technician's kitchen. But he was left only with chi, whose alcohol content was very low.

Aritomo didn't want to drink tons of it.

He turned away. Servants cleaned his room. The dead man had been brought out, but the traces of the struggle were still obvious. The Japanese marched into the washroom, which the time travelers had built themselves, with a stone basin, only roughly hewn out of a rock, and a simple wooden pipe that provided water in four different places above the basin. There was a real drain that also could be closed. In theory, the pool was large enough to take a bath in, and building a proper bathhouse was one of the plans the Japanese have been pursuing since they moved in. They made themselves really comfortable. Their own rooms, kitchen, bathroom, a courtyard for sporting activities, their own guards and their own assassins, who chased you at night.

Aritomo opened the water inlet. The cool water came from a tank, filled three times a day by servants, who brought the water from a nearby reservoir. He washed the blood off his hands, then carefully cleaned his blade, which he had picked up from the floor and which had been strangely difficult to carry, as if the assassin's death tugged on the blade and pulled it down.

The steel was excellent and would not rust quickly, but there was no replacement for the foreseeable future. The knife had saved his life, and for that reason alone it deserved intensive care.

It also helped him collect his thoughts and calm down. When the blade was clean and dry, he felt a little more relaxed than a few minutes ago. The weapon was now easier in his hand, cleaned of the murderer's spirit. He missed a mirror in which he could look at his unshaven face. The only real glass mirrors remained in the boat as a special treasure. The Maya knew polished metal, mostly silver, which the wealthy used as a mirror. It was an interesting thought that these were much more valuable than the Japanese specimens, if only because of the material used to produce them. He had one in his room from which he shaved.

Aritomo found himself thinking of his few remaining razor blades and what he would do when the stock ran out. It was by no means unusual for a naval officer to grow a beard, which was easier to prune with the local knives. Would that make his eternally childish full moon face more masculine?

And why should he waste unnecessary thoughts on it right now?

He finished his cleaning. When he stepped outside, it was still dark, although it wouldn't be too long before dawn. His blood pressure had calmed down, and he felt that he could actually lie down again, but the thought of returning to his tainted room filled him with reluctance.

He stepped into the courtyard. There were now only Mayan warriors and two Japanese, both armed, who had taken over the guard. They only nodded to Aritomo, and he waved it away. No need to make a report. They were good for the night.

He sat on a stone bench and looked into the crystal clear night sky. No one else seemed to share his restlessness. The noises of the night were clearly audible again. At dawn, the King would get an idea of the situation and, Aritomo suspected, warriors would visit the noble whose servant had been the assassin. Mayan justice was sometimes very quick, and the punishments did not include too many gradations. Those who did not speak were tortured until they admitted everything, including that what they had never done.

This thought made Aritomo shiver that night.

2

Helmut Köhler felt the bile rise inside him. He clung to the railing, stared into the roaring abyss of the sea, felt his stomach crawl up his throat, as the *Gratianus* slid deep into the trough, and then the familiar gag came, and he opened his mouth. Almost nothing came of it, since he had completely sacrificed his stomach contents to Neptune an hour ago, but the violent, cramping nausea didn't want to subside. His desperate moan subsided in the roar of the storm, and when the cramp let off and he opened his eyes again, which he had tormentedly closed, he stopped trying to empty something that was long empty.

He took a deep breath, felt the current weakness ease somewhat. Köhler was not the only one on board the expedition fleet's flagship who fared so badly. This was the third day they were stuck in the storm, and even the most experienced sailor was beginning to push his limits. There was little sleep, and when he tried to find some, he was restless, always interrupted, in violently rocking hammocks that threw you against the comrade or the wall and sometimes with force on the floor. There was hardly anything to eat, and when there was, it was cold, often wet, and those who felt sick hardly managed to eat anything solid anyway. Yesterday, Köhler had dipped ship rusks in thin wine and swallowed them somehow, but an hour later they came back up,

Everyone's strength was weakening. They all prayed for calm weather, if only a break in the constant romp and roar. The ship was in better shape than its crew. In any case, the *Gratianus* showed no signs of not being able to cope with the forces.

Köhler looked up and saw Navarch Langenhagen, who was standing on the bridge next to the gubernator, tied up like all of them, because it often happened that a breaker struck the rail with great power and tore an inattentive crew member with him. Screams, cries for help went down in the deafening rustle of wind and waves. But the tightly woven ropes that everyone had to secure himself with and which slid along the guide rails next to the railing had already saved many a life. It was still the case that most seafarers could not swim and deliberately did not want to learn it in order to exchange the torture of a slow death in the sea by drowning as quickly as possible.

Köhler was able to swim.

And he never wanted to give up either.

His stomach felt the same. He sensed another cramp coming. He straightened up, stuck his face into the spray, felt the cold dampness smack against his skin and an icy shiver run down his body. He was wet to the bone, no matter how much he tied the thick leather coat around his body. The masses of water that flowed down his collar were enough to soak him completely.

The nausea in his stomach subsided again. He closed and opened his eyes, wiped his wet face with his wet hand, which did nothing but feel like he had done something, a senseless gesture, expression of weak defiance. Then he felt someone pull on his arm.

Magister Aedilius stood next to him. The ship's doctor, he was one of the graduates of the Medical Academy of Ravenna, the forge for medical staff that the doctor of the *Saarbrücken* had founded and which trained the best healers in the world. Aedilius was no longer a young man but of strong stature and had served on many ships before being assigned to the expedition. His gray-brown beard was damp, and he was wearing a hat that encircled his bald head like a second skin.

He did not say anything. He should have screamed to make himself understood. But his eyes expressed concern and a little pity. Aedilius held out a leather bottle to Köhler, with the opening closed, and when he took it, he felt a pleasant warmth in his hand, refreshment enough without having to uncork it. Warmth and dryness. There was little that Köhler wanted more at the moment.

The medic nodded to him promptly. Köhler knew what was in the bottle—a perfidious herbal drink that everyone said was the most disgusting thing they had ever drunk. Köhler had had enough of disgust that he had so far successfully avoided the doctor's approaches. But now Aedilius had caught him.

There was no escape.

He grimaced and tried to shake his head one last time, but the doctor looked at him firmly and raised a warning finger. Then he made a pouring gesture in front of his mouth. Aedilius was in command of everything related to health. He was even allowed to give orders to Langenhagen.

This was an order. Köhler was a soldier. He followed orders.

He lifted the cork, closed his eyes, and took a deep sip. Better to get it over with and die a dignified death, manly, without fear.

The burning, rotting liquid flowed down his throat. He felt his stomach rebel almost immediately. He didn't know which was worse, the utterly disgusting taste or the caustic feeling when the drink combined with his upset stomach acid. He immediately felt the gagging sensation start and put the bottle down, ready to do it all again …

But nothing happened.

Köhler's eyes widened, and he listened to himself. A strange, numbing warmth had settled on his battered stomach, and the nausea was just a lurking feeling somewhere below, covered and anything but acute.

He was almost … fine.

Aedilius looked at him knowingly, smiled, made another, pouring movement.

Köhler did not hesitate a second time.

He had been a fool.

He raised the bottle and took a deep sip. It was still an unspeakable brew, but now he drank it without fear and bad expectations. It made things easier. The warming, numbing feeling in his stomach was intensified and it pushed back the nausea until it was almost imperceptible.

He handed the bottle back to the doctor. Köhler could not gauge whether his expression was adequately communicating the gratitude he was feeling, but it seemed as if the message had arrived. Aedilius nodded to him, gave him a smile, and turned. A boatswain stood a few meters further and, in a high arc, put a meal that was not even slightly digested into the waves. The wind was unpredictable. With stoic calm, Köhler wiped a chewed chunk off his sleeve. Seconds later the spray had completely cleaned him.

Aedilius ran to the boatswain and presented him with the bottle. According to the facial expression of the sea sick, this candidate had previously also been rather reserved about the doctor's brew. A mistake, as Köhler was now ready to admit. He regarded with pleasure that the boatswain submitted to the doctor's request, and shortly afterwards the same pleasantly touched facial expression that Köhler had just shown was visible on his features as well. The man took another sip almost hastily.

Köhler now returned to his place next to the Navarch. Another senior officer, Adrianus Sextus Cabo, stood on the foredeck and gave the necessary orders. The night black sky and the spray roaring over the rail made it almost impossible to see from here what was happening in the front part of the ship. It was late afternoon, but the sun was only a faint glow behind the thick banks of clouds that a mighty wind was pushing across the sky. There was not much to issue orders for – almost all of the sails had been dropped, only a small storm sail hung from the front mast. The control of the ships was possible primarily because the steam engine was running at full power, and thus gave the ship enough propulsion to actually influence the course with the rudder. The gubernator was a muscular man who was almost as tall as Köhler, although he did not descend from the generally taller time walkers. He clutched the rudder wheel with strong fists, despite the fact that it was currently tied. The storm came directly from the west, and they steered the fleet against the wind. Without the steam engines, this would be an extremely difficult undertaking. It was problematic enough. The ships were built robustly and had ridden the storm without problems. As always, it was the human factor that started to wear off.

Helmut Köhler could say this with some certainty, at least for himself.

"How are you?" Langenhagen shouted against the noise of the

storm and turned his wet, shiny face to Köhler. Next to the rudder hung two storm lamps, which swayed to the left and right on short iron chains and undeterredly cast their pale light on the ship's command deck.

"Aedilius!" Köhler shouted back. He waved in the direction of the medicus, who was just now giving his herbal drink to another sailor swaying like the storm lamps. Langenhagen grinned and nodded, having overcome his fear of the brew from the start and set a good example. In fact, Köhler had watched him eat ship's biscuit, cheese, and hot wine without giving everything back.

Köhler decided to no longer unnecessarily question his trust in Aedilius.

"Where are we?" he asked.

"Far off course!" Langenhagen back. He pointed to the sky. "We won't know until it clears up properly."

"What's your best guess?"

"Three days are over. The longest storm I've ever seen was five. I think we'll be through soon."

Langenhagen sounded confident and looked that way. Köhler nodded and clung to the railing that separated the quarterdeck from the rest of the ship. Only the most essential crew remained on deck. The Boatswain regularly checked that everything was lashed tight and counted whether all the people who were supposed to be there were onboard. The rest lingered inside the ship and did little more than wait for the torture to end.

Köhler remembered that the first two weeks of their trip had been absolutely trouble-free and peaceful. They had entered the Atlantic, and it seemed as if their expedition had started under a good star. Favorable winds had accelerated their progress, the ships had stayed together without any problems. The mood among the men had been excellent, full of curiosity, a great desire to explore and discover. When the skies closed and the storm announced itself, nobody had expected such a catastrophic and constant change in the weather. Nevertheless, they had endured it all with great confidence. Weren't they the best seafarers in the Empire? Weren't their ships the best of the entire fleet?

16

But now the mood began to change. Köhler hoped that Langenhagen – who actually had the rank of Navarch, but liked to see himself primarily as the captain of his ship – would be correct with his forecast.

"Go below deck!" Langenhagen shouted. "I want to know if everything is okay. And eat something. Aedilius' drink really helps. You need strengthening. Hot wine, slightly diluted. Something solid on it."

Köhler only nodded. Now that the herbal potion had taken effect, he felt a different kind of rumbling in his stomach. Hunger. Clearly recognizable desire for food for the first time in three days. He immediately followed the order.

He was grateful when he closed the companionway. It was a little quieter down there than on deck, the roar of the storm fading somewhat into the background. He saw sailors looking at him, nodding, often sitting tired against the wall or curled up in hammocks, in different phases of exhaustion, boredom or illness. But there was calm, a little fatalism, and only a few conversations. No dice game. No noise except the muffled roar from outside. A certain discipline in exhaustion. Good enough for Köhler, good enough for the ship.

He entered the galley. The ship's cook, called Smutje in the language of the time-wanderers, looked at him expectantly. It was significant that the only man who was completely unaffected by the storm was of all people the master of supplies. He showed his gaps in his teeth when he grinned at Köhler and gestured at his supplies with a sweeping gesture. The man was his best customer and always chewed on something. Even now, his mouth moved not only according to his words, but also to work on food. This sight had recently made Köhler nauseated, but now it triggered something like anticipation in him.

"A fresh start, sir?" The man was dripping with hypocrisy.

"Still an iron stomach, Vitelius?"

"Bronze, like our brave machine. Some wine?"

"Water and rusks."

"The very big risk, sir. You are a brave man, an ornament of the fleet, an image of Roman masculinity."

"Stop talking rubbish."

The Smutje grinned and handed him what he wanted and watched with a certain lurking look what was going to happen. He was genuinely impressed when Köhler ate the food with methodical chewing and then pecked some soaked crumbs off his coat. The Smutje smiled knowingly. "Our dear Medicus' herbal drink."

"Clever man."

"I swear on the stuff. Haven't drunk anything of it yet." The cook patted his stomach. "Bronze, as you know."

Köhler gave the man a disparaging look, but was as happy as a child that the rusk in his stomach made no move to reappear.

"Are you all right down here?"

If anyone could answer that question, it was the Smutje. He was one of the few who still looked at everything with open eyes. And very much amused in most ways.

"With drawbacks. I think some are almost bored."

"As soon as the wind subsides, we set sail again to save coal. Then there will be more than enough to do."

"But that doesn't apply to legionaries. Not only are they sick, they absolutely don't know what to do with themselves."

"There's a lot of cleaning up to do upstairs. We will put together work details. They're going to be busy, too."

Vitelius nodded and scratched his ear. Apparently he found something, looked at it for a moment before immediately put it between his busy jaws. Köhler was reasonably certain that behavior like this couldn't be healthy.

"How long?"

"The Navarch thinks no more than two days."

"And are we heading further west?"

"Indeed. I prefer not to say anything about whether the storm has broken the fleet apart. We have had no contact with the other ships since the winds started. Only noise on the shortwave. We'll have to wait here too, and see what the end of the wind will bring us."

"Two days?"

Köhler smiled.

"Is it getting too much for you? Despite a bronze stomach?"

"I haven't cooked anything decent in three days. I am filled with pity and care for my starving comrades. They have to get some proper food between their teeth."

Köhler agreed. However, he assumed that the Smutje did consider primarily his own teeth with his remark.

"Just be patient."

Köhler raised his hand in greeting and turned away. A short passage below deck confirmed the cook's statement. Everything was quiet, as far as one could really speak of calm with these violent waves. He answered a few questions – roughly the same ones he had just discussed – and spread more confidence than he felt.

But he was an officer. Always smile and wave.

When he finally struggled back up, he closed his eyes, almost blinded. The beam of light that had briefly shone down on them through one of the thick cloud banks had disappeared just as quickly as it had appeared – but his heart leapt when he saw the light dancing over the violent waves.

A good sign.

Langenhagen nodded to him, grinning happily. Even the helmsman looked relaxed, although he was still clutching the steering wheel as tightly as when Köhler had last seen him.

The wind didn't let up. A deep wave trough made Köhler's stomach go up again, but this time everything was under control.

It got better.

Everything was getting better now.

3

Of course, he had to make an example.

It was no different.

The former king of Saclemacal was no longer very pleased. The main reason for this was that Inugami had separated the man's head from his torso with his sword, with a quick, targeted and powerful stroke of the exemplary sharpened weapon. The body had bled to death in a red pond, and the head from which the feather headdress had fallen rested a little further.

The man had behaved appropriately, and Inugami was able to show respect for that. When they had conquered the city – after a short but fierce struggle in which the defenders quickly realized the hopelessness of their situation –, the King had subjugated himself to the conquerors. Inugami didn't know if he had hoped for mercy. But he hadn't been in the mood to let this wonderful opportunity for a symbolic act pass away. He certainly didn't have to kill every king he got hold of, but it was a necessary, useful sacrifice at least for the first time.

So the head fell. The King had immediately recognized his fate and accepted the judgment without complaint. Therefore Inugami had left him the headdress, the sign of his dignity. It had only made the act of killing stronger. The crowned head fell before the eyes of everyone, the conquered as the conquerors. The Mutalese cheers had been loud and contained real enthusiasm. For them, Saclemacal was a haven of treason. The just punishment had been pronounced and executed. The messenger of the gods had taken the King's head, and his wondrous sword had described such a beautiful, clear bow and had carried out his work so smoothly and quietly that the magic of this weapon had made the warriors' hearts beat faster.

A worthy deed. A necessary act.

Inugami turned, sword still raised. Next to him stood Chitam, the king of Mutal – a title that lost value every day, and this was not only the view of the Japanese. In fact, Inugami was in the process of contesting the power behind it. To be more precise, with the severed head of the inferior ruler, the captain had also cut off a lot of Chitam's power, and he waved his bloody sword like a scepter.

Finally he lowered his arm with the blade and left the top of the temple building on which he had carried out the execution. All sorts of rituals would follow that had to do with the Mayan religion and into which Inugami was disinterested. He sensed that he could not maintain this ignorance forever if he wanted to achieve Mayan loyalty on this spiritual level as well, if he wanted them to follow him with body and soul in all things. But he first had to reform the Mayan religion. The practices that did not help him had to go – human sacrifice, for example, the decision to wage wars according to the status of the stars and not when it seemed strategically wise. He had to reinforce the religious aspects where they were useful to him, but everything had to be more efficient. From now on, every conquest would upset the military practices of this people. In former times, Saclemacal would have been conquered, one would have set an example – just as Inugami had just done –, and afterwards, Mutal would have left with a promise of tribute after installing a new ruler, someone, from whom it was hoped that he would not cause any trouble during his lifetime. Sometimes that worked and sometimes it didn't; indirect exercise of power depended heavily on the victor's enduring prestige and ability to maintain a permanent threat. As memory faded, it became more likely that the once defeated developed the opinion that their defeat should be seen as a historic event and that there were no political consequences involved anymore.

Inugami would not allow that. Saclemacal would not be free again. The smaller city and its outskirts were the first building block of his new empire. He would appoint a governor who would always do exactly what Mutal ordered him to do. The road between the two cities would be expanded, and he would set up a daily messenger service. The couriers would walk but would exchange the latest news and orders every day – orders that were supposed to be executed, otherwise the consequences would be felt immediately. A new state could not be erected on any non-binding agreements.

Saclemacal would thus remain firmly in the grip of Mutal. The city's warriors would fight alongside Inugami. The way was mapped. Other cities had taken part in the attack on Mutal, and other royal heads had to detach themselves from their shoulders. The counterattacks were legitimate; no one in the neighborhood could blame Mutal.

Inugami had no illusions. As soon as word got around that the conquered cities would be firmly incorporated into the Mutal's dominion, resistance would increase. Then, he knew, the real war would begin, the war about absolute supremacy in Central America. Inugami knew the risks. It could, of course, go wrong. He needed the help of people who were fallible. But if he didn't try, he would throw away his life here in the distant past and live an undignified existence. Others might get used to it, get an Indian girl pregnant, and grow old and fat. Inugami was not ready for this.

He did great things.

He made history.

Or at least he would die trying.

He walked along the ranks of his warriors, silently taking their testimonies of honor. The men would be rewarded. That night was theirs. Inugami would let the reins slide, close his eyes. No looting, no rape – but everything was allowed up to this limit, and the city had to make the warriors feel good.

The good mood of his soldiers was in the interest of those who were controlled by them.

He disappeared into the palace of the King of Saclemacal and left the crowd behind. Here, in the chambers of the dead, only his bodyguard and the servants of the executed king awaited him, submissive and ready to carry out his orders.

Achak, the general of the King Chitam, also waited here, and now, Inugami wanted to accept that, his general, intoxicated with victory and Chi, whom he had plentifully awarded himself after the triumph. His face was red. He had cleaned his armor, his long obsidian knife, with which he had devotedly sliced open the bodies of his enemies. The man was far from young, but the battle seemed to give him unprecedented energy. He had driven through the ranks of enemies like a wisp and had taken one life after another, with such a fervent enthusiasm that even Inugami had been scared for a moment. It was as if he had released a demon on his enemies who had devoured, with the greatest devotion, the blood and suffering of his opponents, insatiable and full of strength.

Achak was a good general. He had prepared the battle thoroughly and was always ready to learn even more effective methods of murder. He had used the small spear catapults with enthusiasm. He was already talking about larger models that could be used to fire more than just spears, gravel, many pointed stones that drove through the ranks of the enemies like a cloud of death, slitting their skin, mutilating their faces and making them blind with pain, willing recipients of the deadly blow from the hands of soldiers who only had to finish what the projectiles had started.

Achak had painted this with a passion that the Japanese didn't fail to recognize. In fact, after the victory celebrations, they would start building more weapons, thereby strengthening their capabilities. Anyway, the old general was his man, in every way. His loyalty to the king, to Chitam, was only on the surface. His heart belonged to Inugami, as long as it gave him the opportunity to shed the blood of other people in battle.

Inugami wanted to give that to him, and plenty of it.

The general fell on his knees.

"Lord, I greet you. It is a time of triumph."

"That it is. Raise."

Inugami waved and everyone left the room except Achak, who finally sat on a stool. He was a little shaky on his feet, had been drinking well, and the intoxication of the fight had started to turn into an intoxication of alcohol.

"What is your plan, sir? What's the next step?" he articulated with the great care of a man who knew he had to be very focused to be able to speak clearly.

"Tayasal, general, just as we discussed it."

Achak's eyes shone. "The enemy will crawl in the dust before us. The head of the King of Tayasal will roll over the floor. Nothing and nobody stands in our way. Another grand victory, another defeat for the enemy. This is Mutal's time, and you, great Inugami, are the prophet of that time."

The Japanese smiled. He quite liked Achak's attitude.

"You have the full list of casualties?"

"Lord, we haven't lost a hundred men. The army is sure of victory and ready to march."

"Tayasal is small."

"And Yaxchilan is big and close. It may be that the new king comes up with ideas."

There had to be a new king, that was clear. Such a large city did not remain without a ruler for long. They still didn't know anything about him or his plans. That would change in the foreseeable future.

"He lacks warriors," Inugami said.

"He may also lack stupidity. I advise keeping the Saclemacal garrison as small as possible."

Inugami sat down too, his expression thoughtful.

"I'm afraid of an uprising, General. We are doing this differently now. We conquer and secure, we manage and keep. Do you understand that, Achak?"

"You explained it to me. I think 500 men will be enough. None of your warrior slaves coming from this city. They might be inclined to rethink their loyalty. We'll take them with us on the campaign."

"We'll take them all to Tayasal. Five hundred men. Who should be governor?"

Achak had apparently not thought about it yet. He frowned and was obviously trying to find a clever answer to the question. Inugami did not push him, took the break to fill a plate with fruit. The battle had made him hungry, and the table was richly covered. He found it remarkable that the old general, although he had every right to do so, did not himself ask for the post equivalent to that of a king – as long as Inugami was not present. Achak was not someone who wanted to rule – his only goal was to create the military basis for such rule.

"We have two options, sir. We elevate someone from here and put a general of ours at his side to keep an eye on him. The other alternative would be to promote one of ours and completely ignore the local nobility. Both options have their risks."

"What is your advice?"

"You are striving for a new kind of rule, new bonds of loyalty, and a permanent connection between the cities. An empire, as you called it. You must be certain of the loyalty of the people who rule this empire for you."

"What does Chitam say?"

Achak seemed surprised at the question. During the whole conversation, he obviously hadn't considered the King of Mutal, who was now actually King of Saclemacal. Inugami thought that was a good sign. It showed how unimportant Chitam was becoming in the eyes of his most important followers. The time was near to depose the King and put an end to this charade. Soon, very soon.

"Chitam hasn't said anything to me yet. He may think and act like his ancestors, elevating someone from the city who swear allegiance and promises tribute – and then marching off again. Those times are over."

"Yes, my lord."

"I want to appoint one of our men to be governor."

"So be it."

"I need suggestions. Someone with intelligence who knows his limits. Loyal, as far as we can be sure."

Achak hesitated long enough to arouse Inugami's suspicions.

"What's the problem, general?"

"My lord ..."

"Speak up."

"We cannot actually be completely sure of anyone at the moment. There is ... not everyone speaks and acts freely, not everyone clearly shows where his loyalty actually lies. Lord, you will find the safest candidates for such an office among those who are personally loyal because they know what treason means to them – and what wonderful reward they can expect if they remain loyal and do what you expect."

Achak didn't say anything else and looked at Inugami, who immediately nodded thoughtfully.

The old man was of course absolutely right.

In this situation, his choice was indeed limited. Very limited. But he could make the best of it. He wanted to use his own people as governors, in the larger cities, which were further away and could not be controlled directly. Aritomo would be king one day, though he had no idea yet. But not so close to Mutal. That would be a waste of limited resources. Saclemacal was easy to get to, quick to punish; it was a small town with limited resources, not a potential center of resistance. Basically only important because of its symbolic value as the first building block of the new empire but ultimately as a settlement of negligible importance.

Inugami nodded and stretched.

"Did that fellow Balkun survive the battle? The man who saved Chitam's family from the fire?"

"He was brave and unharmed," Achak replied with a knowing smile. The old man seemed to be able to understand and agree with his thoughts. Inugami smiled back.

"Then call him, General."

4

Inocoyotl hated waiting, at least as much as he was used to do it. It was one of the prerogatives of great rulers to keep anyone waiting who was not of the same rank, and no matter how many Mayan kings existed, the number of rulers who were actually accepted as equal was not great. If you were king of one of the big cities, not somewhere in the province but of a real center of military, economic and political power, then lower kings had to endure until they were called, and nobody was allowed to show any impatience. In this, a Mayan ruler was no different from a king of Teotihuacán, and so he endured what was to be endured.

K'uk' Bahlam, King of B'aakal, was one of the great ones. After Inocoyotl arrived in the city and had been received with great respect, he had waited a day for the Lord to address him. During this time, he had been granted the freedom to take a look around this metropolis and quickly learned that there were only a few cities besides B'aakal and Mutal that had achieved this size and wealth. K'uk' Bahlam was a ruler who was very aware of his dignity and power. At the same time, however, it was he who had invited to this conference, and since he wanted something, he was not half as distant as one would have expected him to be. The King of Popo' had arrived before Inocoyotl, and he was of roughly the same rank and standing as K'uk', but the other rulers, although they governed only small spots, were treated with respect and appropriately. Inocoyotl might represent the great Teotihuacán, but he was not a king, and so it was only right that he had to wait.

No problem.

He had used his time.

The rumors about the strange messengers of the gods had been fleshed out during his stay. It was difficult now to dismiss everything as a web of fancies. Inocoyotl became friends with the thought that his gracious divine ruler had sent him here at a time when something very, very strange was happening. He had the greatest respect for his king and had no doubt about his wisdom and foresight. But he would have some questions after his return, if his master was in a good mood. Meztli might even reveal on his own if all of this was indeed mere coincidence or intention. Inocoyotl, at any rate, felt he was in the right place at the right time, and as much as he believed in divine will, he trusted the fact that sometimes a king knew more than his faithful servant.

Maintaining the good humor and mercy of his king depended not least on the success of his mission. Inocoyotl had the problem, however, that he did not know exactly what should be considered a success. He was deep in thought in the waiting room, far from bored when a servant called for him to enter the audience chamber.

He thanked and followed the man.

K'uk Bahlam's chamber was not large. But the king himself was, a massive man with a nose so dominant that Inocoyotl for a moment forgot his manners and stared at them involuntarily. He was not expected to throw himself on the floor. He represented a power that even the highest Mayan kings had healthy respect for. However, the ambassador was not lacking in deference. He bowed deeply and did not straighten up until Bahlam asked him to sit down.

The king was not alone. A clerk sat next to him and would record the most important aspects of the conversation. B'aakal was known for its carefully kept archive. And next to the king sat a second man of dignified appearance, dressed in similarly magnificent feather headdresses. Inocoyotl couldn't be sure, but he assumed that this was the king of Popo', whose name he hadn't heard yet. It was sometimes difficult to keep track of the Maya. They had so many important rulers.

But if the rumors were true, there were efforts to change this.

"Greetings to the envoy from Teotihuacán," boomed Bahlam's deep voice. "Sit down and tell us about your great lord."

Inocoyotl bowed again and took a seat. Since the Lord of Popo' didn't seem to be communicating with him, he turned his attention to the jovial figure of Bahlam. However, he was not fooled by this. Bahlam's body was large and soft, but his will was harder than the best obsidian.

"Noble King, noble majesties, I send you my lord's greetings, and I'm delighted to see you in the best of health. The friendship of my lord and king is unbreakable, and his blessings accompany you. Teotihuacán sees you as a family, and we are united by a bond that stretches through the ages. Thank you for the friendly welcome, the kind hospitality and the opportunity to step in front of you."

K'uk' Bahlam's broad face grew even wider, as his lips twisted into a smile, thus expressing his benevolence. "Thank you, ambassador. It is an astonishing coincidence that you appear here at the exact time when a major crisis is looming, and I have called a gathering of dignitaries to discuss this."

Inocoyotl kept his composure. It was remarkable that Bahlam had exactly the same thoughts as the envoy himself. His respect for the massive man grew a little more. "A coincidence, indeed. I only heard about this meeting on my way here."

"So you weren't sent directly as an observer, as a participant in the deliberations?"

"No," Inocoyotl said the truth. "My mission was of a more general nature. I should strengthen relationships with our friends, the Maya, and visit many cities. It was not my specific job to attend this conference; I knew nothing about it and neither did my master."

He wasn't so sure about the last claim, but of course he couldn't show that.

Bahlam nodded. "But then you hurried here."

"It seemed appropriate to me. Am I welcome?"

Bahlam laughed. It was remarkable what tremors the brief outburst caused on his body. "A lot. The gods look benevolently down at us. We could use the help of our generous friend, your king, someday."

Inocoyotl said nothing and just bowed. He knew that he had extensive powers. His king might support whatever he said here, even what he didn't think was right, just to save his face. In such a case, however, the head of his envoy would no longer be sitting on his shoulders too securely once he returned. Inocoyotl quite liked the current position of his head. He had to be very careful. "I've only heard rumors so far, noble majesties."

"It started with rumors. But it is now much more than that."

"Do you want to inform me?"

"That is the purpose of this gathering." Bahlam rose.

Inocoyotl immediately wanted to do the same, but the king waved him off. The flexibility with which he was able to move was amazing, as if all the fat on his bones were actually muscles. Inocoyotl frowned. Indeed, there may have been more muscles than it appeared. He didn't want to face the man in battle. The outcome could be surprising.

And Inocoyotl was really attached to his head.

Bahlam spread his arms and spoke. "Many weeks ago there were the first indications that amazing things had happened in Mutal. They spoke of messengers of the gods that would have appeared one day from heaven, brought by a strange vehicle, a metal container of impressive size, which the temple crushed among itself. We didn't take these rumors too seriously, they sounded a little ... hysterical."

Inocoyotl just grunted. Who would blame Bahlam? That was his first reaction to the story. Visions of priests who had given themselves to chi too intensively and wanted to impress gullible people to demonstrate their usefulness.

"But then these rumors grew as our own informants began to confirm them in their reports. Indeed, something extraordinary has happened in Mutal. And any doubts we might have had have been cleared up by recent events that you probably haven't heard of."

Inocoyotl nodded promptly. "I'm listening, high king."

"And attentively, as I observe. Good."

Bahlam walked through the room during his lecture, driven by an inner unrest that now seemed to be transferred to Inocoyotl. He had to hold on to himself not to jump up. The one who remained completely uninvolved was the lord of Popo'. He had even closed his eyes. "Our dear brother, the king of Yaxchilan, has always been a man full of ambition and confidence. He used a victory over a neighboring town to fuel enthusiasm for a campaign against Mutal, and he managed to find two valuable allies in this regard, the lords of Saclemacal and Tayasal. An impressive army marched toward Mutal, and although this city is so big and powerful, I wouldn't have given much of its chances of a successful defense."

Inocoyotl said nothing. The Mayan habit of constantly attacking each other was well known in Teotihuacán. His own king was very pleased with this practice. Mayan kings in battle meant that none of them could ever pose a serious threat to the Eternal City. So they should keep pounding each other's skulls. Inocoyotl found this a very reasonable attitude. The description presented to him thus so far corresponded to what he had to expect from the current power politics of this region. "What happened?"

"Mutal prevailed. The king of Yaxchilan is dead. Thousands of prisoners have been made."

"One hears a lot about the power of Mutal's warriors," Inocoyotl said, unable to hide the fact that he was somewhat proud. Mutal's current dynasty was founded by a noble Teotihuacán who had led one of the last great campaigns in this region. It seemed that some of his people's energy and ability had been transferred to his offspring. If a Mayan state was honored by Teotihuacán, it was Mutal.

Bahlam knew that, of course. And he was a polite man. "Indeed, envoy. But all reports speak of magic weapons that brought great destruction to the attackers, thundering sticks from which invisible arrows shot, and large fires that spontaneously spread like magic. They speak of men in strange robes who have conquered the ear and heart of the King of Mutal and a metal vehicle that rests on one of their temples."

"These reports sound ... embellished."

Bahlam laughed again in his shattering way. The sound came deep from his body and felt like a volcano was preparing to erupt. There was something contagious as well as terrifying.

"My spies are men of the greatest reliability, I expressly admonish them to only report what they hear and see and never to try to interpret these things."

Inocoyotl believed that the king was extremely careful when selecting and instructing his agents, especially those in Mutal. He was concerned that the truth did not seem to be far from the visions of drunken priests.

"That's how you called this important conference," Inocoyotl concluded. "In the visit of the messengers of the gods you see a danger, not a blessing."

"I doubt it's messengers from the gods. I have no doubt, however, that they are a danger, except for Mutal itself, and I don't want to come to a final judgment there either."

"What is the danger? How do you want to deal with this? Do you wish to attack Mutal? Who should support you?"

Bahlam laughed again, and Inocoyotl imagined hearing respect in the laughter. "Everyone at this conference once wanted to conquer Mutal. Even the mighty Teotihuacán, if I remember correctly."

Inocoyotl shook his head mockingly, grinning. He started to warm up for this king.

"The problem is not whether and when we attack Mutal, but rather where the king of that city, supported by the messengers of the gods, is now turning his eye. The last thing we heard today, delivered directly by messenger from one of my spies, is this: King Chitam of Mutal's troops have set out to punish Saclemacal for participating in the attack on Mutal. And everyone agrees that this city will not be the last to fall victim to the campaign."

"It doesn't sound unusual. Saclemacal is actually owing tribute to Mutal and has committed treason. That's how you would act, noble Bahlam, if one of your tributes should orientate himself otherwise."

Bahlam laughed again, but this time it sounded happier. "I don't blame Mutal. One small detail bothers me: Chitam, it is said, is now determined not to just punish Saclemacal, to humiliate the king there and replace him with a more pleasing one, to plunder properly and to take slaves – no, the intent is to conquer the city. Permanently. Manage its affairs directly, with no intention of ever granting her independence again."

Inocoyotl understood. He understood Bahlam's fears too well. And he remembered why Teotihuacán was so happy that the Mayan kings were fully occupied with their own repetitive trades. Because if this wasn't the case …

"Chitam is ambitious," Inocoyotl said finally.

"He or those who stand behind him," said Bahlam.

"Yes, these strange alleged messengers of the gods."

"Supposedly or not, the fact that someone with special powers is fighting for Mutal is undisputed."

Inocoyotl nodded. "And what plan do you have, my king?"

"An alliance."

"An alliance against Mutal."

"An alliance to march against Mutal, join forces before it marches against us."

Bahlam leaned forward, eyes narrowed into narrow slits, and fixed his eyes on the ambassador, who knew exactly what was coming.

"This is a potential danger for the mighty Teotihuacán too!"

"My master is undefeated and invincible," Inocoyotl said almost automatically, but he still felt a little out of balance. He didn't want to believe much of what Bahlam was saying. On the other hand, the king was apparently not one who was prone to hasty alarmism. He seemed to be a careful ruler who knew how to assess risks. It was clear that he believed the reports of his agents. And Meztli had sent him, his ambassador, here at that time. The conclusion was overwhelmingly clear.

"Your city is powerful, more powerful than all of us," Bahlam admitted, trying to sound somewhat respectful, an effort that Inocoyotl rewarded with a smile. "But if this attack on Saclemacal succeeds and turns into a tidal wave, it might be too late for all of us. After Saclemacal, Mutal will logically attack Tayasal or Yaxchilan, one of the other two cities that were involved in the original attack against Mutal. So we have a little time to make our own preparations and to position ourselves."

"Then we have to think of several strategies at the same time," Inocoyotl heard himself say, and immediately noticed the satisfied smile on Bahlam's heavy lips. But now there was no going back for him, he was part of the discussion, and he wasn't sure if that was wrong at all. There was a feeling of a threat, the magnitude of which could not yet be properly estimated. As diffuse as it sounded, the fear that came with it felt real.

"What do your ideas look like?" Bahlam asked.

"First of all, I will send a messenger to my master with all the information you have just given me. I may have to tell him myself at one time so he can see the urgency of the matter."

"I want to provide an escort for this man, and he should travel quickly," Bahlam said, nodding.

"Then I have to inform myself about these things before I recommend my king to join an alliance against Mutal. I cannot step before my master, only armed with second-hand information. I have to see."

The fat king's nod again. "I can understand that. It will not be too dangerous if you only act as an interested ambassador for Teotihuacán. In Mutal they are aware of your common history and feel connected to you. Chitam will speak to you, and you will be able to look around. I'll give you the name of one of my agents, you can meet him on site, and he can tell you his view of things."

"A good idea, noble king, and I am grateful for it. But you should continue and consider how you try to defend yourself against Mutal. If an alliance is your target and you want to attack Mutal to avoid the looming danger, you need a commander-in-chief. You can imagine yourself taking this office?"

Bahlam looked pensive as if he had never paid attention to this question. Inocoyotl, of course, didn't believe that for a moment. "B'aakal is the most powerful of the cities that gather here. Popo' alone can be regarded as equivalent, but the noble ruler has already indicated that he intends to leave the overall command to someone else."

Inocoyotl's eyes fell again on the quietly seated man who hadn't spoken a word before and nodded to him. He got a slightly bowed head to answer.

The ambassador thought that he would not really be able to figure that man out.

But he had expected Bahlam's answer, and it was now up to him to deliver bad news to the king.

"Noble Bahlam, your request is logical, because B'aakal is the first among the cities we are talking about. Of course, I don't know yet whether my lord will join this alliance, but let's assume he sees the danger as you do. When he declares himself as a full member of your alliance, it is clear at the same time, and I say this as someone who has served both him and his father for many years: My great sir will not accept anyone's command except his own – exercised by himself or through one his generals, whom he will certainly send if he participates in this campaign."

Inocoyotl bowed his head in a gesture of respect. It was better to address this unpleasant fact straight away than to trigger conflicts later which, if everything was as urgent as described, could have very negative consequences.

Bahlam looked at Inocoyotl, looking neither angry nor disappointed. "Ambassador, you must think I'm a fool."

"Not even remotely!" Inocoyotl replied.

The rumbling, erupting laugh of the king was heard again. "I have the impression. I assure you, I am not. I am clear about who the king of Teotihuacán is and what rank he occupies in the structure of the world. If … I say it very clearly … if your Lord decides to march against Mutal together with us, I will leave him or his general in command and pray with him to all the gods, ours and yours, that they may give us victory – all of us."

Inocoyotl felt relieved and confirmed in his good judgment of Bahlam. Truly not a fool. And he had already considered this question very carefully. He bowed again. "A wise decision."

"I don't claim wisdom. Security is my goal."

"Should I take part in your consultations?"

"I don't make that decision. You are, of course, invited. Your word will have weight. But if you have to make sure that everything I've told you is correct, you should leave while there is still the possibility of traveling peacefully."

"That sounds wise again."

"And again it's all about security – yours in this case."

"The mighty Bahlam's concern moves me."

The king liked to laugh, and so he did it again. However, he seemed genuinely amused and clapped his hands.

"Excellent, Inocoyotl from Teotihuacán. You will be attending my banquet that I will be giving to all my guests tonight. And then do as you see fit."

"I'm traveling, but I'm leaving one of mine as an observer. He will not speak and take no position, but he will be my eye and my ear."

"So be it. Now you are wise, my friend."

Inocoyotl smiled softly.

"I just want to be on the safe side."

Bahlam laughed loudly, with violent tremors in his body, and even the silent King of Popo' managed to smile. Inocoyotl bowed again and found that the matter had gone well.

Then he left.

5

Lengsley touched Sarukazaki's shoulder. He was allowed this confidentiality. He had been working side by side with the technician for weeks, and it was as if two related souls had found each other. Across all linguistic and cultural differences, the two men shared a common passion for everything related to technical devices. Be it the complicated machinery of the boat, be it the much simpler things they tried to convey to the Maya, it was all engineering, and everything was equally important. There were some among the Maya who shared this passion, a strange mix of builders, artisans, scribes, and some young people who might not have been all of these, often sons of influential nobles. They had formed an informal circle around Lengsley and Sarukazaki, a group of students and teachers, because even the time travelers had to understand what their hosts knew before they could set out to teach them anything useful.

It was always in the evening, and it was not always the same number of Maya who gathered around the two men, but the changes were minor. Lengsley and Sarukazaki had started to come up with something like a curriculum to be able to convey information in a targeted manner. Since this was entirely in line with Inugami's wishes, who generally did not think much of the achievements of Mayan culture and saw a massive need for development, there was no danger of causing the Captain's dislike.

They had started to learn the numbers of the Maya themselves and how they did the math. In some areas the Mutalese were very advanced. Lengsley was only beginning to get an idea of what astronomical knowledge existed, but he was already impressed. He found understanding listeners as he began to work through formulas and calculations that he slowly introduced and ended his explanations immediately when he found that someone already knew the answers and could do it much better. In this way, he succeeded in exploring the scope of Mayan mathematics, which in many ways was the basis, above all, for the introduction to mechanics.

Otherwise it was just fun. It was a pleasure to work with people who wanted to know something and who were able to use their previous knowledge correctly and build on it. Sometimes the evening discussion wandered and they left the topic that they had intended. As a rule, it remained with technical-scientific discussions, also on topics where even Lengsley and Sarukazaki had to resign at some point, since they knew little more about it than the Maya. But they were not resented for it. The questioners steadfastly probed the depth of their teachers' knowledge, and soon they seemed to have gained an impression of where further inquiries were worthwhile and where not. Their respect didn't seem to shrink. Of course, the teachers lost the nimbus of infallibility, but since neither the British nor his Japanese colleague had ever seriously tried maintain such and did not attach any importance to it, this did not particularly matter. With each lesson, apparent and actual differences blurred a little more.

However, their lessons got a special quality when one evening Prince Isamu appeared with them, along with his teacher, the old Sawada. Lengsley did not lack respect, but Sarukazaki immediately became stiff, terribly formal, and hardly dared to look the boy in the face. Sawada just sat with the Prince, and they both listened to the conversation. They said nothing, and at the end, when everyone left the fire to sleep, Sawada came up to both of them and said, "The Prince will be attending your classes in the future, Brit. He needs instruction, and I'm busy with many other things that Captain Inugami told me to do. You will include His Highness in the conversation, and he will learn."

The way Sawada said it sounded like an order. Lengsley had no major reservations, Isamu seemed to be nice enough despite his parentage, and he had already learned a lot of the Mayan language. Sarukazaki, however, only turned pale when he heard Sawada's words, and the first two evening sessions showed how uncomfortable he was, tense, excited, and unsure of how to behave properly. Lengsley was concerned about this and wasn't sure how to help his colleague. Sarukazaki was of little use during these lessons.

It was their Maya friends who solved the problem. The younger ones included Isamu in their conversations, first carefully, then with greater courage when the Prince was ready to respond to her request. This broke the ice for Sarukazaki, too, and since the Prince never complained when someone turned to him without being asked or even corrected him, the soldier relaxed visibly.

Lengsley knew that Sawada was playing a dangerous game. Inugami had specifically ordered that the Prince be kept as far away from the "savages" as possible. He wanted to make the boy a god emperor, as Aritomo had explained to the British, exactly as he was meant to do, and in the spirit of the old shogunate – as a puppet and symbol of a power that was actually in the hands of the shogun, and who in turn intended to hold this office, there was no doubt for Lengsley.

But Sawada seemed to want to use the opportunity that Inugami was in Saclemacal for his own plans. Since none of the crew dared to contradict the Prince and his wishes – an effect that the Captain may have underestimated –, he was able to gradually ensure that the Prince's isolation was removed. The evening lessons with the intellectual elite of Mutal were as much a part of it as some other arrangements that Sawada had made in a subtle way.

Aritomo didn't seem to notice or didn't want to notice. Lengsley assumed that he did not want to, since he had to enforce his orders in Inugami's absence, at least in theory. And there were probably those for whom the first officer did not feel the necessary enthusiasm to enforce anything.

Isamu thawed more every night.

And it happened what Sawada would have intended.

He found a friend – a young man, a year or two older than the prince, the son of a nobleman, who attended every evening instruction with his friends and had never been absent, and whose intent was no doubt to be more than just a member of the elite the city. His name was Ichik, and he was one of the first to speak to

Isamu. The Prince discovered a fascination for Mayan architecture with him. One day when Lengsley saw the two boys standing in front of the Jaguar Temple as Ichik explained the intricacies of the building to him – and shortly afterwards the intricacies of some of the noble daughters of their age passing by –, it was clear to the Brit that there was no way back into isolation for the Prince. How would Inugami deal with it – and what drastic measures would he be ruthless enough to take in order to restore the status quo? And if he admitted, to think how would he take revenge on Sawada or even him, the suspicious Gaijin?

This said something about Sawada that he hadn't asked him beforehand, knowing that any possible consequence would hit him at least as hard as the old teacher. Both were, of course, indispensable to the captain in their own way. But that didn't mean Inugami couldn't make life very difficult for them. He was a calculating but also a vindictive man who did not shy away from violence in any form. There was a reason why King Chitam had sent his family to safety far from Mutal, out of the captain's reach, and before they left for Saclemacal.

Lengsley found himself thinking about his own escape options. It was not a good sign.

It was one evening, the day the news of the triumph at Saclemacal reached their ears, when the group had been smaller than usual and lectures ended earlier. A violent tropical storm had wreaked havoc, and most of the usual guests had been busy repairing until the dark, so tiredness had prevailed over eagerness to learn. But Isamu, and with him his friend Ichik, had not missed the opportunity to attend Sarukazaki's presentation of a model of a water mill. The Maya relied heavily on the strength of their muscles and had achieved something outstanding with it. But since they didn't even use wheels for vehicles, they had underestimated hydropower, and Sarukazaki had made it its business to change that.

The presentation went well; there had been questions and a request to repeat it again the next time everyone was there. The Japanese had been satisfied, and Lengsley had little to contribute as this was the technician's show.

He helped Sarukazaki disassemble his carefully constructed water mill and to safekeep the model for another demonstration, and only realized when they were done and the Japanese left with his treasure toward the accommodation that Prince Isamu and Ichik had waited until the end.

The Brit felt almost alarmed against his will. He took a deep breath and smiled. "Is there anything else I can do for you, Your Highness?" Lengsley said with a respectful tone. He couldn't take the risk of claiming too much freedom. As a stranger among the Japanese as well as the Maya, his position was special, and he had to use the credit he had obtained on both sides with great care.

"Mr. Lengsley, I'd be happy if you just call me Isamu – when we're among us."

Ichik was apparently included in "among us," and the fact that the Prince spoke to him in English – which he knew surprisingly well – was a sign that he was serious.

"Good, Isamu ... whatever you want. But if I accidentally ignore certain elements of expected etiquette, then –"

"It is already forgiven," the Prince replied, smiling.

"So what can I do for you?"

"I would like your opinion as an outsider."

Lengsley pressed his lips together briefly. Isamu did not act diplomatically, but on the other hand this word corresponded exactly to the thoughts he had just had himself. So why should he blame the young man? "My opinion on what?"

"To my fate."

Lengsley immediately felt overwhelmed, and the alarmed feeling returned. The question was asked so clearly, without any self-pity, and there was a great deal of uncertainty behind it, but at the same time there was also self-knowledge about his own role – it was so much that he did not know at which level he should answer and why he was actually chosen to deal with this topic. He had, of course, talked to Aritomo about the Prince, and they had both agreed that Isamu was a poor guy who would find it very difficult to assert himself in the face of all the forces that were pulling at him. The boy had also started talking to Aritomo a few weeks ago, and Aritomo had told Lengsley about it in a nutshell. The Prince was looking for advice old Sawada obviously couldn't give him.

But was he, the Gaijin, capable to do so?

The Prince seemed to think so. Or he was desperate enough to try to talk to anyone who was available to him.

"Let's sit down again," Lengsley murmured. The nighttime fire around which they had gathered had already started to go out, so he added some branches. "So your fate – I can't see the future, my prince."

Isamu looked into the flames and nodded. "Nobody can. But I would like to know what you would advise me, which way to go."

"It depends on your wishes and ideas."

"I thought of my duty."

Lengsley nodded. "When fulfilling your duty is your wish –"

"What is my duty?"

"Good question. If we believe Captain Inugami –"

"That's my problem," Isamu interrupted. Lengsley saw the otherwise controlled and motionless mask that the Prince always seemed to wear getting crumbly. Emotions became visible, and they had to be quite violent. "I do not believe him."

Lengsley didn't know what to say. It was difficult for him to internalize the Japanese concepts of discipline and obedience. After all, it wasn't just about belief. Many may have doubts about the Captain's plans. But no one admitted it openly, except perhaps Aritomo, who was high up in the hierarchy itself. Lengsley was not a soldier, but he knew what the Japanese thought and what alternatives they had if they tried to break the cycle of obedience and discipline. Often enough, only dishonor or even suicide remained. His comrades were too quick at hand with death for Lengsley's taste.

Isamu knew all of this much better than Lengsley, because he had been trained that way all his life. If he was willing to cross these invisible barriers, the limits that Japanese society had placed around him, the Prince's despair must be greater than Aritomo had assumed. And often desperate actions grew out of desperation. The fact that Isamu spoke to Lengsley – well considered – certainly had its meaning.

"I don't want to rule over these people, Mr. Lengsley, neither by name, as a mere symbol, nor seriously. They have their own dynasties, as venerable and old as those I am from. I have no right to do so. And I do not share Captain Inugami's attitude, who treats the people here like things or pawns like they are just tools with which to accomplish his great plans. I know that I will never see my home again. And you know what? It doesn't matter to me. I do not long back to the court, I do not miss the rules, the stiff ceremony and all the expectations that have been imposed on me without ever having a realistic prospect of sitting on the throne. I see this journey as a way to freedom."

Lengsley nodded slowly. "But the captain blocks this path, Isamu."

"That's the way it is. I cannot and will not accept that."

Lengsley was surprised at the Prince's intense speech. Put forward in well-spoken words that betrayed both his intelligence and his education, he had not turned clouded his true feelings and aspirations. Ichik sat next to him and probably understood more than enough of what his friend had just said. Lengsley felt a great burden placed on his shoulders with the Prince's trust. If Isamu revealed his true feelings and intentions to him and Aritomo, wasn't there a great responsibility for both of them? And how did one want to do it justice? The hope of advice and assistance was clearly evident from the Prince's words. Lengsley was still clearly overwhelmed with it.

To say this to the Prince would cause too much disappointment. Then who else did he have to turn to?

"Have you spoken to Aritomo Hara about these things?"

"Once and not so clearly. It's difficult for him too."

Isamu had put the first officer's dilemma in one simple sentence. That he said this spoke of his ability to observe. And it became Lengsley's burden. Isamu, in his perception of hierarchy, obedience, honor, and discipline, had come to the conclusion that Aritomo Hara, with all his goodwill and understanding, had his hands tied in many ways. But Lengsley …

Lengsley was the Gaijin, even at the best of times one who was on the margins, outside, who didn't belong, couldn't belong at all. And Isamu, in his thinking, with his doubts and hopes, felt more like a stranger, more and more so, and apparently believed that Lengsley was most likely to be the one who would understand … and help him.

It had a certain logic, but it didn't help the British very much.

"What do you expect of me, Isamu?"

The Prince nodded slowly, gave Ichik a long look. He took a deep breath.

"I know that it sounds insane and dangerous, Mr. Lengsley. But I want to do what I can only accomplish before the golden cage around me is completely closed. I want to run away, Mr. Lengsley." He stared into the Britishman's eyes as if this would prove the seriousness of his intentions. "I want to run away as soon as possible, and I want you to help me with that."

6

Ixchel's sister Nicte cried quietly. Aktul put a hand gently on her mouth, which immediately silenced the girl. Ixchel narrowed her eyes after nodding encouragingly at her sister. Nicte didn't cry out of fear, but out of exhaustion. Ixchel would never dream of reproaching her for that.

From the edge of the forest they could see the first farmsteads that surrounded the city in a wide circle. It was early morning, the chill of the night was still in their bones. They had waited for the darkness on a tree, sitting in the mighty branches, half asleep, half awake, a reason for Nicte's exhaustion and her helpless reaction to it. They had already been on the road for days to make sure that pursuers kept their distance. They had fed on what the forest had provided, and Aktul was an experienced hunter-gatherer. They weren't hungry, but they were dirty, tired, and especially the little one cried often. A bad environment to deal with the violent death of one's mother, the shock of flight, the struggles, the insecurity, and fear. Ixchel dreamed violently every night when she got some sleep, and the horror of the visions terrified her. Nevertheless, she did not wake up crying but with a quiet determination not to suppress the violence of these images, but to use it instead. Her goal had to be to use the power behind it to turn it against those responsible for their misery.

And she had to be strong for Nicte. Strong for the old Aktul, who struggled admirably with the sudden responsibility for the two princesses, but who could not use any additional crying or despair. Ixchel had to show him her strength so that he could use his moderately. Her survival was dependent on this.

And thus the precondition for Ixchel to be able to inflict terrible revenge on the murderers.

She had her guess who those might be.

Her legs and feet ached. It was incomprehensible to her how old Aktul had mastered the strength to march so extensively, often with her little sister in his arms. Unimaginable energy prevailed in the warrior, who now had to take care of the two girls and didn't even complain or seem to struggle. He was very determined and had given Ixchel several suggestions for a safe haven, which she had all considered well. Last but not least, it was the news that her mother received shortly before she left that prompted her to make a decision.

Now it would prove whether it was the right one.

"How do we do it, Aktul?" she whispered. The door of a mud hut was knocked aside, and a woman stepped outside, an empty calabash in one hand and in the other a little boy, who was still rubbing sleep from his eyes. The woman looked around, seemed to take in the peaceful morning before heading for their own well, which spoke of the wealth of this farmer. It could even be a low noble, considering the size of the hut and the adjoining buildings, definitely someone of a certain rank, who had built so generously out here at the city limits, because he was also watching the border for his masters. From here the road went straight to the center, and a fast runner could quickly announce any visitors – peaceful or hostile.

"We have to prevent people from not taking us seriously. We look like homeless people, like vagabonds. And we have to gain access to the right people. So we only have one chance."

Ixchel did not say that not only did they look like vagabonds, that was basically what they were, an insight that, a thought which, however, would not strengthen their confidence.

"Will he listen to us?"

"If we get the chance to speak to him in person –"

"It shouldn't be that difficult."

Aktul laughed softly. "He's a fickle man, I heard. Your grandfather wasn't always sure if he could trust him. He delivered both truth and lies. It was not always easy to separate one from the other, as I've heard."

"Still, he remained in my grandfather's service."

"He somehow did, one way or another."

"Then he's committed to Mutal."

Aktul shook his head. "I don't think he has ever felt really committed to anyone or anything. Besides its own convenience and safety, maybe. We're a threat to both, Princess."

Ixchel understood that. But there was no alternative, and they had decided. "You speak."

"That won't be enough." Aktul fixed the girl with a steady glance. "You will have to convince him, my dove. It depends more on you than on me."

Ixchel nodded. She was not afraid. Since the death of her mother, she felt full of a holy determination, a strong courage. She would remove all obstacles, that was her goal. A fickle spy who sometimes served Mutal and sometimes his actual masters, and who did not consider loyalty an outstanding personality trait was not an obstacle, not even a challenge. He was no more than a flight of stairs on their way up, toward the completion of their mission, her retaliation.

If the step turned out to be brittle, she would simply skip it.

"Then we shouldn't wait any longer," Ixchel decided, and the old warrior bowed instinctively. There was no doubt in his mind that she was the princess, his master's daughter, and no matter how big the age difference, he knew that Ixchel was an extraordinary young lady.

And that had become even clearer in the days of flight than before.

He seemingly served her with joy.

They left the edge of the forest and went into the open. They walked the first hundred yards without paying any attention, but then the woman saw them both as she looked up from the well to watch the little boy who had started his morning toilet. The sudden distrust in her eyes was somewhat alleviated by the fact that Ixchel's little sister hurried straight to the well without further ado, crouched next to the astonished looking boy and used the water to wash the sleep from last night out of her eyes – and the dirt that spread across her face.

Children had something soothing. Nevertheless, the woman opened her mouth and shouted, "Agun!"

Aktul and Ixchel stopped near the woman, at a safe distance so as not to appear threatening. The woman's eyes saw the weapons, the man's spear and his atlatl, then, with astonishment, not only the girl's atlatl, but also the strange apparatus she carried with her, the messenger's magic killing device.

"Agun!" The shout had been a little more urgent this time.

"Don't be afraid, woman," Aktul said softly. "We are friends of Agun and would like to talk to him."

"Friends?" The distrust was so clearly audible that it almost jumped at the visitors. "At this time ... what friends?"

"Let me talk to –"

"What's happening?" came a male voice. "I'm not awake enough to –"

All eyes turned to the entrance of the mud house, from which now came a wiry, slightly leaning forward man who was a good ten years older than the woman, only dressed in a cloth that he had wrapped around his loins. The man interrupted himself, came out completely, and then walked fearlessly toward the visitors. He might be older, maybe as old as Aktul, but he shared the watchful gaze and the almost dissecting powers of observation with the soldier, something that Ixchel saw as a good sign. No one who panicked about anything.

"Who are you?" he asked and stopped in front of the two, not unfriendly, but with a good deal of suspicion in his voice.

"They want to see you, Agun!" the woman said, shaking her head from behind.

"Me? Who are you?"

The question was addressed to Aktul, who bowed slightly.

"My name is Aktul, warrior of the Chitam, protector of Ixchel, the king's daughter."

"Mutal?" The question had come in a whisper, and Ixchel watched the man's nimble gaze flick to the right and left, the way his wife put a hand over her mouth, and took her boy by the hand.

"Mutal. We have to talk, Agun."

The man's gaze now focused on Ixchel and her sister, and recognition shimmered in his eyes. "You are the princess – you are both the daughters of Chitam, the daughters of Lady Tzutz."

"Why don't you let us in, Agun?" Ixchel said, also not unkindly, but in the attitude of a young woman who might one day have the right to ascend the great throne of Mutal.

The man looked at his wife, then nodded hastily.

"Quickly, before the neighbors wake up. Your visit is surprising and, above all, disturbing given the news one hears from Mutal."

Aktul took hold of the man's forearm. "Wait until you hear what I have to say, Agun from B'aakal. Your surprise will increase, as will your dismay."

Agun looked at the warrior first, then at Ixchel. "So you need my help."

Ixchel smiled cheerlessly. She hadn't missed the lurking in the man's voice. She followed him inside the hut and knew exactly what was going to happen. It was, as always, when people appeared at court and had something to offer that their grandfather might have wanted but couldn't force.

Negotiations started.

She would not need Aktul's help for that.

She could do that herself.

7

"You can rejoice, the victory is complete!"

The messenger's face showed his joy and pride in bringing this wonderful news to Aritomo. It was at that moment that the officer realized for the first time that he had secretly nurtured a little hope, even hidden from himself – the hope that Saclemacal would have defended himself better than expected and that a lucky throw from an atlatl or the targeted hit of a powerful warrior would have killed Captain Inugami.

Aritomo closed his eyes as if trying to savor the feeling of triumph. Instead, he tried to ignore the disappointment that this highly dishonorable hope, contrary to all the rules of his professional existence, had remained unfulfilled. And his disappointment that he did not intend to suppress this emotion.

"Thank you. Thank you for this good news. I hope the honorable Inugami is doing well?" He wrestled with the question and the messenger's radiant smile widened.

"He is fine! He distinguished himself in the fight, searched for and found the enemy! Now he sits on the throne at Saclemacal and dispenses his justice."

Aritomo knew how to classify the nuance. Chitam was not seated on the throne of the conquered city personally, if there was one at all. Of course, Inugami would continue, at least for a while, to maintain the illusion that it was only acting in accordance with the ruler of Mutal. But the messenger, whether wanted or not, had already torn off the veil in his report and said what more and more of the Maya thought – and many of them, apparently, with the ardent enthusiasm of a belligerent people who were committed to the imperial vision of their new savior.

Aritomo had to admit that Inugami was on the right track. And even if he did not show great appreciation to the Maya, he still seemed to have kindled a fire in them. The question was whether he could keep it under control.

"Did the honorable Inugami say anything about his future plans?"

"Not to me, but I'm bringing this letter and its instructions to you. But everyone knows that Tayasal will fall next."

The messenger produced a carefully folded sheet of paper, which he gave to Aritomo, bowing. It was covered with the thin, printed characters that were characteristic of Inugami's handwriting.

"I thank you. Now go and rest. I'll call you if I need your services."

"My Lord!" The messenger bowed and disappeared.

Aritomo was well aware of the curious looks of the other Japanese who were with him in the courtyard of their shared accommodation. The letter would contain no response to the first officer's last letter to Inugami after the assassination attempt. This may arrive soon, and Aritomo was afraid of the orders that followed. Depending on Inugami's mood, especially his anger and contempt for the "savages," his reaction was completely unpredictable, and if he asked Aritomo to make an example, it would pose considerable problems. The nobleman who had instigated the murder had been arrested and imprisoned, and Chitam's return was awaited for his trial. Aritomo could have ordered a punishment himself – nobody here would have seriously opposed this –, but he shied away from the beginning of a cycle of violence and counterviolence. It was difficult to wage a war both externally and internally, but he wasn't sure whether Inugami would see it that way.

He unfolded the letter completely and read.

The captain's words were tight and businesslike. He reported victory, listed losses, and described the resources of the much smaller city of Saclemacal with even greater contempt than his attitude toward Mutal. The messenger hadn't exaggerated. The struggle had been one-sided, victory was absolute, and Aritomo raised his eyebrows in astonishment when he heard about Inugami's staffing decision. He had appointed Balkun, the savior of Chitam and his family, to the position of governor of the city, giving him honor and office ... to an extent that Aritomo would never have believed possible.

He dropped the paper, ignoring the expectant looks from the others.

An interesting move.

The officer always had to remind himself not to underestimate his captain. Indeed, this had been unexpected. Aritomo remembered the way Inugami reacted to Balkun rather dismissive, critical, and degrading. But sometimes it was the right decision to put such a man in a position that would make him stand out from the crowd and create commitment.

In the best case.

Aritomo continued reading.

Then Inugami came to his future plans. Encouraged by the recent victory, he decided to continue the campaign immediately and not to return to Mutal. The next town on his list was Tayasal, a little further from Mutal, which would prolong his absence for some time. Only after that did he intend to take a break, to take a quick look at affairs back in Mutal before he finally incorporated the biggest chunk, the metropolis of Yaxchilan, which was only a little smaller than Mutal and which had had enough time to prepare for a defense. Possibly, however, if Tayasal turned out to be quick to conquer, the march toward Yaxchilan could be connected directly. He would inform Aritomo in due course.

Inugami's letter ended with the instruction to continue "holding the ground" in Mutal, including "firm and determined action" against "inappropriate submissions" by King Chitam, who would now return to his hometown after defeating Saclemacal.

Aritomo dropped the letter. Chitam therefore would not participate in the continuation of the punitive expedition.

Had the King given up? Did he think he was wasting his time if he continued to be used as a symbolic figure for Inugami's military maneuvers? Or did he want to take the opportunity to turn Inugami's absence into an advantage for himself? And if the latter was true – did he expect Aritomo to stand on his side and possibly openly rebel against Inugami?

Aritomo felt dark clouds brewing above him, although the day was pleasant and bright. Decisions that he had put off for a long time cast shadows on him. Aritomo had to be sure of his allies and see where his enemies were. However, he was not so sure whether the two could be so clearly distinguished from each other. Neither did he want Chitam to become the captain's puppet, nor did he want to combine his own fate with the wishes of the Mayan king.

He pocketed the letter without reacting to the curious glances of his comrades, refrained to inform them of its contents. Nobody would ask, they were all respecting the iron discipline of hierarchy. What the Captain told the First Officer was only for him until they got their orders. This kind of devotion protected Aritomo, who was faced with the possibility of having to or want to break this discipline.

He looked up.

"All is well. The captain was victorious and will continue the war. We have to continue here and await Inugami's orders."

Everyone nodded and looked satisfied. There were only a few here who questioned the Captain's plans.

Aritomo frowned, as he got up and left the accommodation. He wanted a different approach. He could make it very easy for himself. Just obey. Participate in Inugami's imperial plans. He would rule. It was inevitable that part of this empire would fall to him as a territory in which he could control and act as he wished. A very promising thought, and he was a little surprised that he did not immediately fell to this temptation.

When he left the building, four guards – two Mayan warriors and two members of the submarine crew – immediately joined him. They carried two of the few weapons they had, loaded and ready, determined to get rid of any potential threat. But today was obviously a peaceful day, for the crew of "messenger" anyway – Aritomo still had his problems with this term –, and so far no one was hostile to or behaved threatening.

His path led him to the palace, where, in the absence of the King, a council of nobles was in charge of the normal public affairs. Aritomo was familiar with these personalities in different ways, but knew that the informal presidency was occupied by the high priest Itzunami, who had been the first to receive English lessons and whose skills in that language had grown to a remarkable level since then. Aritomo, too, had not neglected his language lessons and was busy studying Maya. He didn't know if he was actually progressing as well as his teacher – an old, weathered writer who had been sent to him personally for this purpose – always claimed. But he found himself in the situation of being able to understand more and more of everyday conversations, and had already started reading simple texts that his teacher repeatedly presented to him with patient persistence. So he actually learned something, and this knowledge brought him satisfaction.

Aritomo attended the council as a silent observer. He was asked his views often enough, but he was wise in holding himself back. He deliberately did not want to act like Inugami and left the daily business to those who in all likelihood knew a lot better about it. Today, however, the preparatory work was on the plan, with which the submarine could possibly be taken from the pyramid. It was becoming increasingly apparent that the ruined temple, the never completed tomb of Chitam's father, would not withstand the constant pressure of the metal body for too long. At some point the building would sag, and there was a risk that it could cause major damage. This had to be prevented. It was not yet clear where the boat would ultimately go – maybe first into the large lake south of Mutal, at least this was the most likely solution –, but it had to get down from the temple, and as soon as possible. The other alternative was to build a new, more stable support structure under the boat, making it the city's landmark forever, an option that Lengsley and Sarukazaki now secretly preferred.

The Maya did not shy away from this challenge. They were grandiose builders who thought on a large scale. They may have underestimated the weight of the boat, but they did not consider the operation to be impossible. The plans that Lengsley, Sarukazaki and their Mayan colleagues had drawn up were reminiscent of the construction of the Egyptian pyramids, with a trundle bed made of tree trunks, with many ropes and flanges, a lot of collective muscular strength from hundreds of workers, and a gentle lowering of the boat along the slope of the ruin until it came to rest on the large square in front of the building. Not a very ambitious plan, but one for which all kinds of preparations had to be made. In the end, it wasn't even Aritomo who had to make the decision – as long as Mutal's men were mostly deployed outside the city as warriors, there was a shortage of workers anyway. Those who were still here had to take care of the endless cycle of sowing and harvesting, because this time the losses due to the absence of the soldiers would not be offset by rich tribute of conquered cities. Inugami wanted to rule, and he knew very well that it did not help his legitimacy to deprive the subjects of what was necessary, especially to expose them to hunger. Therefore they couldn't expect corn deliveries to Mutal, and accordingly the city had to continue to take care of itself.

Aritomo could easily enter the palace. Nobody dared to stop one of the messengers of the gods.

When he stepped into the throne room, which despite its pompous name seemed rather narrow and sometimes oppressive to the Japanese, some of the council members were already waiting. Aritomo immediately noticed that something was wrong – there was excitement, some faces were openly horrified, and others were angry, wildly determined to do something without being able to steer this determination in any way. When the congregation recognized Aritomo, High Priest Itzunami pulled away from the group and hurried toward him, his face covered in sweat, although it was comfortably cool here, protected by the thick sandstone walls.

"Master … have you heard the message?" he asked a little breathlessly.

"Which message? What happened?"

"The Queen! The lady Tzutz! The princesses – they're all dead!"

The Japanese paused and took a moment to digest the words and make sure that he hadn't misunderstood. Itzunami repeated, no less excited, and then Aritomo was sure to understand correctly.

He stared at Itzunami, unable to utter a word. He looked for a lie on the priest's face, but there was nothing to be seen. Dead. And

Chitam was already on the way back after defeating Saclemacal, could arrive here every day, and what only …

Dead.

"How did this happen?" he managed to say. Itzunami wrestled with his hands, an expression of pure despair.

"Murder! An assassination, a robbery! All were slaughtered. Travelers have discovered the bodies on the road, and there are other traces that they were carried into the jungle. Blood there, too. It must have been days ago, because the corpses have already been digested by animals. Some are unrecognizable."

The scope of this news rested on Aritomo like a heavy weight, and he closed his eyes for a moment.

"Are you sure they're all dead? Nobody escaped?"

"We don't know exactly how many people the Queen had with her. But her body is clearly recognized. We fear the worst for the children, but their bodies have not been found. Perhaps there is still hope and they have only been abducted. Mutal's enemies, that's for sure. But …"

Aritomo nodded. Itzunami didn't have to say anything else. The Maya were willing to wage war against each other at all times and took advantage of these occasions when the time was right for them. But the kidnapping of children, the arbitrary killing of women without directly gaining political capital – and without prior provocation? This was rather uncommon, and in Mutal's case, it was the first event of its kind. Aritomo had used the city's historical records to improve his writing skills, and also his teacher had a soft spot for history and was happy to talk about the subject extensively.

That didn't sound like the Maya.

But if that was the case, there was only one terrible alternative.

Aritomo had to sit down. But he couldn't show any weakness. He was a messenger of the gods. They never got dizzy.

"The King must be informed immediately," Itzunami said. "We're sending messengers to Saclemacal!"

"The King is already on his way back here," Aritomo answered weakly. "But yes, send the messengers, he must know as soon as possible. Are there any clues as to who is responsible for this act?"

Itzunami nodded grimly. "Yes, my lord. We found remains of clothing on site, two dead warriors who were not part of the Queen's entourage. They wore traditional costumes and symbols from those of Yaxchilan. The dead king of that city still reaches for his enemies from the underworld. There must still be scattered subjects of this unworthy man on the way, hidden in the forest, probably the exact same people who set fire to the palace. All of this fits together too well to be untrue. But we won't rest until the culprits are found. The King himself will not rest, not a minute. We're going to search the jungle, we're going to hunt them down, and we're going to wage war on anyone who gives them shelter." Itzunami looked at Aritomo inquiringly. "May I hope for the help of the messengers? Are you at Mutal's side during this difficult hour?"

The first officer made an approving gesture. How could he have refused this request? He could only dispel or confirm his own, much more terrible, suspicions if he found out the truth.

"We want to do what we can do. But don't expect miracles, priest. I am as horrified by this development as everyone else, and I am just as perplexed and desperate. The Lady Tzutz was an honorable and smart woman. Your loss weighs heavily. The King will descend into a very dark mood. Itzunami, you have to stand by his side and make sure that he doesn't make any hasty decisions. He can be very impulsive. The warriors are out of town. He has to be careful."

Itzunami laughed bitterly. "He listens to you more than me, messenger. You are the one who should speak to him. But I agree with you. Without Mutal's military power, vengeance will not be possible. Inugami himself has to take matters into his own hands and restore the city's honor."

Aritomo nodded silently.

But what if it was the same Inugami that had soiled this very honor?

A speculation, certainly nothing else. But the gnawing doubt remained. He trusted the Captain to order the death of the royal family to upset Chitam – or to blame someone who hadn't done it. Yaxchilan. How fitting. Another, even stronger motivation to take care of this metropolis, to prove the dishonor of the enemies and the moral superiority of Inugami. A double punishment, a just revenge, there was nothing better to push all of the city's warriors to their best – and with a grand victory, mapped out by the gods, initiated by the new shogun, to cement the Captain's legitimacy in a way that nobody would be able to do anything about it anymore.

Aritomo chided himself as being too hasty, too suspicious, and a fool who took conclusions out of thin air because they met his fears, perhaps also because he secretly wanted Inugami to be the man he thought he was.

This could lead to dangerous misjudgments.

"I'll write a message to Inugami myself and send a messenger," he said, and the priest nodded, obviously pleased to have someone else do the job. "You discuss everything else here, I'll go back to our house to get it done right away."

"We'll let you know as soon as we know something new."

"I'm grateful for that."

Aritomo felt dismissed, although no one would have told him so. He saved everyone the embarrassment of having to look for more words of horror or sympathy, but said goodbye immediately and hurried back to the Japanese residence. His bodyguard wasn't even surprised when he came out so quickly. The news had by now reached the soldiers, and while the two Japanese accepted the matter with equanimity, the Maya showed their dismay as well as their displeasure quite openly.

They hurried back.

Once at his destination, Lengsley was waiting for him. He too must have heard the news by now, because he immediately got down to business, pulled Aritomo aside, spoke in a lowered voice.

"What do we do?"

"Call Sawada. We have to hold council of war."

"We have to."

It took less than five minutes for the triumvirate to gather. Aritomo didn't know how to start, so he didn't object when old Sawada spoke first. His head was still buzzing. It was good if the others initiated their deliberations.

"It's a disaster," the old man said, clearly dismayed. "Inugami is going to be outraged."

Aritomo frowned. Inugami would be outraged? Even if he was not responsible for this act, he would not be particularly angry about it, but would only try to do everything in his favor.

"The death of Lady Tzutz is something that particularly infuriates the Maya, and Chitam might become completely unpredictable," he said. "We have to be careful not only of the political consequences but also of becoming victims ourselves. The assassination attempt on me shows that we don't have only friends in this city."

Sawada and Lengsley stared at Aritomo in disbelief.

"What are you talking about?" the Brit finally managed to ask.

"If Lady Tzutz was not murdered by the men of Yaxchilan –"

"I beg your pardon? The Queen is dead?" Sawada interrupted, eyes wide.

Aritomo suddenly grew cold. He took a deep breath. "Good. I notice that we may be talking past each other. I just learned that the Queen and her daughters were subjected to a cowardly attack. The Queen is dead, her daughters have disappeared. It suggests that Yaxchilan men are responsible for this act, and maybe that's true. If but –"

He paused when Lengsley grabbed his upper arm. "Aritomo," said the Brit with an urgent undertone. "It's all terrible, sure. But Sawada and I have something else to discuss with you!"

"What? What else?"

The old man raised his trembling voice. He looked so battered that Aritomo involuntarily feared that he would collapse. But the teacher kept himself with iron self-discipline.

"Isamu has disappeared," he finally said.

"I beg your pardon?"

"With notice," Lengsley added. "I wanted to tell you, but I didn't expect the Prince to act so quickly."

Aritomo groaned and put his head in his hands. The third blow. He felt things slip away from him in such a fast way that he seemed to loose whatever he wanted to hold on.

"Lengsley," he said half-desperately, half-reproachfully.

"I know. He spoke to me about it two nights ago. I only took it half seriously, the reverie of a young guy who wants to feel freedom. I wanted to discuss it with you in time, really, but there is so much to do, and we barely came across each other ... it sounds like a bad excuse, I know ..."

Sawada raised a hand and waved it off.

"If anyone is to be blamed, it is me. I have known the Prince longest and best of all of us. I should have recognized the signs much sooner. In retrospect ... yes, I see it. But before that – I should have done something earlier."

"But what?" Aritomo murmured softly, remembering his own conversation with the Prince. "But what could we have done that would do everyone justice?"

Sawada screwed up her lips.

"The Prince has duties. What his personal wishes are is second to his duty."

Aritomo sighed. That was exactly what had led to this catastrophe. But it wasn't helpful to argue with the old teacher, who, in his way, had only the best in mind for the boy.

"It worked in Japan but not here. It is not clear if what we consider to be our duty is actually valid," Lengsley said. Aritomo nodded. Sawada was not happy with this answer, but that was exactly the problem.

"When did he disappear?"

"Apparently at night. His bodyguard only noticed it now that he didn't show up for breakfast."

"Where? Are there any traces?"

Sawada and Lengsley shook their heads.

"Is he traveling alone?"

"No. His friend Ichik appears to be with him."

Friend? Aritomo hadn't even noticed Isamu had made friends. He scolded himself a fool. What stupidity. He had been careless.

And yes: Inugami would be outraged.

"We're sending search teams," he said hoarsely. "We ask the Maya for help. Sawada – we will return to the council meeting immediately."

60

"But Captain Inugami ..."

"He has to wait. We mustn't waste time now."

Sawada was silent, bowed his head, rose with Aritomo.

They hurried away. And both of them already suspected that all their actions would be in vain.

8

Inugami looked at the worm consisting of soldiers that was moving out of Saclemacal before his eyes and felt a great satisfaction as well as anger. His satisfaction was fueled by the fact that the occupation of the city had developed very well, the population was ready to accept the new rule without complaint, and Balkun, his governor, after he had overcome his surprise, proved to be active and sensible. Inugami didn't trust the man for a second and had made it clear to him that any failure, any appearance of betrayal would result in his death and that of his family in Yaxchilan, a city he was planning to conquer as part of this first campaign.

Balkun would be very careful, eager to fulfill his new master's wishes. His family was his weakness; he had spoken of them and expressed his longing once too often. Inugami was excited to see how this experiment would develop. He had to learn how to draw loyal servants to him, and he really didn't care what motivation led to their loyalty as long as it worked. Saclemacal was relatively insignificant as a city. He would be ready at any time to make an example of it if something went wrong.

Unfortunately, Inugami was bothered by the fact that Chitam did not want to participate personally in the continuation of the campaign and had already started the return journey to Mutal a few days ago was certainly one of them. Inugami knew that the King was unpredictable. As soon as he heard of his wife's death, which Inugami had threaded to fuel the Mutalese's anger at the enemies in Yaxchilan, his own suspicion would stand in the way of drawing the right conclusions and driving the war forward. In addition, the captain was not sure whether Aritomo Hara would be able to keep the king sufficiently under control. Aritomo might have been a decent officer, but he lacked bite, toughness, ruthlessness, and the self-driving discipline that every day helped Inugami focus and do the necessary things, including those that were a bit uncomfortable.

Hara, on the other hand, was not able to do this, at least not as the situation sometimes required. He had too much sympathy for the Indians, even took them really seriously, much more seriously than they were entitled to. They were children who needed guidance and a strong, punishing hand. Aritomo Hara, however, seemed to show more than reluctant respect for some aspects of their culture. That made him vulnerable. A clever Indian could take advantage of this to sneak into his trust. And then there was the Brit, this Lengsley, who had made friends with him. He didn't understand the kind of discipline Inugami thought necessary, and he infected Hara with European ideas that would only keep him off the right path.

The captain had therefore decided to do something about Lengsley. The Briton had valuable knowledge, so it would not be appropriate to simply eradicate it. But he would find employment that was appropriate to his abilities and far away from Aritomo Hara. The more his empire grew, the easier it would be to find a good opportunity to do so.

Everyone belonged in his place. And it was Captain Inugami who determined where that was.

To achieve this, Inugami first had to position himself in the right geographic position – and for that he had to push his conquest plans faster and more intensively. His devoted troop of warrior slaves would help him. Their loyalty had increased. He had allowed them to acquire personal wealth from this city's loot. He gave them young women for pleasure. They now realized that devotion and bravery paid off for them, and when one of theirs was appointed governor of this city, the bond of loyalty was tied even closer. You could go up high if you served the divine Inugami, you could be like one of the kings, achieve a position that for most of them was beyond imagination. And if the campaign went on like this, there were still many towns and villages to be distributed that needed the zealous, the submissive and above all the absolute administration, and who would Inugami entrust with these tasks other than his most loyal warriors and followers?

That's how Inugami planned it, and that's how he implemented it.

Now it was Tayasal's turn.

It had been quite amusing so far.

He had a messenger from this city executed as soon as he heard that the new king of this city asked for peace and agreed to pay great tribute. Inugami didn't care for tribute. He wanted power, and every other king was just in his way. If Tayasal surrendered without a fight and completely submitted, he would prove to be merciful and thus send a message to all other Maya: You do not have to suffer and bleed for your king. Give up, surrender and nobody should die. He was even ready to spare the king himself. In Saclemacal, he had shown that he was tough. He also had to show his mild side every now and then.

The news would make an impression, he was absolutely certain of that.

Inugami was not bloodthirsty. Unlike his general, he wasn't particularly happy about killing people. Since he would be forced to take part in the fighting himself until further notice, there was always the risk of falling victim to a lucky thrust with a spear. This was something the Captain was happy to avoid. After the conquest of Yaxchilan, he calculated, he would no longer have to lead from the front. Then his nimbus, his reputation, would be so strong that he could afford to truly take the commanding position and direct the army instead of going to battle himself.

But first of all Tayasal, which, if everything developed positively, should fall into his hand like a ripe fruit from a tree.

"My lord!"

Inugami felt startled from his daydreams. He didn't particularly appreciate that. When he worked intensively on his plans, it was sometimes like falling into a trance in which everything he was going to do became very clear. He enjoyed the anticipation of his triumphs, and then being confronted with the not so advanced reality from outside was sobering. He had to control himself not to react gruffly. He stood here watching his troops leave for Tayasal, and it was his job to be inspiring and focused, to be with his men, and not to let them see that they were little more than slaughter animals to him.

The noble who had approached him had been appointed commander of a group of messenger runners by Inugami, the core of a signaling company he was planning to set up, a special unit whose sole task was communication. It was imperative to incorporate into the new army the level of division of labor and specialization that was necessary for effective warfare, as measured by Japanese imperial standards.

"My lord!"

It was a little embarrassing that Inugami's imagination was wandering again. Oh, there was so much to think about ... "What is it?"

"A message from Mutal, my lord, from your servant Aritomo."

He was given a paper. It came from the submarine's meager supply. He stripped the leaves. The narrowly written lines in Japanese, in Aritomo Hara's well-known handwriting, were a comfort to him, simply from the sight of them. But when he started reading, his expression darkened visibly. It was not the death of Lady Tzutz that made him angry. It wasn't even the failed assassination attempt on his deputy that got him going. That was to be expected. Whoever exercised power became a target, especially when others saw their position at risk. The security measures had to be tightened and he trusted the first officer to do so, out of self-interest.

It was the last, the most important message that made Inugami's blood boil. That this warped, unwilling, stupid, characterless brat had dared to stray from the predetermined path of his life and actually believed that it had something to decide for himself – that was what shook Inugami and made him really angry.

Outwardly, he showed a mask of absolute self-control.

"Go!" he told the man. "Leave me alone!"

He was obeyed. And in this the savage was better than the noble-blooded offspring of the Emperor, who did not want to accept that his life meant accepting obligations. Obligations! What did Sawada have, what had the other teachers taught Isamu? Did nothing of it stuck in the little idiot's head? Hadn't he understood that he was a tool of higher powers, that he was the basis of a new empire, that the journey through time, their appearance here in Central America, was predetermined by the spirits in order to achieve great things?

How dare he! How dare he!

Inugami clenched his fists, crumpled the paper of the letter in his hand, and suppressed a tremor. He would teach Isamu a lesson as soon as he found him. If the animals of the forest hadn't eaten him beforehand or if an illness hadn't taken him away, which wasn't even a bad prospect anymore. And he wouldn't lift a finger to help him if the enemy got hold of him and turned to him with blackmail. No mercy for stupidity, no help for lack of discipline, no understanding of romantic ideas of freedom. He hadn't been like that at that age, his father and after him his uncle had already taken care of it, and the two strictest regiments had hardened his mind and body. There was no other way, there was no better way. He had expected nothing less from a prince of the highest blood and that was what made the disappointment he now felt so strong and penetrating.

But Prince Isamu would sooner or later learn this lesson, and it would be a very, very painful learning process, Inugami would make sure of that.

But just the thought ...

Inugami took a deep breath. He couldn't let himself go like that. Anger should not take possession of him this way. He resisted the first impulses, such as immediately traveling to Mutal himself to see that everything was done right. He had understood something very early on once he started to cement his plans for this country: he could not be everywhere. He couldn't handle everything himself. He had to surround himself with loyal followers for lower responsibilities, for the delegation of tasks, and as much as he was hurt by this knowledge, it could not only be his fellow Japanese. On the one hand, their number would be far too small if his empire continued to grow, on the other hand, despite their racial superiority, they were simply overwhelmed with tasks of rule and administration in terms of education and origin. He had to carefully select, test and deploy from the Mayan noble families, from the prudent and capable men of his warrior slaves. Inugami wanted never to lose sight of the big picture and not to get lost in small things. Isamu's disappearance was certainly not a petitesse, but on the other hand, it was just a boy who, like the captain himself, was beginning to detach himself from the habits of the time where he started this journey.

Seen in this way, Inugami stated with a certain irony that the boy's behavior was similar to his own. The captain created something new, and Isamu wanted that, too, but only for himself. The two of them were not dissimilar.

That didn't mean he wasn't going to spank the boy hard as soon as he got hold of him, prince or not. Nobody snubbed him in such a way. He found it remarkable that he also resisted the spontaneous impulse to punish Sawada or Hara. He hadn't given any special instructions to guard Isamu, which might have been a mistake.

Nobody did what you didn't do yourself. And yet he had to delegate. It was a permanent contradiction that he would never be able to resolve.

He left the roof of the building from which he had watched the marching troops. His own departure could no longer be postponed, and Tayasal was a few days away. It would be a long time before the fight for the city could begin seriously, and he couldn't go back now. He considered writing a letter to his deputy immediately but rejected the thought. Only if he returned to Mutal with the strongest prestige and the highest legitimization, before his decisive campaign against Yaxchilan, would he personally take care of this concern, and then with determined hardness and the strongest will. At that time, he had decided, the task was to eliminate Chitam and finally put Mutal under his rule, if not as a shogun then as an emperor.

For Inugami that was ultimately the same.

9

"We lost them, but we're on course."

Langenhagen dropped the binoculars and handed them to Köhler. Both had struggled to keep an eye out for the other ships in their small fleet, looking in all directions for the past half hour, and neither had seen anything.

"We will try to contact them as soon as we have the shortwave transmitter back in operation," Köhler said confidently. "If they all pass on their location, we can arrange a course that will bring us back together."

The storm had not only torn off the antenna of their radio, the entire, complicated structure had been dismantled by the two radio operators before the start of the heaviest waves and stowed in boxes lined with wool. The extremely sensitive tubes in particular, which were currently handcrafted with a reject factor of 90 percent, were almost irreplaceable, so that their fate was not left to chance. It took a while for the device to be reassembled and tested, and it would be no different on the other ships of the expedition. The storm had swept them apart, despite the better controls the steam engines allowed. Köhler and Langenhagen only hoped that all ships had survived this hurricane without major damage.

In any case, the *Gratianus* had proven to be stable, the crew professional and disciplined. There had been minor injuries to the ship and seafarers, but nothing that could not be remedied quickly using on-board means. The calmer weather, the occasional sunshine, and the realization that the storm would only add a few more days to the crossing, which they had estimated to be around twenty-five days, had contributed to the overall positive mood. Everyone congratulated themselves on their bravery. The relief was almost palpable. The storm had welded crew and ship together, especially integrating the many newcomers on board. Seen this way, the hurricane had been a good thing, Köhler was ready to admit.

But one shouldn't wish for too much of a good thing either. If the journey would now end without further problems, Köhler would not complain. Although he was now convinced of its effects, he felt no need to taste the murderous herbal drink of the ship's doctor again. He wanted to keep this pleasure for very special occasions.

"Then we should hope for good weather for the rest of the trip. We can't do anything else anyway," said Langenhagen, packing the valuable binoculars into the leather case. The development of the optical industry had made a really big leap with the arrival of time-wanderers. The glass that was made in the empire was no longer a privilege for the super-rich, but was increasingly becoming the everyday commodity from which windows and containers were made. Small businesses founded by graduates with excellent training had settled near the Ravenna Academy, and two of them had specialized in the manufacture of binoculars, primarily for military purposes, as well as spectacle lenses. So far, not many people with short-sighted or far-sightedness could afford a corrective lens, the production was still too complex for that. But here too everyone was confident that developments in the future would make this blessing generally accessible to all those with poor eyesight. Köhler knew that Langenhagen put on such a glass when he had to read longer texts, and otherwise kept it carefully padded in his cabin. As someone who had grown up near the Academy with his father and who had trained in it as a naval officer, Köhler was used to always being confronted with the latest developments. Others, especially those in the more remote provinces of the empire, were only gradually enjoying these changes. This led to resistance and fear, and persuasion was not always successful. It was an arduous process that faced many challenges.

That would change once the railroad started operating. When Köhler left the empire, the first track from Ravenna to Rome was about to be completed. A second from Ravenna to Milan was planned. It was probably already in operation when he returned home. Once the provinces were connected to this new form of transport, social and economic change would take place very quickly.

And, Köhler was also certain: the empire would start to stink badly. As someone who ran a steamship, he knew pretty much what to expect.

He took a deep breath and took in the spicy sea air. Better to enjoy this while he could. He cherished the blessing of the steam engine, but anyone with any degree of observation had to acknowledge that as soon as the cities were full of them, they would pollute the air. Even his father, a great fan of progress, had enough in the last years of his life. They had left the growing industrial belt around Ravenna and bought themselves a beautiful house in the country, peaceful and secluded, calm – and without any stench other than the exhalations of humans and animals.

Köhler, who had inherited the building together with his siblings, quickly decided with them to keep the beautiful country house. It was now used by the whole family as a refuge from the rampant conglomerate of Ravenna, where most of them, however, continued to make their living. Horst's older sister Annelie worked as a teacher at the Academy and was considered a great specialist in plants, married to another master of the same specialization. They had a graduate of their studies on board this expedition. And his brother Josephus had gone into politics and was currently serving the empire as ambassador in Aksum, the empire in northeast Africa, which had proven to be a very reliable partner of Rome over the past decades – and whose upswing was almost as meteoric as Rome's, partly due to this friendship. The officer hadn't seen his brother in years. He hoped he was fine. He heard that Aksum had also started to stink since the first Roman steam engines were put into operation there. It was obviously a process that no one could stop.

"Is your stomach okay?"

Aedilius had joined him while the captain had gone below deck. The doctor seemed to enjoy the fresh breeze and the pleasant weather as much as the first officer, and he was long through with his first round of treatments for the injured. Köhler admired the medicus' stamina. He had worked hard the whole time and hardly rested, and yet he was not only in a good mood but also exuded untamed energy. Köhler could only show respect for the older man.

70

"I'm fine. All meals stay where they belong," he replied with a smile and nodded to Aedilius, who himself held a steaming mug of hot but diluted wine. "I can only thank you again."

Aedilius smiled back and shook his head.

"But that's not enough for me. I demand that you take my medicine right away in the next storm. You're an old seaman, Köhler, and I can't quite believe that you've been on the ropes in every storm in your career so far."

Köhler tried to exude an appropriate sense of guilt. "No, but I had seldom seen such strong hurricanes. This is my first major voyage outside of coastal waters. These are storms of a magnitude only a few Roman seamen have been allowed to experience so far. I am sure that our comrades who navigate to Asia and around Africa will also be surprised by many unforeseen things."

"The time-wanderers described the weather conditions in detail in their notes. And my esteemed colleagues on the other expeditions have the same resources as I do – just hopefully less stubborn shipmates."

"It is one thing to read a text and to imagine reality, the other to experience it."

Aedilius nodded and took a sip of wine. "That is probably true. So what kind of reality will we confront in America?"

Köhler was grateful for the change of subject. It was no pleasure to be constantly reminded of one's own stupidity. "If we believe the reports of the time-wanderers, which are scarce on the subject, the indigenous population is most developed in the central part of the continent and in the south. That is why we are heading for Central America."

"That's not what I meant. As I said, I read it too. But as you said, the time-wanderers also admitted that they knew very little about that region during this time. So we're real explorers."

"We surely are."

"So what do you expect?"

Köhler shook his head. "Medicus, we have supplies on board, horses, maps, and we are very well armed. We expect the worst and hope for the best."

"No personal thoughts, first officer?"

Köhler didn't know how to deal best with the mockery in Aedilius's voice. The man was known for his wit and his jokes were not always clearly recognizable as such. And not everyone understood his sense of humor. Köhler was ready to laugh, but he considered himself to be a very serious person. Perhaps this was the reason why the doctor liked to try his jokes on him: to lure him out of his cage of seriousness. Köhler appreciated the attempt, but he found that the medicus was better off to choose another victim, an opinion he kept for himself. He would probably need Aedilius one day, and it was better if the man who held the operating knife liked him.

"I have a lot of personal thoughts, Aedilius," he said in a steadily friendly tone. "But to share them is not my intention. They do not guide my actions or my motivation. I live in reality, in the now, and when the future comes, I will deal with it. I am part of a large crew, and our commander is an intelligent man. I will give my opinion on facts, but I will not get lost in speculation."

"Those who are able to deal with different facets of the future are mentally prepared for surprises." Aedilius said this with a certain tone, he seemed to think it was his motto in life.

"If one has enough imagination. If speculations are based on experience, they either remain vague or too predictable to serve as preparation."

"You lack imagination?"

"I lack experience. I have no comparison. Every imagination seems idle to me, Medicus. What about you? Are you imagining all the terrible diseases you will be confronted with?"

Aedilius laughed. "No. On the one hand, I already know many of these diseases, because the time-wanderers had traveled widely and their medical manuals, which Magister Neumann came up with, describe symptoms and causes in great detail. On the other hand, I rather hope for the positive: new medicines, new active ingredients, new ointments, new treatment methods. I am not only on this expedition as a doctor, my friend, I am also here to learn." He slapped Köhler on the shoulder. "But I like your perspective. It calms me down."

72

Köhler raised his eyebrows. "That surprises me."

"You are the first officer. I expect you to calm me down."

Köhler patted his stomach. "Then I owe you something."

The doctor raised his cup. "Life is business, my friend. And a money lender never forgets a loan. Even if he never claims it back."

With that, he turned and walked across the deck.

Köhler watched him and shook his head. Getting to know this man was as interesting and unpredictable as the journey to mysterious Central America.

10

Une rose, suddenly torn from sleep. She wiped her weary eyes, in which sleep and the remnants of her tears mingled. Her heart pounded. Since the queen's death and the disappearance of her nieces, she has slept very restlessly, battered by wild dreams, by sudden bouts of fear and foreboding. She felt the sweat on her neck and on her forehead, which was now getting cold, and picked up a cloth that she kept next to her bed, moistened it with water, wiped her face. She didn't know where the dreams came from and whether they meant anything. So far, she had hardly told anyone about it.

The guards in front of her apartments had been reinforced, all reliable men, but she just couldn't calm down. Was she simply scared? It seemed to be more than that. The picture of Tzutz stood before her eyes as if she were still alive, and from every corner, in every room, she thought she heard the laughter of Ixchel and her little sister Nicte. It had been a mistake not to escape the city with Tzutz, she told herself, even though she couldn't have done anything against determined assassins. In fact, she had behaved correctly and survived, but instead of bringing joy to her, the insight led to reproaches and feelings of guilt that she could not explain. So she slept badly, cried often, sometimes all of a sudden and out of the blue. The fact that she had been able to fall asleep last evening was certainly due to the comforting presence of Lengsley, who visited her every free minute and often just held her in his arms in the past few days, giving her silent reassurance. What should he have said or done anyway?

It was hard enough that everyone had started whispering about her relationship with Lengsley. Une Balam was not married, so the relationship was basically tolerated, especially since her people had a more relaxed relationship with sex. Nevertheless, she was a princess and currently the highest of her family in the city. If Chitam died, too, she would be the natural successor, the new queen, and that was possibly the perspective that made her most afraid. She had never had to seriously consider this perspective in her life. She would probably let one of Chitam's brothers go first if it got that far. She was not a queen. And she had no king. Her eyes fell gently on the sleeping figure of the Brit.

Of course, that wasn't true. She had a king, but the Maya would not accept him. Women of their class married the highest nobility or the princes of other cities. The status of the messengers was not yet clear. They worked and sweated like normal people, did not behave like exalted nobility. Lengsley, in particular, was tirelessly seen in the workshops and construction sites, giving advice, lending a hand, driven by the need to pass on his knowledge and experience to those who were eager to learn. Une Balam heard the grumbling of some priests who spoke of the "old ways" and "good traditions," but so far Lengsley had never interfered in spiritual questions. He did not think about these things very much, and that was his luck, because he hardly offered a target for the most important group of the Mutalesian nobility, the clergy. One day, Une expected, the messengers would find a place in the hierarchy of Mutal, their nobility defined, their role embedded in the structure of the universe. Then it would no longer be unusual for a princess to be close to such a man.

But now they didn't make a big deal of it. Everyone knew about it. Everyone tolerated it. Who would speak openly against the messengers? The assassination attempt on Aritomo showed that in case of doubt, the displeasure was not expressed in words. Nothing that helped soothe the fear in her heart. She was young. She was in love with a strange, fascinating man who knew things and thought in a way that she found absolutely irresistible. She didn't want to lose any of that. She wanted a happy future, a big family. She wanted children, ready to learn from her father all the secrets he knew. A very, very extraordinary family, a spectacular perspective, a nobility of a special kind, the nobility not only of origin but of knowledge.

Une Balam took a deep breath and let it escape intermittently, not yet a sigh but a discharge of tension and pain, and foreboding. Not quiet enough to protect Lengsley's sleep, who moved, turned, blinked, and saw in the dim glow of the nocturnal log fire the outline of Une's sitting upright and apparently staring into space.

"Bad dream?"

He still spoke her language awkwardly, although she studied with him at least as often as they did ... other things.

"I just woke up," she lied halfheartedly. It was difficult for her to lie to him. Until further notice, his still weak language skills helped her, but at some point she would no longer be able to use it as a shield against her feelings. Her otherwise convincing acting skills sometimes failed with this man, or they simply weren't enough. At least that was true for those phases when she felt really bad. Suddenly her ability to steer the man on the path she wished him was taken away.

Lengsley frowned, raised on one arm, and cocked his head as he continued to look at her. "You're scared, and there's nothing I can do about it," he said in English now. Une had learned this language much better than he did hers, and it became the basis of her communication when the man wanted to communicate more than his need for food, drink or to be allowed to touch her breasts. "I feel pretty helpless. I'd like to make promises to you, but I'm bad at it. I can't guarantee your safety, nobody can. I can only tell you that I will protect you as best I can."

Une smiled softly. She appreciated Lengsley's honesty, a quality that made him feel right in comparison to many other men she had met. However, she had to admit that as a member of the royal family she had met only a very limited number and above all a limited quality of men, as everyone saw in her the sister of the king and far less a woman for whom one would have to express feelings. The latter was inherently difficult for men anyway, and Lengsley was no exception. It had taken a while for her to get him so far, at least once in a while, to verbally step out of himself. He was still not very good at it, so she enjoyed the few moments when he succeeded.

"I don't expect miracles from you."

"But I'd like to do some."

"The gods are responsible for that."

Lengsley put on an expression of mock indignation.

"I am a messenger of the gods!"

Une laughed softly and shook her head.

"Unfortunately, that's not enough."

Lengsley grimaced and sat down properly, hands on his lap. Both looked out of the window at the same time, which here, from the second floor of the building, afforded a beautiful view of the sky.

"The sun is going to rise soon," the man said, stroking Une's bare back, but more absent-minded, like an instinctive activity, with no purpose. "Chitam is expected to return. What are you going to tell him?"

Une looked at him questioningly.

"Do you think he'll need my advice?"

Lengsley shook his head as if he couldn't believe she was asking such a question.

"That's what I'm expecting. He will be overwhelmed with anger and grief. He'll look for someone to exact his revenge on."

"Yaxchilan is to blame."

Lengsley nodded slowly, cautiously, not enthusiastic enough for Une's taste.

"You doubt it?" she asked.

The Englishman said nothing at first, then softly: "I just wouldn't be so sure, Une."

It was an answer that troubled her and drove any tiredness out of her thoughts. She knew Lengsley well enough to understand when he was serious or something was bothering him. But in such situations it was sometimes difficult to persuade him to be open.

"What do you suspect?"

"I don't have anything tangible. I'm just afraid that ..."

"Speak."

"It's hard for me."

Une turned so that she could look directly into his eyes without turning her neck and saw that her bare breasts were not drawing his attention. Something had to worry him a lot if he didn't respond to what he usually couldn't get enough of. She took a deep breath, but that didn't trigger the expected response either.

Now she was worried, too. Really worried.

"What if those from Yaxchilan are not responsible – but someone who would like to blame them in order to increase the motivation for war?", he said.

"That ... you can't mean ..."

"You are as clever as you are beautiful."

"Inugami? I don't want to say it out loud."

"It's better to whisper."

"But such an act ... if Chitam should find out ... Inugami endangers everything he has built up in mutual trust and loyalty!"

Lengsley sighed and lowered his hand, which was still caressing her back.

"This man doesn't think that way. He wants to eradicate Chitam as a political factor. A lonely king, tortured by the pain of his loss. Someone who only thinks of revenge and nothing else. Inugami as a level-headed, clearly thinking military leader, as someone who combines revenge with a plan, forges the idea of an empire. Chitam as a puppet, as a symbol, eventually as nothing at all. Of course, Inugami has to deal with the disappearance of Isamu, whom he wanted to build as a replacement. But on the other hand, I trust him either to make himself king – or to use another symbolic figure."

Lengsley gave Une a long look.

"A weak woman, for example, who is just regarded as someone looking good, able to perform rituals, to bless the leaders, and to give birth to obedient children."

Une put a hand over her mouth as if frightened by something. "You don't talk about me?"

"I say what I think. It's difficult enough for me. But you should be dealing with certain things that I cannot protect you from. Inugami has power, and if he conquers Yaxchilan, he rules four cities – and it won't be the last. If his army of warrior slaves grows – and he'll make sure of it, I assure you –, he'll have a power base that is insurmountable. The other Mayan cities have nothing to oppose this type of organized, large-scale and long-term strategic warfare."

"They don't?"

Une Balam frowned. Lengsley was not like Inugami and some of his comrades. He neither looked down at the Maya, nor did he consider them to be savages. His love for Une had certainly made a big contribution to this. But he still seemed, perhaps subconsciously, to underestimate the Mayan abilities.

She put a hand on his arm and looked at him seriously.

"The kings of the other cities are no fools. They will watch closely what is happening here. And they will react. Inugami doesn't even know what kind of storm can build against him. I would not be surprised if a first alliance of the other cities is already discussing countermeasures at this moment. Mutal is full of spies. They will have reported everything, in clear language. And then there's still a player that Inugami is definitely not considering."

"Who could that be?"

"Teotihuacán. The city from which our dynasty originated. The city to which I can trace my own bloodline. The biggest, the most powerful city of them all."

Lengsley looked at Une in confusion. "I have never heard of it."

Une didn't like to believe that but realized that there had been little reason to direct the conversation to it, especially for Lengsley, who usually dealt with other things. For Une, Teotihuacán was part of her own history and anchored as an eternal constant in the minds of many Maya.

"You will hear from it, I will bet on that. It may take some time fort hem to become aware of what is happening here, but once the King of Teotihuacán's eyes turn to us, your Inugami should have a power base that is really worth it – otherwise we will be crushed under the feet of the soldiers from the big city before we can blink, fire sticks and the metal ship or not. The armies of the Divine Ruler are not known to shy away from challenges, my beloved. Their will is strong, their weapons are deadly, and they are many. Inugami's greatest danger would be if Teotihuacán allied with other Mayan states. Such an army the world would never have seen before."

Lengsley shook his head slowly, incredulously, as if he did not want to admit the terrible scenario Une Balam was presenting to him.

"You keep thinking, and you're smarter than I thought," he said softly, pulling the princess' body toward him. "I have to apologize to you for both my arrogance and my lack of trust."

"We're still getting to know each other."

"You would be a great queen."

"You would be a perfectly acceptable king."

Lengsley laughed. "I would be an appalling king."

"The structures of your rule would be more stable," she said with a serious expression. "You shouldn't underestimate that."

Lengsley kissed her cheek. "The sun hasn't risen yet," he whispered. His attention was now back to where Une Balam had been expecting it all the time, as soon as he had spoken about his worries and opened up to her.

She found that he deserved a reward and moved his right hand invitingly to her chest.

And Lengsley was ready to be rewarded.

11

Mutal was big, and in a way it was home.

Inocoyotl smiled at the thought, as he saw the first outline of the metropolis through the morning mist. They had marched hard, and the soldiers of the Divine Ruler had proven themselves worthy companions. No word of complaint had come over her lips, no groaning or shaking their heads when Inocoyotl had ended the all too short night's sleep. It was clear to everyone that the ambassador of the Divine was among them. Because of his position, he could have insisted that he be carried in a palanquin, but Inocoyotl felt neither sublime nor frail enough for it. So if the old man set such a pace, who should complain about the hard march?

It had become clear to everyone that the more general exploratory expedition to maintain neglected diplomatic contacts had become something else and that their protégé, commissioned directly by the God King, did not drive them forward for no reason. His success was their test, and not one of the men under Queca's command wanted to be accused of failing to meet expectations.

As if the officer had noticed that Inocoyotl had thought of him, he appeared next to the ambassador.

"Should I send a messenger ahead?"

"No. Let all the signs and banners be raised, let us march loudly and audibly, and let us show the greatest discipline. Teotihuacán does not announce himself. We once conquered this city and appointed its ruler, whose successor is now on the throne. This city owes us respect, and if it doesn't show it, we'll know where we're at."

"Yes, my lord!"

This answer was entirely to Queca's taste, Inocoyotl could see that. With this approach, he took a calculated risk. If these strange messengers of the gods reigned the city indeed, their reaction would show whether they were willing to take political considerations into account or whether they acted in a grandeur that gave an outlook on their future behavior. In that case, there was only hope that they could get away alive.

When they approached the city at a steady pace and the first families on the outskirts of the city were awakened from their sleep by their march, Inocoyotl was able to take a look at the mysterious object that was perched on a pyramid in the city center that had not yet been completed. At first, the view was only occasionally possible; when they entered the wide access road that would lead them straight to the center, it was hard to miss. It spoke for the men from Teotihuacán that they neither stopped and showed confusion, nor began to question their orders. Their march did not slow down and the discipline did not weaken. The searching looks that kept falling on the mighty, black appearance were filled with doubts and sometimes fear. Inocoyotl himself felt a certain feeling of anxiety. It was one thing to be provided with agent's reports about this miracle and the seemingly fantastic development, it was quite another to be able to convince oneself of the truth. No exaggeration but reality – and it didn't need any verbal decoration. Even the king of Teotihuacán, Inocoyotl was now certain, would be impressed by this ... thing, whatever it was supposed to represent.

And it became clear to him that until now he had been secretly hoping that the rumors and stories would turn out to be exactly that, only rumors, which on closer inspection turned out to be absurd. A hope that he had not become aware of and that he now noticed where it was disappointed. It would have made everything a lot easier if the King of Mutal had simply become a little megalomaniac. One could got along with that.

The closer they marched, the more the damage from the fight against the soldiers from Yaxchilan was visible. A lot had been repaired, and construction sites were still recognizable. Of course, there was destruction during a battle, but the fact that entire walls of palaces had collapsed ... that was rather unusual, unless the builders had already made major mistakes in the construction, which Inocoyotl did not want to expect from Mutal.

A great force had left these traces and once again underpinned the reports he had read. His disappointment was now almost palpable.

Then the first men in the city came straight up to them, some with sleep in their eyes. Inocoyotl recognized priests and high-ranking nobles, hurriedly dressed up to receive the noble guest, and an honor guard who was seen to have been recruited from a night watch and was in urgent need of rest as well.

Inocoyotl hid a smile. The effort deserved respect. He had wanted to provoke this or a comparable reaction. And it was probably not the intention of the city's elders to immediately throw him to the gods for food. That was comforting.

He saw only the familiar faces of Mutal's residents, no one unusual. There was apparently none of the messengers among the small group of notables that greeted him. Of course, he didn't know exactly how to recognize them, but the agent reports said they were distinctly different from the Maya.

Maybe they waited in the background.

Maybe they just hadn't woken up yet.

Messengers of the gods who got up late and enjoyed sleeping in immediately lost their spiritual significance.

A lean priest came to meet him, bowed low, and spread his arms.

"Itzunami from Mutal greets the visitor from Teotihuacán!"

Inocoyotl nodded slowly. "Inocoyotl, Messenger of the Divine Ruler, greets the children of the city!"

Itzunami didn't even flinch when Inocoyotl called him the "child of the city." Even though Teotihuacán's sovereignty over Mutal was based only on historical events that had long been forgotten by many, it was clear that someone at a higher hierarchical level visited one below him. This did not mean that a King of Mutal would take any orders without good cause. It just said that the protocol was followed as long as it didn't cost too much.

In any case, Itzunami seemed to be of the correct opinion that politeness was not a major investment and that one could therefore dispense it freely, an attitude that Inocoyotl shared.

"Your visit is both a joy and a surprise," said the priest, waiting for his companions to complete all of their bows before continuing.

"Our king is out of town. In his absence, this council rules. I can speak for him in all modesty. But soon Chitam will return, and you can confer with him directly. Until then, let us cater for you."

Inocoyotl nodded. The notables that had met him here were not just nobles. They were the city's current rulers. But what role did the messengers of the god play? Had the spies exaggerated in their descriptions?

"I'm coming unannounced but not unintentionally," Inocoyotl replied, waving toward the black device beginning to cast a shadow in the morning sun. "The news of strange events has reached the ear of the Divine Ruler," he lied on, without flinching. "I was sent to marvel at the miracle and report to my master. I hope Mutal will not be burdened with that."

"How can a visit from our older brothers be a burden?" Itzunami replied smoothly, picking up on the family issue the emissary had started with, just with the nuance that he made the residents of Mutal not younger children but younger siblings, a note that Inocoyotl didn't miss. He smiled contentedly. The old priest did not play the game badly, and he was always happy when he came across a worthy interlocutor. He bowed out of genuine respect for the delegation. Indeed, these were Teotihuacán's children.

"I'm ready to be enlightened about the events by you, if you like to," he said. "The king is gone, you say?"

"We expect him back every day. He was on a campaign against our neighbors in Saclemacal. You must have heard of the cowardly attack by that alliance led by cursed Yaxchilan. Saclemacal was one of them and received the just punishment."

"I'm glad to hear that," said Inocoyotl in a neutral tone. When Itzunami uttered the name of Yaxchilan, his hatred had been clearly audible, neither masked by diplomatic restraint nor by courtesy to the guest. Whatever had happened here, Inocoyotl was certain that Yaxchilan was due and that no one would be able to prevent the Mutalese from executing their revenge. There was nothing wrong with that – as long as the previous customs were adhered to. Conquer, loot, appoint a subservient ruler, agree on a tribute, withdraw. If

84

nothing more than that happened, Mutal was in its rights and didn't need to be blamed.

"You are warmly welcome in the new palace. It is still under construction, but we will definitely be able to offer you a suitable guest quarters."

"The old palace –"

"Has burned out and will be destroyed."

Inocoyotl raised his eyebrows. This detail hadn't been in the reports, so it must have been recent. "A fire got out of control?"

"Arson."

"What happened?"

Itzunami made a face. "A first attempt ultimately failed. But a second attempt was successful. We mourn the death of the queen and the disappearance of the two princesses." He looked openly at Inocoyotl. "When the king returns, he may not be in a good mood, and it may well be that his company is not as pleasant as you expect. If this happens, I would like to apologize for it already."

Inocoyotl was calm. Events developed quickly and obviously not going for the better. It was the right decision to travel here and get an idea of the situation.

"I offer my sincere condolences to the people of Mutal," he said and tried to give his thoughtful expression a glimpse of grief. "A shameful act, and I pray that the cowardly perpetrators will be brought to justice."

"Thank you. If you want to follow me."

Inocoyotl, along with Itzunami, trotted toward a large building, some of which was still under construction, which gave an idea of the likely outline of its completion, but which still had a lot to be done. After all, in addition to the still blackened remains of the burned-out part, a new audience hall had been erected, and Inocoyotl saw with satisfaction that the city leaders had used the welcoming conversation to press ahead with the preparations for his reception. In any case, a new guard of honor was selected, and the scent of the opened kitchens suggested that work on a proper meal had already begun.

They entered the audience room. Like all Maya rooms, it was relatively narrow. At its head was an orphaned throne waiting for its king. In addition to Itzunami, some members of the welcoming committee had gathered, while Inocoyotl had only asked for Queca to come with them. He gave up a bodyguard as a sign of his trust in his family here in Mutal.

And then he met the first messenger of the gods – or rather two, who were also waiting in the hall and who were immediately recognizable as strangers by their appearance and clothing. Inocoyotl was introduced to a young and an old man, both of whom wore tight-fitting garments that precisely encircled their limbs. The young man's clothing was additionally decorated with all kinds of symbols that hardly interrupted the monotony. The old man wore black robes that were devastatingly uniform and gave him a very austere appearance. Both of them demanded respect by their appearance alone, but Inocoyotl was warned not to attach importance to such things too much.

"This is Aritomo Hara, second of the messengers of the gods. His master, the captain of the black vessel, is on the campaign that I have already told you about," Itzunami introduced the younger one. The man named Hara bowed, showed insecurity in the presence of the guest, and didn't look half as superior and powerful as one might have imagined.

"The messengers fight for Mutal?" Inocoyotl said. He did not miss the brief hesitation before the priest answered.

"Yes, they fight with us and have brought us victory, twice already," Itzunami said then, and although it sounded honest – and according to the envoy's knowledge it was –, Inocoyotl felt that this was not the whole truth.

"Here is Master Sawada, the great teacher," was the old man's turn.

"I greet the envoy from Teotihuacán," the man said in slightly broken Maya, and bowed. "I'm excited to learn about your city."

Inocoyotl felt no distrust here. If Sawada was the great teacher, then he was also the great student, because he believed that one went with the other. Sawada's interest was sincere, and Inocoyotl's only problem was that these "messengers" pretended to know nothing or very little about his city, a fact that was really hard to believe. Teotihuacán was known, respected and feared all over the world. What kind of gods were they who didn't even give their emissaries the most necessary information along the way?

"I'll be happy to answer your questions," he said with a noncommittal tone and was finally asked to sit on a stone bench.

Itzunami knew exactly what was expected of him. In the emerging silence, he began to describe the events of the past weeks and months before the visits. He tried to avoid overly wild exaggeration. His voice remained calm and composed, even when he described the battle for Mutal and the share of the messengers in the victory over the men of Yaxchilan. Inocoyotl listened without interrupting him even once. He did not get the impression that the priest was prone to lies. The fact that much of it absolutely corresponded to the contents of the spy-reports that had been presented to him only reinforced this impression. The priest was finished after half an hour. He looked at the ambassador, as if he expected a lot of questions, but the man thanked him kindly for the report and immediately turned to Aritomo Hara and Sawada, who had remained silent and unmoved. Since they had not protested the priest's descriptions, Inocoyotl had to assume that they were in favor of the priest's point of view and that he believed that he had told everything accurately.

He knew that a response was now expected from him, and he struggled with it. All of this was disconnected from all of his previous experience, and he had no idea what his ruler would do in this situation. Only if Mutal turned against the divine city with the messengers leading them did the matter become clear: Nobody attacked Teotihuacán with impunity, nobody who was reasonable would even try it.

Inocoyotl looked closely at Aritomo and Sawada. They looked like people who knew what they were doing. Both made a calm and deliberate impression, and if they spoke at all, and in contrast to Itzunami, they apparently did not like to relate to deities, providences, and apparitions. Aritomo reminded him, in a way, of Queca, with his pragmatic and goal-oriented manner, and Sawada, in turn, reminded him of his own teachers, who were generous with their knowledge but otherwise left it up to their students to draw the right conclusions from what they had learned.

Yes, they were all quite sane.

Inocoyotl urged to ask a question, but not here in public. It would be interpreted as blasphemy, and he was already known for his critical attitude toward his own deities, tolerated because he was useful, but certainly not here in Mutal, where he apparently walked in the presence of heavenly figures.

He would ask his question once the opportunity arose.

Nevertheless, he now reported from his city and satisfied genuine curiosity. What happened in and around Teotihuacán was important, and it was gratefully accepted to be brought up to date. What the envoy had to report was not half as exciting as what Itzunami said, but out of courtesy no one dared to interrupt his presentation. Since Inocoyotl was not prone to praise his master consistently and kept the report short, the exchange was soon over.

It almost surprised him that his request for a personal conversation with the messengers was accepted without any problems. But since they did not refuse, the Mutalese were probably not able to guard their access to the strange visitors. Something like jealousy sparkled in the eyes of some councilors when Sawada agreed to take Inocoyotl to the metal vehicle of the messengers and allow him access. The envoy knew he had to be careful. Under no circumstances should he give the impression that he wanted to take "their" messengers away from the Mutalese.

Still, he would ask Sawada if they really were emissaries of heavenly powers – or if there was a more profane explanation for their origins. He didn't know if the old man would answer him, but the question had to be asked – just not in public, and certainly not in the presence of a priest who obviously owed his exalted position to the fact that he was particularly well connected to the mysterious visitors.

Before another discussion could develop, a servant burst into the session, drawing everyone's attention. He only showed the absolutely necessary minimum level of courtesy when he threw himself on the floor in front of Itzunami. The fact that a highly respected guest was present seemed to have escaped him completely. But before anyone could reprimand him for his behavior, he already told what he had to report.

His message was not alarming or unexpected, but it ended the conversation quickly, which Inocoyotl found accommodating.

King Chitam had been spotted approaching the outskirts of Mutal with his retinue and bodyguard. It was as if the envoy's presence was forgotten, and everyone could see the nervousness caused by the king's arrival. He returned to the city, which had now been stripped of her queen, and no one could foresee what state of mind he was in. Preparations for the envoy's reception were therefore immediately changed to those for the appropriate greeting of Chitam, and Inocoyotl considered it advisable to withdraw into the background and not stand in anyone's way. He and Queca were not asked to leave the site, but no more attention was paid to them.

He was pleasantly surprised when Sawada spoke to him.

"My lord Inocoyotl, it will take more than an hour until the king arrives here and is available to you. Do you want to follow my invitation and take a look at the boat?"

The envoy was somewhat irritated when Sawada described the divine vehicle with a word he would have given to a simple dugout, but he would not be discussing it now, therefore agreed eagerly, a little bit happy to escape the hustle and bustle, and when he did so, he asked to be allowed to grant Queca this honor, too, a request which was immediately granted. Sawada led the two men out of the audience hall, and they soon found themselves confronted with the ascent over the ruins of the temple, up to the makeshift platform that had been built to the side of the tower, which Sawada said led inside the black monster. Inocoyotl looked up and felt respect, a little fear, and curiosity at the same time. It was no wonder that this vehicle was attributed to the gods. Had it appeared in Teotihuacán, it would have been given the same meaning. How would Meztli have reacted?

They stopped at the top of the platform. Inocoyotl looked down at the square. He touched the black metal with one hand, it was warm, like a living animal. His eyes fell on the huge, iron atlatl, which had caused so much destruction, and here, in the immediate vicinity of the apparition, he began to believe the stories. This was out of this world, and so the question remained, where did it actually come from?

Certainly not from the gods. With every minute he talked to Sawada, his conviction solidified that he was not dealing with heavenly messengers here but with ordinary mortals, of mysterious origins, but otherwise no flesh and blood like himself.

So it was certainly not wrong to speak to him directly without being in danger of being instantly struck by lightning.

"Master Sawada," he said after a pause. "You are not really messengers of the gods, is that correct?"

Sawada looked at him and it seemed as if he wanted to smile, an emotion that he suppressed at the last moment. Then he nodded. "Our friends in Mutal get along well with this idea. Whether everyone believes in it or whether it is just a simple explanation of a much more difficult reality to describe – I will leave that open."

"Itzunami believes it?"

"He believes what suits him."

"What benefits him."

"It's about the same thing, I think."

Inocoyotl was now the one who smiled without wanting to hide it. Whether sent by gods or not, the man was to his taste. In any case, he did not look threatening, although the envoy knew that such an impression could easily be deceived.

"So no messengers of gods?"

Sawada gestured with his shoulders.

"Ultimately, a strange fate brought us here. If one assumes that such incidents were predetermined by heavenly powers, as a test or purely by divine arbitrariness, we are in a way sent, but without a message, without a mission and, I honestly say, without supernatural powers." He slapped the metal body of the boat with the palm of his hand. "This is a fish without water. We built it, with our hands, with tools that we left behind in our homeland. It is a craft superior to everything the Maya and, at the risk of insulting you, everything your people know."

90

"You are not insulting me," said Inocoyotl. "But don't say it too loud when my king is around."

"I'll remind myself."

"So tell me the truth, and I don't want to hold it against you: Where are you from – and how did your fish fall out of the water onto the roof of a temple?"

Sawada told him in clear words, and Inocoyotl was amazed at the level of ignorance the "messengers of the gods" showed about the circumstances of their arrival. They came from a distant time, and it was unclear to them how they had made the trip. They were victims of the circumstances, toys played by an inscrutable fate, and as far as the gods were concerned, they had not yet taken pity on explaining the background – or even the rules of the game – to mortals.

Inocoyotl had no reason to doubt Sawada's account and felt his mistrust of the official interpretation of what had happened confirmed. That didn't make things easier, of course. If the newcomers were normal people, only blessed with exceptional knowledge and sophisticated weapons, it was dangerous, because they did not follow divine advice but made their own plans. Inocoyotl was old and smart enough to know what that was going to mean. Sawada was very careful about the intentions and plans of the messengers of the gods and repeatedly referred to their leader, the man named Inugami.

For some reason, Inocoyotl worried even more.

Then he entered the inside of the vehicle and found it to be tight and oppressive. The strange smell was irritating, and although Sawada explained many things to him, the meaning of it all eluded him. He admitted that he was happy to be back outside after a short stay. To actually accomplish a long journey in such a thing, he imagined as laborious and dangerous.

When they had brought their conversation to an end, the envoy was at least able to state that Master Sawada was a sensible and intelligent man who himself had no ambition to unsettle the world and to question the order that had been established for centuries.

Even if their meeting inside the boat would had not reached a natural end, they could not have continued, because the column moving toward the central square was now clearly recognizable as the King's retinue, and from a distance Inocoyotl could make out his precious feather headdress. He looked sideways in surprise when Sawada suddenly held a black thing in his hand and handed it to him. It had two holes for the man to look through, and it took a short briefing before the envoy was intrigued to realize that he was holding something that brought distant things close to his eye. He quickly learned to fix the sight so that it became clear, and suddenly King Chitam's face jumped at him, and its details were clearly visible.

Inocoyotl involuntarily flinched. It was unexpected and the most magical thing he had met here.

Truly they were not holy messengers, but the things they had were strange qualities.

Inocoyotl was eager not to detach himself from the object, and when he finally lowered it, he felt loss and disappointment. His desire to have something like that was piqued.

But then he remembered the expression he had seen on the young king's face, and all other thoughts and desires were gone.

What he saw there was disturbing. There was a storm of emotion in the man that could break out at any time, and it was not clear who would be the victim of this eruption.

He was certain that the coming days would bring a lot of variety. And this change might prove dangerous, at least very tiring.

Inocoyotl decided to stay as far in the background as possible. If he had learned one from his own king, it was wise reluctance to encounter royal mood swings.

Because these could be quite fatal to the environment.

12

K'uk' Bahlam, King of B'aakal, was known as a patient man, almost kind, although this impression could not deceive any of his enemies. He was ready for any cruelty necessary to secure his city and his rule, but that was the important limitation: the necessity had to be quite evident. If it failed that test, he would not shed blood and was ready to be generous and kind. He had known the old Agun for a long time, because it was well known that he spied for Mutal, and K'uk' Bahlam occasionally fed the man with information that he knew would end up on his rival's lap. That Agun, on the other hand, encouraged by some precious gifts and a friendly invitation to the palace, was quite willing to trace the events of his occasional trips to Mutal – quite in detail and literally, which led to Bahlam having possession of a very decent city map – helped to continue the tolerant attitude toward the spy. Agun's death would have been of no use to anyone and cause a lot of damage, so K'uk' Bahlam had only been pleased when the old man came to him and asked for an audience.

His joy turned into a mixture of amazement, horror, and perplexity when Agun showed up with someone else and after he found out who it was.

Following the minute-long description of the spy, supplemented by occasional statements by a very respectful old warrior who had put his gnarled hands on the shoulders of the taller of the two girls, the King of B'aakal was silent at first, because he had to digest what the gods had presented him with unexpectedly. The old warrior was respectful, but his demeanor showed that he was ready at any time to stand between any danger and the two girls – Mutalese princesses, by the gods! Bahlam did not want to test his heroism. Such an attack belonged into the "not necessary" category, and so he tended to be generous.

"Bring benches. Bring food and drink. Prepares fresh clothes. Prepare a bath."

The orders came suddenly and quickly, and their tone left no room for hesitation. Servants hurried away to do their master's bidding as fast as possible. While the bath and clothing were being prepared in the neighboring rooms, benches and small tables were set up in the presence of the king, and as soon as possible they were filled with food, straight from the royal pantry and thus nothing that Bahlam – abundantly – didn't himself ingest. It was only fair for princesses, and both looked hungry.

Bahlam didn't think it was a good idea to be hungry. It made aggressive and led to hasty action. He did everything he could to avoid this emotional embarrassment and took the opportunity to have a second breakfast.

He nodded to the visitors. Of course, Agun felt included in the invitation and served himself vigorously, even though he had only just had breakfast himself. Bahlam tolerated it with a smile. Agun had just proven useful and someone who was able to make the right decision. He wanted to reward him with a full belly.

Bahlam watched the visitors eat, hesitantly at first, then encouraged by his approving nod, and wherever a plate emptied, it was refilled by servants, and where cups were running low, someone was ready, calabash in hand. Bahlam showed no sign of impatience, closed his eyes, took a little something himself, all to convey the message that there was no need for haste and that he had something very important to contemplate anyway. This was quite true, because the question of what it meant for him and his allies to have two Mutalese princesses in custody was of considerable importance and needed careful consideration.

Bahlam came up with the best ideas when he chewed.

"Ixchel is your name," he said to the older of the two girls. She might still be young, but whether it was the signs of stress of her escape or of an emerging toughness of a future ruler, she did not make the impression that she wanted to have her toys back. Bahlam did notice that she carried an atlatl, and the way it was held indicated that she could handle it. He hadn't humiliated his visitors by taking everything from them, and the room was filled with his warriors, who kept a close eye on everything. Ixchel looked determined.

Only determined to do what?

"I am Ixchel, daughter of Tzutz and Chitam, the royal couple of Mutal," she said firmly, but not without respect. It was not surprising that she named her mother first. Her violent death still had to be very fresh in the daughter's memory.

"I want to tell you that your mother's death makes me very sad," Bahlam said now. "She was known as a wise woman, and everyone expected her to be an excellent advisor to her husband. Her demise is a loss for Mutal, a loss for all of us. Even as my enemy, I would have paid her that respect at any time."

Ixchel bowed her head. Her little sister, reminded of the mother by these words, hid her face in the robe of the old warrior, who put a protective hand on her head.

"Thank you, noble Bahlam. I know that Mutal and B'aakal have not always agreed on everything in the past. In fact, my grandfather said that war between our cities was inevitable. Nevertheless, I am here as a supplicant and beg you to listen to me."

That was well said, as the king thought, and he noticed the pride in the eyes of the old warrior, who ate but did not lose his watchfulness for a second.

"You don't have to plead, Princess," Bahlam said, raising a hand. He almost felt a fatherly affection for the brave girl. He was the father of seven children, not all of them well-behaved, but none of his daughters showed such self-confidence, which had less to do with rank and position but more with real conviction and determination, which he still wasn't able to classify properly. "Speak to me, what is your request!"

"A stay and safety for me and mine."

Bahlam nodded. "It's risky. Mutal could assume that my hand had been visible in these events."

Ixchel seemed to have expected this answer, for she accepted it with a slight bow that was not lacking in grace. Then she turned to her only servant. "Aktul!"

The old warrior stepped forward. In his hands he carried an elongated object wrapped in large sheets. Bahlam had thought it was an atlatl, along with a few shells, worthy of a powerful fighter. But when the old man unrolled the leaves, a strange something appeared beneath it, made of a dark fabric, with wood at one end and the appearance of a threat.

Bahlam looked at it closely, and the looks of others in his court also focused on the thing that the old man now put at the king's feet. Then he remembered the reports from Mutal, the descriptions of his spies, the findings of his investigation, and the reason why Teotihuacán's envoy had gone there.

He pressed his lips on each other, mulling, before he spoke. "This is a weapon of the messengers. You brought it with you from Mutal?"

If Ixchel was astonished because the king knew what her souvenir was, she did not show it.

"Never would one of the messengers have left this to me. You know what happened in Mutal?"

Bahlam made a vague gesture. "One hears things."

"I'm sure you know more than just rumors."

"I heard about this weapon. It is said to be very lethal, more lethal than anything we have. Am I wrong?"

"You are not mistaken."

"Where does it come from?"

"Aktul stole it from one of the attackers who killed my mother."

There followed a period of silence in the audience room. Bahlam tried to understand the implications, but in that short time he only came to the conclusion that all of their difficulties had apparently only begun. Difficulties, however, that brought opportunities. He licked his lips. This was actually promising.

"The messengers are interested in your mother's death? Did she insult them, attack them, or only criticized them?"

"Nothing of the sort!" The daughter's answer sounded a little desperate as she didn't understand why the mother had to die and also showed a bit of betrayed affection, as if the messengers at first left a different impression on her and had afterwards misused her naive trust. Bahlam understood that. First they saved the city, then they killed the queen of that same city. Where was the logic in this? But looking at this from a ruler's perspective and not that of a god, this suddenly made sense. However, he still lacked some important information.

What he knew, however, was enough to see that Mutal really became a problem and that the alliance he had established was forced to act, the sooner the better.

He nodded to Ixchel. "I grant you shelter, you, your sister, and your warrior. I promise you protection and safety, and if I march against Mutal, you should find out why your mother died and who is responsible."

Ixchel smiled slightly, and it was not an expression of gratitude but again one of determination that radiated from her. "I do not want to claim too much of your grace than necessary, dear lord of B'aakal, but allow me to ask that you extend the favor by an important point."

Bahlam nodded. He was curious. "Speak, Princess Ixchel."

"If you march toward Mutal, I will march with you. I throw the atlatl like the best of your warriors. And once we have reached my home, I judge and condemn, not you."

Her voice had been sharp like carefully cut obsidian, and Bahlam was surprised to find that a cold shiver ran down his spine as her words reached his ears. It was more than determination, it was the strong, indelible desire for vengeance, bloody vengeance, and preferably from her own hand.

Bahlam had to be careful.

This girl was never to be allowed to take the throne of Mutal. She would probably be even more dangerous than these strange messengers of the gods.

But he wanted to fulfill her that one wish beforehand. Because he liked it that way.

He raised both hands.

"So be it, Ixchel from Mutal," he said. "You should march with us."

And it was as if the whole court had held their breath until that moment. The murmur and the meaningful looks that were suddenly noticeable spoke for it. Bahlam smiled. All of this would develop to its benefit.

All that remained was to hope that Inocoyotl survived his mission. Whoever killed a queen would not shy away from an envoy from Teotihuacán, the king was certain of that.

13

The march to Tayasal became a march of triumph. For Inugami, halfway through the well-developed connecting road between the two cities, it was clear that there would be no battle. The next messengers from Tayasal had met them the day after the death of the first, a group of frightened men who threw themselves on the ground in front of the vanguard of the warrior slaves and were immediately taken to the general and master of the holy messengers. They had brought a second letter from the new king of Tayasal, in which he promised to the Lord of Mutal unwavering loyalty and eternal tribute if he would only spare his family and refrain from attack. The subtle difference to the first message: He spoke of loyalty and submission, not just of tribute, which showed that the lord of that city had understood where the new wind was blowing from and what reaction could possibly save his neck. Inugami had done nothing to keep the events in Saclemacal secret. He hadn't stopped anyone who was planning to leave the city after the battle. Many hurried messengers should have carried the news of the city's fate to Tayasal and hopefully to Yaxchilan.

The news of the death of Lady Tzutz had now officially spread among the army of Mutal. He himself had helped in that, careful to ensure that his interpretation of the events was immediately conveyed. It was Yaxchilan's fault. At least among Mutal's warriors, hatred of the enemy had grown immeasurably. The doggedness with which these men followed him on this campaign was evident. Inugami was very happy with himself.

And now the second letter from Tayasal.

It was a good start. Inugami did not reply. His inclination to respond to the new king's requests was great, at least as far as sparing lives was concerned. There was no point wasting one's own strength, and when the city was opened to him, everyone should be disciplined enough. Only one would have to vacate his place: the king himself, as Inugami knew no tolerance. He did not have to die – if he surrendered immediately, Inugami wanted to keep him in exile in Mutal, where he could continue to live –, but his throne belonged to an appointed governor who was no longer a divine king but simply an administrator.

He would insist on that. He would enforce that. And he was reasonably certain that the lord of Tayasal would prove to be reasonable.

When they were halfway there, more messengers came, a little more desperate than the first. They were surprised that their colleagues were still alive and were allowed to march as guests, since they had expected that the angry messenger of the gods would wipe them out. When they were convinced otherwise, they were immediately more relaxed, but this did nothing to detract from their submissiveness and the urgency of their mission. Another letter from the King of Tayasal, again the readiness to refrain from any struggle, and for the first time the indication that one would be ready to abdicate and deliver the highest person if the family and the children were spared.

Inugami was surprised. Mayan kings were not known for simply evacuating their throne, which was given to them by the gods. But this one had not been in office for long after the death of his predecessor, who had not taken part in the battle against Mutal but was overthrown after the great defeat. He had probably had slight doubts as to whether the gods had actually chosen him as ruler or not someone else – someone with magical weapons and a damn big, pretty victorious army, for example.

Inugami's willingness to show grace grew. The king shouldn't be killed, he decided. And he kept that decision when he marched into Tayasal days later, a small town like Saclemacal, completely open, with a fearful and expectant roadside population, few soldiers, and a king standing in front of the city's main square who threw himself in the dust before Inugami and his leaders, and with him the whole court.

100

As it was supposed to be.

For a few moments, Inugami let this affect everyone, the residents of the city as well as his troops. It was a symbolic act full of messages, and it was intended to strengthen his power, his legitimacy, and his charisma. And the impact was huge. He felt everyone's eyes on him. He felt the triumph and satisfaction of his men, Achak first and foremost, to whom the disappointment of not being allowed to spill blood spoiled the mood somewhat.

"Rise, King of Tayasal!" the captain called out. He hadn't even bothered to memorize this man's name. He was no longer part of the history of his city. His name was therefore completely unimportant.

The young man did as he was told.

"You have begged mercy, and grace is to be granted to you!" Inugami said aloud. "The city is spared. Your family will be spared." He looked straight into the relieved face of the king. "You are spared."

The first timid cheers sounded. Inugami raised his arms, and it fell silent again.

"You shall be my guest, in Mutal, the queen of all cities, the center of my power, and live there with yours until the end of your days. But I take your throne and your rule from you."

The king bowed his head and covered his disappointment. He had hoped for another one after the first round of good news. But in this important aspect the messenger of the gods did not want to meet his expectations.

But he wasn't in a position to argue with Inugami.

"I obey your will, messenger of gods," he said aloud, so there was no doubt about his intentions. "The city and the country belong to Mutal. I will withdraw as you ordered."

Inugami smiled graciously. It went better than expected, almost perfectly. This process had to spread like wildfire in Mayaland. Everyone should know that there was an alternative to fighting, a way that everyone could protect their lives. He hoped that other rulers, especially in smaller towns, would take this as an example. It would be annoying to have to conquer every autonomous place piece by piece. He was not allowed to split his strength like that, did not yet have enough confidence in his commanders to be able to commission them with their own operations. Some would possibly remember their old loyalties or come up with the idea of replacing one dynasty with another – personified by themselves.

Control was everything, at least for the time being, until loyalty to him had passed into flesh and blood, became a habit and a matter of course that no longer seriously questioned. The moment when Inugami ordered and everyone obeyed him had to become normal. Then he could distribute authority and be reasonably certain that no matter how far Mutal was, there would be no questioning of his supremacy. Only then a loyal cadre of capable administrators could develop who he could entrust with tasks without constantly keeping an eye on everything. Until then he had to improvise, just like in Saclemacal.

Now he needed a governor for Tayasal, and he felt that it would be necessary again to look for a suitable candidate in the ranks of his warrior slaves. He knew what he was doing. With small steps, he transformed his slaves into a new nobility, who pushed the old one aside and who had a new legitimization, not appointed and led by the gods but by Inugami, the new shogun or, if it came to it, the new king. The emperor. They owed their exalted position to him alone. He was the source of their existence.

The longer Inugami thought about this perspective, the more his heart warmed to it.

He looked at the deposed king. He would not humiliate him any further. His people would make sure that he packed up his belongings and left for Mutal as soon as possible. Inugami sighed. He would have to write another letter to Lieutenant Hara, with detailed instructions on how to deal with the Tayasal man.

At least he knew the Mutal affairs in reasonably safe hands. Chitam had returned safely by now. Inugami did not envy Aritomo the task of having to deal with the angry and suffering king. It was to be hoped that the men he trusted, who had eliminated the queen, would no longer attract attention and have sufficiently covered their tracks. He didn't know if everything had really gone smoothly. But the details would clear up when he returned triumphantly to Mutal.

102

He set out to enter Tayasal's rather modest palace. It was important to perform certain symbolic acts. He would sit in the deposed king's place, listening to the blessings of the priests. He would forbid blood to be shed in his honor or to attune the gods to the new times. He was determined to drive this barbaric custom out. When two priests in Saclemacal had insisted that as the new ruler he had to submit to a ritual during which he was expected to use a needle to poke through his penis' foreskin in a secret, sacred chamber, half underground, he had refused to puncture his organ, catch the blood and consume plenty of chi. He didn't need visions, fed by pain and alcohol, to know what to do. The Mayan gods were silly decals of true spirituality, dolls with absurd habits, perversions of human abysses, a wonderful pretext for rituals that had no other purpose than to place a priestly caste in a privileged position. There was only one privilege in Inugami's new empire, and that was to find recognition and mercy in the eyes of the new ruler. That was the true nobility, and wherever the gods had their hand, Inugami was imbued with the conviction that only rational action and faithful fulfillment of duties made one person more than just another tool.

Those who refused to fight for their own purpose immediately agreed to serve the purpose of others. That was Inugami's conviction, his sacred creed, his conviction, and a motto he followed in live and action.

He entered the former king's chambers. A certain exhaustion caught him. The long marches, the excitement, all of this took its toll. The old king's servants had left everything impeccable, and it was Mutal's soldiers who were now taking care of their leader to avoid unpleasant surprises. One never knew if there wasn't someone around after all who disagreed with the new power in place. Inugami did not believe that there was a great danger, but the news of the failed attempt to assassinate his deputy had made him even more vigilant.

When he entered the bedchamber, he found a large bucket of hot water, as he had ordered. Personal hygiene was extremely important, and his obsession with cleaning himself with boiled water and the soap he had brought with him from the boat had already given rise to rumors. The Maya were generally not aware of the connection between poor hygiene and infections, and Inugami admitted that these findings were still relatively new in his day. But that shouldn't stop him from paying close attention to this aspect. He noted with satisfaction that his followers had become particularly enthusiastic about this habit. It was behavior that he only approved of being spread quickly.

In addition to the water and a small buffet of freshly prepared food, three young girls were waiting for him; none of them were older than sixteen. They sat in a row on his couch, were dressed up according to local standards, made up and obviously intended as a kind of personal welcome gift for the new ruler, to cheer him up and to recognize the advantages of Tayasal. Inugami smiled as his eyes rested comfortably on the three expectantly smiling women. Indeed, whoever was responsible for their selection had shown good taste. The young ladies were of a pleasant build, no fat village tromps, and their brown eyes showed dedication and willingness. Inugami looked at the prepared meal, then at the water, and decided to delay the meal. After all, he wasn't really dirty either. He had only sweated to the usual extent, the effort to separate a head from the torso had been spared. Indeed, he began to like this city, and even though he knew that this was an attempt at manipulation, he was quite willing to accept it.

He was the new overlord, the creator of an empire – hadn't he more than earned certain amenities?

Inugami smiled and undid the buttons on his shirt.

As if this was a call to action, the three girls rose and began to assist him. Within a few moments, the covers had fallen, only moments later the women's clothes were on the floor, and the firm, supple bodies of his concubines were pressed against his own. He felt the immediate excitement, enjoyed how slender hands gripped his manhood and began to massage it gently, then demanding. He let himself be drawn onto the bed, felt soft breasts, the nipples pressed against his mouth, and how warm kisses began to wet his skin everywhere. Arms wrapped around him, pelvis pressed against his thighs, he felt the scratching of pubic hair, the moisture of their

104

loins as it began to spread over him. He sucked in the earthy smell of their skin, listened to the soft whispers with which the three women encouraged each other to divide his body like a battlefield between themselves, everywhere at once.

Inugami released a moan, half relaxation, half excitement, and closed his eyes, stretched his arms and let the young flesh slide over his body, stimulate his limb to relentless hardness, always charming, withdrawing again and again, a joyful game of promise and hesitation that he was only too happy to succumb to.

This was his reward, this was his right. He was Inugami, the lord of the Mutal Empire, the new Emperor of America. And all who served him did so with dedication, lust and the strong desire to give him the greatest satisfaction.

He had arrived where he belonged. This was his place. All of this was predetermined, Inugami was absolutely certain of it right now, more than ever. All doubts were gone.

He felt tongues and lips press around his member, cool, strong fingers wrapped around his shaft, and groaned again. The little sluts would fight over his semen, the effusion of a messenger of gods, the new ruler over everything that is, and they would still lick him when he was long exhausted ...

Then his neck was pulled up and something wrapped around it. He opened his eyes and groaned. One of the young women was suddenly behind him, put his head on her thighs and put a band around his throat – and started strangling him.

Inugami began to fight back, but the other two girls lay heavily on their arms and legs, clinging to him like drowning people, paralyzing him with the sheer weight of their bodies. He saw their faces very close now, staring at him with beautiful brown eyes, and there was no more admiration, no passion, nothing of devotion, there was only cold lust for murder, the determination to kill someone, and that with combined strength.

Inugami mobilized all his power. He jerked his head to the side, tensed his arms and legs, tried to turn his body. It was the over-whelming mobilization of agony that caused one of the girls to slip out of balance. Suddenly he had one arm free, which immediately went up, his hand clenched into a fist, and he struck the face of the assassin, who had a firm grip on the garotte.

A cry of pain. Something cracked and cracked again. His hand ached and got wet. He must have hit her in the mouth, broken out one tooth or more. The grip loosened, he gasped for air, took another swing – but the girls never let up. The woman he had pushed aside threw himself on him, clutched his free arm, paralyzed his movement. And the victim, whose blood now dripped onto his forehead and emitted a slightly metallic smell, overcame her pain, tightened the band again, and Inugami had to fight for his breath again.

He did not find the strength to raise himself again. He felt his defenses weaken, how he could do nothing more than a quiet wheeze, and then how the blackness fell around him, and he realized that it was not easy to be a god.

Especially when you weren't.

14

"Chitam, I'm sorry."

The king looked at Aritomo. His eyes were rimmed red. He had gotten drunk senseless the last night, now that all the city's chi stocks were at his disposal. Or sensible, depending on one's point of view. He had slept until noon and had woken up in a mood that could only be described as murderous. But Chitam was not a man without self-control. The silent rage boiling in him and the horrific mood he showed never went so far as to harass his subordinates to let his feelings out on them. Aritomo feared, however, that those responsible for the murder of Tzutz did not expect a pleasant fate if Chitam ever got hold of them.

The worrying thing was that the King of Mutal had just opined that he didn't believe for a second that scattered Yaxchilan attackers were responsible for this cowardly attack. He had said this with deep seriousness, self-assurance that came from a great deal of conviction, and Aritomo got serious about his fear.

"I even believe you, Aritomo Hara. I believe you that your grief is real. But I don't believe anyone who tells me that those from Yaxchilan killed my wife. Don't get me wrong. I trust that the fanatical followers of dead Tatb'u are capable to do everything, including that. But I know more. I know of things we never talked about. And I didn't want to bring it up so soon. But now the developments have led me to a decision. It is good that you can listen, and I trust you to do more than blindly follow your Lord. That is why what we are now discussing is particularly important."

He looked at Aritomo so intensely, as if he expected the officer to guess what he was talking about by looking at it alone. And Aritomo wasn't far from doing just that. He was reminded of his own suspicions that Inugami was behind the attack. It fit too well into the behavior of the captain, who was unable to stop on his way to power and imperial glory.

But Aritomo was silent. Chitam would explain. And when he said what was to be feared, the time came when the Japanese had to worry about fundamental questions of loyalty – much faster than he wanted to.

Much, much faster.

Chitam was sitting on a stone bench in the audience room, and no one else was present. Servants would certainly appear when the king called, but none of them could be seen. They spoke a mixture of Maya and English, and while both of them were challenged in that, they refrained from asking Itzunami or Sawada for help.

"Before I left for Saclemacal to witness your commander's grand victory ..." Aritomo was certain that there was a trace of sarcasm in Chitam's voice – and a good deal of envy. "... I had an interesting visit. One of your warrior slaves spoke to me, someone you know well. I don't give his name, but it should be clear who it is."

Aritomo had a very precise idea. He leaned forward slightly, the expression on his face concentrated. That promised to be interesting. The arson attack ...

"This man had seen something that night and witnessed a conversation that occurred at my palace just before the fire started. A very insightful conversation and with explosive consequences."

"Speak up, Chitam. Get to the point!" Aritomo was amazed at his own angry tone, as if he suspected that he wasn't going to like the truth and didn't want to admit it. Loyalty was a complicated thing when it put one to the test.

"Someone gave the man the order for the attack. It was one of the messengers of the gods, one of the men with the long metal fire pipes protecting your prince." Chitam smiled. "I heard the prince escaped this protection. That is extremely unfortunate."

Chitam's tone showed that his regret was limited. Aritomo didn't even resent that. Their previous efforts to find out anything about Isamu's whereabouts had been unsuccessful. Whatever the two young men were doing, their actions were better prepared than Aritomo had expected.

"Let's talk about Isamu later," Aritomo muttered, who had heard what he feared secretly. He tried to keep a neutral expression on his face, but the emotionless mask didn't seem to work.

"You don't look surprised," the king immediately demonstrated his powers of observation. "You knew about it?"

Aritomo never missed the sudden coldness and distance in the ruler's voice. "No," he hurried to answer. "But I was afraid of it."

Chitam relaxed a little. "Your Inugami is playing a dangerous game. It could be that his charades would soon be his undoing."

Aritomo nodded, said nothing.

"If Inugami ordered the arson, why not murder my wife? After all, our death has already been his will. It is logical. It fits his behavior. I cannot accept anything else. The conclusion comes to mind."

"You don't know if Inugami gave this order. It wasn't him that your source saw, was it?"

Chitam made a snapping sound that expressed either contempt or unwillingness. "That's true. But did your soldier act without orders and just promised the arsonist the highest honors and titles out of a whim?"

Aritomo listened to the details of what Balkun – and only he could have meant – had heard that evening. No, no matter that Inugami didn't appeared personally, it all pointed to him. And he, Aritomo, had the opportunity to finally resolve this matter.

He stood up. There would be no use delaying the inevitable any longer. "My king, I will go now and investigate."

Chitam also rose and looked almost pleased, as if Aritomo's actions met his expectations. "I think that's necessary. What will you do if it turns out that my guess is true?"

"Then I'll go back to you in need of your advice."

Chitam looked a bit surprised at Aritomo. "My advice?"

"How should someone behave who realizes that his master is completely wrong and threatens to destroy everything?"

"Destroy?" Chitam laughed, it was a cynical laugh, a sound of despair, as if to express all his piercing thoughts that had been torturing him for days.

"What a naive man you are, Aritomo! What kind of destruction? Saclemacal is conquered. Tayasal should already have fallen. I have no doubt that Inugami will also win Yaxchilan. And then what? Who wants to stop him? My house may vanish. But Mutal becomes the center of an empire that the Maya never saw before. It's not a downfall, it's a beginning, someone building something big!" Chitam laughed again. "How did I press my father in the past to show Mutal's power in the world, to put neighbors in their place, to strengthen the city's fame, to let the warriors march. He didn't want to, wasn't a man of permanent war. I didn't despise him for it, but I never understood it. I dreamed of the glory of the battlefield and kings kneeling before me."

Chitam paused and sighed.

"Inugami achieved what I dreamed of back then. That particularly worries me. He achieves a lot more, thinks differently than we do in our run-in ways. He pushes me and mine into the darkness of oblivion. His star shines brightly. I stand in his shadow. Soon, I'm afraid, I won't be standing anymore at all."

A good part of this discouragement, Aritomo was certain, was due to the death of Tzutz. But another part simply spoke a truth.

But he did not miss the lurking look that the king now directed at him. Chitam expected a response, more than a promise to take care of it. A kind of expression of loyalty, perhaps, a word that indicated how far the deputy distanced himself from the actions of his commander.

But Aritomo was not ready for such a word. Not yet. Once he had certainty, final certainty, he would speak to Lengsley, perhaps Sawada and Sarukazaki, and after that, a decision had to be made. He felt very uncomfortable with it and knew that he was disappointing Chitam's expectation, who may now be ready to reach for any straw that promised support and confirmation.

But Aritomo was looking for that himself, and he didn't know where to expect it.

He said goodbye to the king, left him alone, a man who had lost the support of his life, who until recently he had never known how much she had kept him on the right track.

He marched toward the Japanese shelter, where everyone who was not guarding the boat was staying. As he entered the courtyard, silence fell over the assembled crew, which had appeared without orders, driven by rumors and the need to learn more. Aritomo would not meet their desire now but beckoned to one of the two bodyguards Isamu's who had stayed here. Even if he wasn't the one who carried out the arson attack, he was sure he was aware of the goings-on of his comrade who accompanied Inugami on the campaign.

The soldier followed silently. With a wink, Lengsley and Sarukazaki joined. They entered Aritomo's room, and the officer got straight to the point.

"Kato! I have an important matter to discuss with you!"

The bodyguard, a wiry man in his early 30s, was met with prying eyes and stiffened. It was, as always, the escape into discipline that made a good Japanese soldier when there seemed to be no alternative.

"Lieutenant!"

"Have you recently carried out a private command from Captain Inugami?"

The man pressed his lips together. Aritomo saw how conflicting feelings worked in him.

"I don't understand exactly what you mean," the man said.

The officer leaned forward. "You were ordered to shut up?"

"Yes, sir!"

"You got an order?"

Kato was silent, staring straight ahead, past everyone and through Aritomo.

The latter nodded. "Lengsley, look at Kato's place. Bring me his rifle and search for suspicious items."

The Brit frowned. Aritomo suspected that the question was what exactly should be regarded as a "suspicious" item, but he did not want to say so in the presence of the bodyguard to not undermine Aritomo's authority. He saluted laxly and turned away.

Aritomo's eyes went back to Kato, who had frozen into a monument. "Kato, who is responsible for the arson attack on the palace?"

He saw the man's eyes widen slightly, only briefly, but it was response enough to tell Aritomo the bitter truth. How could the lieutenant know about this? Clearly, the man considered this question. It didn't matter whether he had instigated the arsonist himself, whether it was his colleague – or another member of the crew who was blindly willing to follow Inugami. The bodyguards were Inugami's closest confidants. They knew more than Aritomo, and that alone was enough in this case.

The man said nothing.

Aritomo didn't blame him. He hadn't learned it any other way, knew no other behavior. That made him a docile tool.

Lengsley came back and shrugged. Instead of letting it go, he leaned over and whispered something in Aritomo's ear.

He nodded imperceptibly. "Soldier, where's your weapon?"

The bodyguard could no longer tense any of his muscles, he was so stiff.

"I want to know where your rifle is, soldier. It is your duty to present the weapon at any time. I want an inspection."

The man didn't move an inch.

"I'll put you under arrest if you keep refusing my orders," Aritomo said slowly. "Not only did you ignore a superior's direct question, you also lost your gun. And before that, if I may say so, your protégé, the Prince."

With that, he had hit the man. Apparently he wanted to say something, opened his mouth slightly but then changed his mind. The fact that the Prince had managed to disappear under his watchful eye had to bother him more than any wickedness he had committed on behalf of the captain.

"No answer, soldier? Not a word?"

Not one, as Aritomo was able to determine. He would not get on like this.

"You're under arrest. Sarukazaki, tie the man up. Collect everything, his sword, pistol, and then lock him up. He remains tied up until the captain is back and takes care of it."

Aritomo had no illusions about what Inugami would do to the man. His freedom was guaranteed. The captain needed loyal and disciplined followers, and the soldier no doubt belonged to this category.

When Sarukazaki started the procedure, Aritomo noticed that he no longer considered himself loyal and disciplined. That made him restless. If he was no longer able to follow the captain unconditionally, as his duty dictated, where should his life go?

Sarukazaki left, and he was alone with Lengsley.

They looked at each other silently before the Brit spoke. He looked restless, excited, had probably figured the case out quickly.

"Inugami is behind everything? The arson attack? The murder of Tzutz?"

"I am convinced of it. He's crazy."

"But could he succeed in his plans?"

"For how long?" Aritomo shook her head. "His empire is built on sand, Lengsley. One day he will overdo it and end up with an assassin's knife in his heart. Then his work will collapse, and we – we fellow time travelers – will feel the revenge of the Maya. We will not even be able to hope for a gracious death. I don't think everyone will differentiate between him and us then. I've already been able to experience this firsthand."

"Not a very nice outlook."

Aritomo smiled weakly. "We're cowards, aren't we? We just want to survive while the captain tries to change the world. We are faint-hearted, Lengsley. Maybe the captain is right, and this is a unique opportunity to write history."

Lengsley didn't look too convinced. He looked at Aritomo as if he wanted to know if the Japanese really meant it. "I prefer to live in peace. I also can achieve great things and change the world, if only by teaching the Maya things that they do not yet know. Such changes are more radical than any conquest. They have a long-term impact. I'd rather be a teacher than a conqueror."

"Says a man from the British Empire, the greatest nation on earth."

Lengsley grinned and ran a hand through his hair. "The Empire is a bigger burden than you Japanese think."

"We want one ourselves."

"It will be your downfall, just like ours, at some point an unbearable burden. I am not a colonialist, Aritomo. I've seen a lot of the world, and I tell you, one day a lot of shit will fly in our faces."

"Another time and no longer our problem."

The Brit nodded. "So what are we doing about our problem at this time?"

Aritomo smiled. "In any case, I want to prevent anything from flying into our faces."

In that, he saw, there was complete agreement between the two of them.

15

It took a while for Inocoyotl to gather all the information he needed, but it was not his first mission of this kind, and he was therefore not inexperienced in such matters. A brief audience with the suffering king had been rather unproductive, if not pointless. Then he had asked around, accepted invitations, moved around the higher circles of the city. He encouraged his soldiers to talk to the farmers, the artisans, the girls who were sent by their hosts to entertain them.

Everyone had reported to him directly, and Inocoyotl had taken note of every detail, rumor, and joke. He encouraged those who turned out to be mouth-lazy by asking questions, and he met others who had a lot to tell with great patience. It was rarely the case that a single source brought complete knowledge. Usually, one had to assemble reality together from its facets. The ambassador was good at that. It was sometimes annoying, often boring, and in the end it became exhausting, but the procedure as such was inevitable.

Everything came together in one picture.

Inocoyotl had concluded that Chitam of Mutal was not the driving force behind his city's expansion, that he was becoming increasingly distant from the messengers of the gods, and that the pain of his wife's death prevented him from clearly seeing the way in front of him. Inocoyotl, an outsider, a man from afar and with only the pain that resided in his limbs after a long day, saw where Chitam's journey was going. Two paths were open to him, no, basically three. Inocoyotl was not quite sure which one the king would choose.

He might have to help a little. That was when the delicate part of his visit began.

Queca listened to his master's monologue in silence. The ambassador had made a habit of using the leader of his bodyguard as a wall against which he threw his ideas and arguments to see if they penetrated, caused scratches, or simply fell to the ground uselessly. Queca was of practical intelligence, although his arrogance sometimes stood in the way. But he sometimes managed to let the wall reflect, as if a ball ricocheted off it, and Inocoyotl particularly enjoyed that. Ultimately, he played a game here, and the rules have always been the same.

"Three alternatives, sir?" Queca asked.

"Three. He can give up and surrender to the dictates of the messengers of the gods, becoming an instrument that will outlive its usefulness at some point. He can immediately abdicate and hope to be able to enjoy a private life. And he can stand up, face the seemingly inevitable fate, and do whatever he can to save his city and throne."

Queca looked at Inocoyotl questioningly. "How should the latter work? If I understand the reports correctly, the Mutalese are enthusiastic about the holy messengers. They saved the city. They expand power and influence, take revenge on the attackers, bring new miracles, and lead the city to a position above everyone else. And many still believe that they are real messengers of the gods and that following them is a sacred duty."

"Very well observed, Queca," Inocoyotl said. They sat in the assigned accommodation, comfortable and equipped with all amenities. It was late afternoon, and they had eaten well. If it weren't for the situation in the city, the threat, the imponderability, Inocoyotl would have felt almost at ease. However, he would only be able to really relax once he had made a decision. Doing so was also one of the goals of his exchange with the officer, though he did not know how he was really helping his master in this moment.

"He'll need allies. He is the king, but he needs allies to win over the followers he still has and offer a real alternative," Queca said musingly.

"Allies like us. Or the alliance that is now forming. If we can get Chitam on our side, it would be a wonderful symbol for their endeavor – and a reason for the Alliance to claim full legitimacy in their resistance."

Queca nodded. He understood these kinds of arguments. Of course, there was only one symbol, one legitimacy, that he would ever follow. But he rightly assumed that the Maya had exactly the same behavior here that drove hi, too. "How can we get him to do this?"

"By giving his revenge a goal."

"Does he seek revenge? He seems to me very introverted, immersed in grief, and ..."

"Anger. Queca. Something is bubbling inside him that is looking for a way to break out. Chitam is an intelligent man and not without self-control. He looks for his way, but may choose the wrong one. Maybe he wants to fight against the messengers all by himself. Or perhaps he believes that Yaxchilan has to fall first, since they are responsible for his wife's death. But does he believe in this connection? Does he doubt the official explanation? His relationship with the strangers is not perfect, that's easy to see. We have to show him a way, Queca. It is in our interest and in the end also in his." It was clear to the soldier that the former was far more important to him than the latter.

"Will he listen to you, sir?"

"I am the Messenger of Teotihuacán. He can't afford not to listen to me."

"Quite so." Queca moved restlessly. It wasn't his way of arguing with a king's envoy, and it had taken him a while to realize that it didn't hurt him. Nevertheless, it could be noticed from time to time that he had to force himself to contradict Inocoyotl in a field of expertise where he really had nothing to say as a soldier. "But are you important or influential enough to convince him?"

Inocoyotl smiled. Queca really didn't need to much effort to come to this simple question. "No. That would also be the wrong approach. I cannot stand and mark the important man from Teotihuacán, who, with an imperious gesture, announces the truth and expects the King of Mutal to take this at face value immediately. Let us not forget that our city was involved in Mutal's affairs long ago. The first rulers may have deliberately referred to us in their buildings and chronicles, but look around. All steles of the dynasty testify that one quickly created one's own identity, which was more in line with the Mayan traditions and did not push the legacy aside, but let it take a back seat. Not disrespectful but necessary. We are the distant brother, the bond of loyalty is weak. I won't be able to renew it with a mere visit, Queca. No, it is my words themselves that have to bear their own weight. Either the meaning of what I'm saying is convincing, or I'll never get to Chitam."

"So you have to choose your words carefully."

The ambassador sighed. "And place and time to say them. Everything is difficult, because the latter in particular runs through our fingers. We can't stay here forever, we have to report to the Alliance and, more importantly than that, I have to go back to Teotihuacán urgently to subject my actions to the judgment of the Divine."

Queca's expression remained a mask, which was only a good thing. As reasonable as her king seemed, it was absolutely unpredictable how he would react to the very autonomous behavior of his envoy – especially when Inocoyotl suggested that he'd participate in an alliance against Mutal, even assume leadership, and therefore a long and in all likelihood a bloody war, the outcome of which was anything but certain. Queca was wise if he didn't identify too much with what Inocoyotl was doing or not doing. If the king disagreed with what his envoy had accomplished, the shadow of his displeasure could quickly fall on the captain. And if such a shadow fell, the very best of fate was slavery. On the other hand, the priests' hunger for suitable victims for the high holidays was insatiable. A strong, handsome man in the prime of his day would do well on the sacrificial stone.

Inocoyotl smiled when he noticed that such or at least comparable thoughts shot through the soldier's head. He did not resent the man's reluctance. Inocoyotl knew that he was dancing on the edge of a very sharp obsidian blade. There were many risks. But with all fear of the arbitrariness of his ruler, the older man was still a patriot and convinced of the size and dominance of Teotihuacán. The fact that this sometimes had to be helped a little was part of the business.

"Queca, I wrote a letter summarizing all the news and my assessments. Which of your men is the fastest and most enduring runner?"

"Tecal is the best. Nobody catches up with him, and he never tires. With light luggage and the seal of the king, he will travel quickly and safely."

The ambassador carried several of these seals with him, neatly drawn on paper. They were considered a passport and a symbol of protection and power. Whoever bore this seal could invoke the Divine Ruler of Teotihuacán, and anyone who disabled or killed a seal bearer would have to expect the terrible revenge of the most powerful city in the world. The Maya were very careful about this. They either did not like the sovereignty of the great city at all or only recognized it by name – Inocoyotl had no illusions about it –, but throwing stones in the way of an official messenger would not occur to them either. Not even their gods would come up with this absurd idea if asked about it.

Inocoyotl handed Queca the carefully rolled message, bound tightly and protected in a leather tube against the hardships of the weather. Then he handed him a strip of paper with the seal, which the officer accepted in awe. Both were hidden in another leather case that the messenger could easily tie with a ribbon around his shoulders. Light luggage, indeed.

"Tecal should hurry up, my friend!" Inocoyotl warned.

"I'll make it clear to him."

"Now go."

The captain bowed, pressed the message to his chest, and hurried away. All similar tasks – the protection of the mission and the support of the envoy –, he would carry out faithfully and with the highest discipline. Queca was a king's man, just like Inocoyotl, and the order had been given by the highest authority. He didn't have to go through every intrigue, but that message would reach Teotihuacán within a few weeks. As soon as the border of the empire was reached, other messengers would take over the transport. The king's men ran day and night when it was necessary and hardly rested. No effort would be spared just so the Overlord knew what he needed to know.

Inocoyotl didn't know Tecal, but he hoped he would survive, if only to get an answer back to him if necessary. However, it was more likely that he himself would be on his way home to report personally. The potential response was the same, whether expressed by message or in person: an encouragement or guidance from the ruler, an indication that he was satisfied with the envoy's actions, an indication that Inocoyotl's family remained safe and no one would lose a body part because he had made a mistake in the distance. No, the current king was not known for such deeds, but like it was with all gods, he was allowed to, he could if he was in a mood.

Inocoyotl watched Queca.

There were moments when he was not enjoying his work.

16

Aktul looked at her doubtfully. "Nobody knows how the gods work, my princess. Let's keep practicing with the atlatl."

The house in which the two girls and their bodyguard had been accommodated corresponded to their high level. The courtyard was extensive. Three servants took care of their needs. It was almost like being at home and their host didn't impose any unreasonable restrictions on them. They could walk freely through the city and talk to anyone. Ixchel was invited to dinner and accepted some of these invitations. She was the Mutalese princess, and everyone wanted to hear her story – and she was ready to tell it. She needed all the support and sympathy she could get, and Tzutz had trained her early on how to behave properly at court. Ixchel remembered each of her words with terrifying clarity. Sometimes she took Nicte with her, because now it was the job of the older sister to bring her up and teach her everything she needed. When she asked for a teacher who continued the studies in writing and numbers, the request was immediately fulfilled.

They were exemplary little princesses.

With small exceptions.

That Ixchel insisted on weapon training every afternoon was taken as a little craziness of a girl in pain. Ixchel didn't care. She practiced for an hour with the atlatl, the handling of which she matured to perfection. She had started training with the ax, although Aktul had been reluctant. Ixchel had had a slightly smaller weapon made to fit her growing body, in size and weight. It was well balanced in the hand. After dancing wildly through the courtyard for an afternoon and scaring the servants, Aktul was ready to instruct her to avoid injuries and to channel the apparently excess energies into constructive ways. The next day, he had brought her a shield and protective clothing like that of a ball player. Ixchel had endured his care patiently and with a warm feeling in the heart. She had to learn, and Aktul was the best teacher in these matters she could imagine. That he sometimes wanted to protect her a little too much did not resent her. She sensed that he felt guilt in himself not to have prevented Tzutz's death. He wanted to make up for it. There would be no point trying to talk him out of it.

Then, today, she had brought out the god's weapon. Their hosts looked at them with unnatural shyness and had only wanted to have them destroyed. Ixchel saw in it an instrument of her revenge. She had seen the messengers deal with it several times in Mutal, most recently when one of these demons fired a shot at her mother right in front of her. She knew where the front and where the back was, and she knew that the little hook under the staff was used to trigger the magic that made the fire pipe speak.

And that's why she wanted to try it out. She wanted to know how everything worked. It would be a pleasure for her to use the weapon against those who had killed her mother. However, she admitted that the idea of splitting the guilty man's skull with an ax promised far greater satisfaction.

"The atlatl can wait," Ixchel said absently. "And go somewhere else. I don't want you to get hurt. The deadly force emerges from this opening, and nobody can see it. You won't be able to avoid it, old man."

"The old man's going to spank your ass," Aktul growled, but still took a step to the side.

"I'm a princess," Ixchel mocked, as she aimed the muzzle of the rifle at the floor. This seemed the safest course of action for her.

"A few blows will hurt you, too, royal ass or not," Aktul replied, staring at the weapon with disgust. For him, this was a dishonorable way of killing, and he wholeheartedly rejected it. Ixchel was less scrupulous, understanding this weapon might help her one day more than the old man was currently able to predict.

"Aktul, your behavior is improper!"

"And your noble highness is stupid. Let's start with the spear, I got you one."

122

Ixchel looked at the old man in surprise.

He shrugged. "You would have somehow gotten one anyway by yourself, Princess. I don't think you want to miss out in any weapon, or am I wrong?"

"Your wisdom is only surpassed by your courage to fight, dear Aktul," Ixchel replied with warmth in her voice and without any irony. The warrior grunted a little, stared at the firearm again, and said nothing more. Ixchel placed it on the leather she had wrapped it in to protect it from moisture. Aktul was right. Just experimenting with it was too dangerous. Until she met someone who explained how the weapon worked, she would just keep it safe.

She also wanted to relax the old man. She didn't like that he felt uncomfortable, quite the contrary.

Aktul watched her with satisfaction. When she was done, he held out a spear. In contrast to the throwing javelin for the atlatl, this weapon was longer, it was suitable both for thrusting and for attacking in a side arc. Aktul was a master at it. He could cut a man's throat with it as if he were standing right in front of him. Strong arm muscles were necessary to use the weapon effectively.

Ixchel looked at her upper arms. The training made itself felt. The old warrior followed her gaze and smiled. "We practice thrusting and repelling blows, Princess. It's the most important way to fight this weapon anyway."

"There are men who hurl the spear without an atlatl."

"There are strong warriors with a trained arm. Ixchel, the fire of a fighter is burning in you, but your body is not yet fully evolved. Even with the best training, a woman will never be able to get an arm equivalent to that of a good male warrior. When we train you, we have to consider the limitations of your body. There is no use in fighting like a man. You have to fight like a woman, and so effectively that you can kill every man. Do you understand me?"

Ixchel's spontaneous reaction was to be a little offended, but the old man's serious tone instructed her otherwise. It was important to Aktul that she was not only able to defend herself well but was also able to finish her opponents off. He was going to teach her everything she needed to know, and he knew what was useful and what wasn't. It would suit her well to submit to his advice.

She grabbed the spear. It was a little shorter than a grown man's weapon, but still longer than the one she hurled with the atlatl. It had been freshly carved, the tip made of obsidian shimmered black and polished, and Ixchel did not have to touch it to know that it was very sharp and therefore dangerous.

Aktul stepped aside and pointed to the goalpost he had set up at the end of the yard. He carried his own spear, a longer and heavier weapon, and raised it with an ease that belied his age.

"I'll show you how to attack. You will practice it. There are three ways you need to know. A slight upward thrust that hits the opponent's chest under the ribs and drives the tip straight into his heart – an effective push that allows you to pull the spear out afterwards, and an attack that, if successful, kills your opponent immediately and lets you face the next enemy."

Aktul demonstrated it with a powerful movement.

"The second strike is head-on, and here you put the force of your upper body into the attack. If your opponent is wearing armor, his upper body is protected, and if you want to penetrate this protection, you aim at your target parallel to the ground. Point the spear at his chest and look for his heart. There is a risk that the weapon will get caught in the ribs and you will lose time in order to pull it out. In the fight against many, you may be forced to give up the weapon. You are small, so aim at the stomach and intestines. You save your spear and condemn your opponent to a bloody, cruel end. But a strong man will find an opportunity to return the attack, and some, expecting their death, will develop unexpected strength. If you don't back away quickly, this can be your undoing."

The demonstration followed, a result of decades of experience. Ixchel looked at Aktul with concentrated attention.

"The third strike. You stand in an elevated position, perhaps on the level of a temple-stair. Your opponent is fighting you from below. If you aim at the eyes, you can bring about quick death, and the enemy will no longer defend himself, but again there is a risk that your spear will be lost. Thrust into the neck from above or through the throat into the chest. I recommend the neck. If you open a vein, you can put your weapon back in use immediately, and the enemy is very weak. The danger is that you will miss the vein. A strong warrior won't give you a second chance."

Aktul moved and pushed down.

"All of these attacks can be fended off," Ixchel said.

"That's right, Princess. I'll show you how to do it and what you can do about it consequently."

Ixchel looked at the weapon in her hands and was faced with the prospect of a long, sweaty afternoon. She took a deep breath and looked at Aktul, who was watching her closely.

"We'll start with the first one."

Aktul nodded.

They trained until the sun went down.

17

"Another week if nothing else comes up."

The woman looked up when she heard Köhler's words and smiled warmly at the officer. She pushed some unruly hair from her face that had loosened from the knot on the back of her head. The wind was not too wild, the weather refreshing rather than threatening, but the wind was blowing from the wrong direction. They both heard the stomping of the steam engine, which drove the *Gratianus* in the right direction, quite against the expressed will of the elements.

"I obviously miss the land less than you," the woman replied with a laugh, pointing to the dancing waves. "I don't mind delays. I research animals. There are also some in the sea."

Köhler nodded. Augusta Clara Terzia, daughter of a writer at the emperor's court, belonged to the second generation of women who had enjoyed the freedoms and privileges their ancestors could only dream of. She had completed a course of study, had been selected for this important expedition, had reached the age of 30, and was unmarried, still difficult for many to digest. If there was a flaw in her way of life, it was this, and no matter how many women of the new Rome tried to get rid of the traditional ideas, this was certainly a process that had only just begun.

Köhler did not believe in this aspect of equality, although he was careful not to say it too loudly in the presence of Augusta Clara. When he watched the scientist from afar, he thought less about her undoubtedly impressive and sometimes intimidating intellectual qualities. What caught his eye first was her sweeping pelvis, which no doubt deserved the term "childbearing" and seemed to invite his manhood to linger. Although Augusta Clara was kind to everyone, she had never voiced such an invitation, neither to him nor to any of the other men. So she behaved completely within the very strict regulations in this regard on board the expedition, and Köhler had to remind himself not to see this as a flaw but as an advantage. Still, he couldn't help looking for Terzia's company whenever he had time. And this, although she always managed to distract his thoughts from the idea of intense clasping of naked bodies and instead shared chunks of her knowledge with him.

Which just sometimes intimidated him.

She stretched a tanned arm westward. Birds could be seen above the waves.

"They seem to be seagulls. Firstly, an indication that you are right, noble Trierarch."

Köhler grimaced. He held the rank of a trierarch, although he only served as first officer. However, since Langenhagen commanded the entire flotilla, he sometimes had to operate the ship alone, especially when they were performing joint maneuvers and the Navarch's attention was otherwise occupied. Still, he didn't like using military ranks too much when talking to civilians, because they created an unnecessary distance.

And distance was not something he wanted to build between himself and Augusta Clara Terzia. His purpose was rather the opposite. An absurd idea on board, and Köhler would never cross this invisible line, no matter how enthusiastic his flirting attempts were. But on land ...

Köhler was smart enough to see why Terzia endured his advances with humor and good-naturedness. As a result, the rest of the crew knew that anyone who approached this woman had a serious and powerful competitor. This had its advantages and formed an invisible protective radius around her, for which she was prepared to endure Köhler's presence. The Trierarch did not feel exploited in any way. Eventually it made her willingly speak to him, ready to play games, if only with words.

She probably even enjoyed it a little.

He looked into her broad smile.

No, he was pretty sure of it.

"Seagulls, yes," he said a little lame, shadowing his eyes with his right hand. "It seems they exist all over the world."

"What did you expect? There will be species that we find all over the world, and species that are only found in certain areas. We now have to find out what the situation is in *Amerika*. I'm sure we'll have some big surprises waiting for us."

Köhler nodded. The records of the time-wanderers about this area had been very sparse, as had the knowledge that the Germans had brought with them in their memory. The captain's small library consisted mainly of technical, nautical and historical works. A great treasure that after careful translation, had already been copied several times by the hard-working typesetters of the Imperial Book Factory and distributed to educational institutions throughout the Empire. But in the aspects that interested Terzia, there was a lack of knowledge from the future, and they were completely dependent on their own research. This was not something that seemed to worry this woman, because she was not walking on paths that had already been taken but was making her own way. It was clear that she could get excited about it. Upon her return, loaded with samples and records, she would be offered a high position at one of the newly founded universities and, Köhler was certain, would write a book that would serve as a standard reference for the foreseeable future. He wasn't jealous of it. If this expedition was successful, his own career in the fleet was unlimited. Upon his return, he would either be promoted to Navarch or offered another important position. In fact, he would simply apply for his own command to avoid being paralyzed by administrative tasks. To mold on land was not his wish. Maybe there would be a second expedition. Langenhagen would be rewarded at least with a senatorial office or a prefecture after his return. The chance that a follow-up expedition would need a new leader familiar with the circumstances was quite large.

But first of all they had to successfully make this trip.

And they had to survive it. Anticipation and self-confidence were still great. That could change quickly.

To free himself from the cloudy thoughts, Köhler's eyes searched the outlines of the other ships in her flotilla. The repair of the shortwave transmitter had resulted in them being able to contact the remaining three ships. After communicating the exact position to each other, determined by the sextant, it had been relatively easy to bring the ships back together. The damage to the storm had long since been repaired. The freighter had weathered the storm well, even the horses that had been loaded seemed to have recovered well. Köhler suspected that they longed for the land, and after the weeks at sea, going ashore would do them good.

"When we arrive, when do we start our first inland expedition?" the scientist asked.

"The Navarch has ordered that we first sail along the coast to explore the situation from the sea and to see which landing site is best. The first shore leave will be made by soldiers who will build a base. We are looking for forest nearby, because we will build a fort to defend ourselves. Only when this base is in place and the Navarch is sure that we can hold it, do we start to consider a first research trip. Please also keep in mind that everything can change if we quickly establish contact with the locals. Then diplomatic considerations are paramount. It may also be that we do not set up a base at all, but instead that the forces of fate immediately lead us to a strange port. Everything is imponderable."

Terzia frowned. That made her lovely.

"So if everything goes wrong," she said, "we can wait a long time for our work to begin."

Köhler shook his head. "I would think that the identification of a landing site that is as ideal as possible, as well as the possible peaceful contact with those who live here, does not fall under the category of 'going wrong.' We don't want to be attacked just because we dare to enter the country too cheekily. Rome is far away, we are relying only on the resources we have with us. I agree with Navarch Langenhagen that unnecessary risks must be avoided. In the end, we should all return home safe and sound. Any knowledge will also be of no use to you if you will never have the opportunity to write it down and spread it at home so that others can also benefit from it."

Terzia seemed to accept the officer's arguments, at least the disappointment was gone from her face. "I'm sure you're right in everything you say. I am of course eager to be able to go ashore to really get started with my work. I have high expectations."

Köhler frowned. From this point of view, he rarely viewed their mission, and then only from a security perspective. The primary goal of the expedition was to find out if time-wanderers had landed anywhere else in the world, at least for the ship's command, which had received clear orders for such a case. There were many other tasks, but that was the main motivation. He hadn't really considered that Terzia was under a very special kind of expectation. He scolded himself a fool. It was understandable. A woman, unmarried, who had left the traditional ways of female life, a member of a minority, often with incomprehension and sometimes even rejection, one of only four ladies on this important expedition – the eyes of her family were on her, the eyes of many other women for whom she was a role model, and also those of people who wished or even predicted failure. She had to and wanted to meet the expectations of many, she had to and wanted to disappoint the expectations of others – and both were inextricably linked. A triumph was double, as was defeat twice. Köhler rocked his head slowly. Although Terzia had smiled lightly at his words and made a lighthearted impression, he now understood the concern and, above all, the pressure under which the woman was operating. And it was a situation in which he could only help her to a very limited extent.

But maybe he could at least relieve her heart a little.

"I promise you one thing," he said. "As soon as we have made all the preparations, the Navarch will certainly commission me to send the first expedition ashore. If we realize that the situation is peaceful and that the risk is limited, I see no reason not to allow a small group of civilians to start working within a certain framework. You will belong to this first group, that's what I am committed to. But don't tell anyone else, otherwise they'll all come running. You are not the only one with expectations."

"But the only one with such beautiful blue eyes."

Köhler grinned. "I have to warn you. Claudia Sculpia, the insect researcher, has breathtaking legs, as the male crew of this ship will be happy to confirm any time."

"So serious competition? I have to keep her away from you."

Köhler nodded seriously. "In fact, I rather assume that she also will belong to the first group. I am a simple man without great finesse, noble Terzia. Too many feminine stimuli cause me great confusion and affect my thinking. As a typical representative of my gender, I tend to find simple solutions that don't overwhelm me. You will certainly understand that."

Terzia laughed. "I want to try to understand. But I have to say that I am not yet beaten in the competition for the most beautiful legs."

Köhler raised a hand in warning and then pointed west. "I am sure that the countries we are now heading to also have many beautiful daughters. I don't want to spoil the fun, but it should be better for everyone involved not to put competition at the center of our attention."

Terzia followed Köhler's outstretched hand.

"That's okay," she said softly. "As long as I'm the center of your attention, I want to be frugal."

She nodded to him and turned away.

Köhler did not even have time to reply in a suitable way.

But it was better that way, because it didn't take long for him to realize that even after a long period of thinking, with the best intentions in the world, he wouldn't have thought of one.

18

Inugami had emerged from under the bodies of the two women only after the guards had killed them. He lacked strength, and he willingly let himself be taken by the arms and carried to the side, sitting down, breathing. He gasped for a while, concentrating on sucking air into his lungs, chasing the black clouds in front of his eyes, and thinking about what had transpired. He felt the moisture on his neck, sweat and blood, and swallowed painfully. He cursed himself and his carelessness, his carnal greed that had made him carefree. Had it not been for his personal guards being attentive and faithful, that night the end of his grandiose plans would have been sealed and he would have been just a marginal note of history, an anecdote, and others would have taken his place.

No, Inugami corrected himself, as he placed a damp cloth on the sore spots on his neck that relieved the pain of the injury. Nobody would have taken his place. Nobody had the necessary format for this. The time travelers would have become an obscurity. Forgotten in later times, their remains unearthed by researchers in the distant future, cause for great wonder and speculation, but irrelevant to the history of mankind.

Inugami closed his eyes.

Or maybe that was even what was supposed to happen. Had one ever heard of a submarine appearing out of nowhere and its crew that reformed Central America and built a powerful empire? None of this was known! Such an empire had to leave its mark on history, the Japanese was sure of that. But if he had never heard of such an event himself, then he might have already failed. Or, if this logic did not necessarily follow, it would change history, and the Inugami that had once lived in the 19th century was not the one that existed now, but a different version and time spread out like the branches of a tree, was not straight and linear. Perhaps there were many Inugamis who were sitting here now thinking about their fate, and others who were strangled on the bed and would not worry about anything. Others who peacefully decided to live in Mutal, others who desperately committed suicide when they realized that there was no return. Infinite possibilities with endless consequences and one as true as the other.

Inugami smiled. He was alive. If these other selves existed, they would have to take care of their own problems.

He looked at the dead women and felt something like regret. Killing such young flesh, those firm thighs, the fine breasts, that was a bit of a waste. But above all those who were behind this cowardly attack and whose punishment was now Inugami's task were wasted as well. These women were unimportant, the bleeding, motionless things were only tools of a higher, a male mind. Whoever was responsible for sending them to his bed to have him murdered had to pay for it. It would not be a quick and merciful death, as it had been given to the assassins. A cruel and painful end was predestined for this person.

It was a shame that the girls could no longer be interrogated. Inugami warned to instruct his guards more carefully. The one who had pulled on the garotte, yes, her death certainly had been inevitable. The others, however, should have been spared to squeeze out any information that might have been hidden in their small and weak brains. Then one would have got rid of them. Or he would have given them to his men for pleasure until they got tired of them. Yes, that would have been an appropriate fate, and fair as well.

Inugami cleared his throat. It hurt. He took a deep breath. That hurt too. But he was alive, and he intended to take advantage of this fact.

"My Lord, are you all right?"

One of the guards now dared to speak to him. Inugami might be wrong, but he heard genuine sympathy from the man's voice. It was irritating on the one hand and encouraging on the other. Despite the incident, it gave him a sense of security.

"I want to know ..." he croaked, clearing his throat again. "... know who did it."

The guard nodded and pointed to the door.

"Lord, do you want to stay in this chamber? We have prepared new accommodation."

Inugami nodded and rose. The smell of the spilled blood was heavy in the room; it would prevent him from sleeping and remind him of his disgrace. He had no illusions: the news of this incident had to spread like wildfire. That was definitely a good thing; that he had survived this assassination was a sign of the gods. But it also had two other ramifications – future conspirators would try harder, and Inugami had to seriously worry about his personal security. That would certainly cost him time and energy that he would otherwise invest in more pressing matters.

But he had to organize this himself. He was never allowed to rely too much on the services of his followers, Maya or Japanese. It was precisely in this matter that he had to establish a new culture of security, and only after its establishment he would be able to sleep peacefully again.

He left the scene and changed his mind on the way. The cool night air promised refreshment and he felt how he was still full of excitement. He was not yet ready for sleep. He ordered the guards to accompany him outside. When he stepped out of a door, he saw the peacefully sleeping city beneath him. It was still dark, but the sky was starry, and there was an almost full moon, bathing everything in a pale white light. The nightly air revived him, and he had the wet towels around his neck replaced. For a moment, he just stood there looking into the impressive sky. At that moment, actually for the first time since he had been marooned in this time, he remembered those he had left behind in his original era. There weren't many. A brother, like him a soldier, old parents whom he rarely visited. Some of the girls in town might remember him as his own memory began to wear off here. He missed the saké and would do everything possible to make at least something similar out of local means. Sarukazaki had promised to do so, but so many things had come up ...

On the other hand, he would be an even easier target for his enemies when drunk. Perhaps the time had come to rethink some of the habits he loved that might turn out to be a security problem. Now that fate had warned him sufficiently, he had an obligation to take care of his own good. If he failed to meet this obligation, there would be no excuses for him should his plans fail. Maintaining himself as the center of change in the world was a top priority.

Inugami decided not to press Sarukazaki after all. It was inevitable that the resourceful mechanic would end up putting something together like a still, and the captain wouldn't say anything against it. But it was no longer an issue to put this project at the top of the list.

"My lord."

Inugami startled from his considerations and turned. One of his slave warriors stood before him, one of the twenty-five officers whose name Inugami couldn't remember now. He nodded to him. "What is it?"

"Lord, the King of Tayasal ..."

"There is no longer a king of Tayasal," Inugami said harshly, his eyebrows furrowing. "He was deposed. Tayasal is now part of the Mutalese Empire."

The soldier winced and bowed his head. "Forgive me, sir, of course. The former king of Tayasal killed himself, sir. We found his body. His wife is dead too, he has cut her throat open. His children have apparently been taken away by servants. Shall we look for them?"

Inugami stared at the man, then made a slow, negative gesture. "When did that happen?"

"It can't be long ago. The wounds are fresh, the blood has not yet clotted."

"Thank you, you can go."

The warrior bowed and disappeared into the palace. With that, the captain realized, it was also clear who was behind the unsuccessful attempt. The fallen ruler had drawn his consequences from the failed attack. Instead of subjecting himself to an undignified execution or starving in long captivity, he had judged himself. Inugami was not satisfied with this. A proper show trial had always, at all times and in all cultures, made an impact, including a public execution, in which Inugami would have been particularly pleased in this case. This had now been denied him, and parading the body of the former king through the streets alone would not have the same effect. Better to just make it disappear.

No. No, he had to disgrace him and spread the story, that he himself, Inugami, had judged the man. Or something similar. A body that disappeared without trace only caused rumors. He had to create facts.

Inugami took a deep breath. His throat still burned, but it was getting more bearable. One would see the traces of the garotte for a long time. Should he cover them or show them openly? He chose the latter. The fact that he had survived and proudly displayed the signs of the attack shouldn't hurt him. He had to capitalize on the matter as best as was possible.

He looked at the city. It would still remain dark for some time. He felt how a certain tiredness was slowly spreading through him again. A little sleep would do him good. He had a lot of work to do tomorrow before planning his campaign against Yaxchilan.

He felt a sudden impatience to act strongly. The attack had troubled him. He knew that his time on earth was limited. It was important to proceed as quickly and consistently as possible. Yaxchilan had to fall.

Yaxchilan. And then?

Inugami allowed himself a fine smile.

There was still a lot to do.

And every setback only made him more determined.

19

"I am grateful for the concern that the Divine Ruler expresses through you," Chitam said, looking at Inocoyotl. They sat alone in the king's private chambers, isolated from servants and courtiers, as far as one could be alone in this building. They spoke in a muffled voice and did everything so that no one could hear what their conversation was about. This was necessary, because the content of their exchange was quite explosive.

"You know that the Eternal City never forgets its children," the envoy replied. "And Mutal is the first among our children. It grew up and makes us proud. But in the end we see you also with concern."

"I am aware of that."

Inocoyotl shook his head. "This worry is greater than the few words I can speak. I have to say it frankly: I do not want to imagine the reaction of the Divine Ruler to my messages and the developments described therein. Your Inugami has conquered Saclemacal, and maybe Tayasal too, most likely – and he has installed governors."

"He did. And he's not my Inugami."

Inocoyotl looked at Chitam closely. His reply came with some vehemence, almost defiantly. He hadn't expected such strong, obvious aversion. But he knew where this antipathy came from and chose clear words again.

"It has not been proven that he is behind the attack on your wife."

"But one of them is responsible for setting fire to my palace."

Indeed, Inocoyotl and Chitam had had a very open conversation so far. The King of Mutal had apparently sought to win Teotihuacán as an ally for what Inocoyotl could only describe as the King's civil war against his own city. It was not something that particularly troubled him, in fact it fit his plans well. But to show this too openly may turn out to be wrong. So he remained cautious in what he said and expressed his doubts. He didn't want to get into a position that looked like he had forced Chitam into rash actions. It was necessary for their plans that the King of Mutal remained to be his own lord, or at least that it seemed to the outside world that way. It would not benefit his position if the impression was given that the Divine City interfered in Mayan matters at will.

"I have got the impression from your descriptions that not all of the messengers agree with their Lord."

"There are differences between them."

"Can you take advantage of this?"

Chitam pursed his lips, looked thoughtful. He wasn't sure, it seemed. "I'll try. Once we agree, I speak to that one named Aritomo. The seeds of doubt are already growing in him. I have to skillfully accelerate their growth. I am still not sure how to do this. But there is definitely one on our side when the time comes, namely the tall man named Lengsley. My sister Une has her strong hands firmly around his balls. Depending on how he behaves, she will massage or crush them."

Inocoyotl found that Chitam's cold, calculating tone hadn't even changed throughout their conversation, even when he was talking about his sister. And he had spoken to "our side," as if an alliance between him and Teotihuacán was already a sealed deal. Of course, Inocoyotl believed that it all boiled down to it. Chitam, however, saw only his goal and all steps toward it as given. That could turn out to be a miscalculation.

Inocoyotl remembered the name Lengsley. It might make sense to remember him again at the right time. He leaned back and pretended to consider the other person's words. In fact, he knew exactly where the conversation would take him.

"What exactly do you expect from Teotihuacán, noble Chitam? I have to remind you that the Divine Ruler has not yet made a decision. He won't be happy with all the things I put on the table anyway. Join an alliance, yes lead it. And the formally responsible opponent, the King of Mutal himself, wants to join in. It's an … unorthodox practice."

138

"Unorthodox things are happening, Ambassador. If there is one thing for sure, it is that."

"Indeed."

Inocoyotl was not quite clear about the king's state of mind. This cold anger seemed to mix now and then with a fatalism that he regarded with concern. Fatalism led to instances where determination was paralyzed in strenuous situations. But if Chitam needed one thing, it was his determination.

Chitam, however, seemed to take Inocoyotl's doubts more seriously than before.

"My expectations are more hopes. Your ancestors from your city once helped my ancestors to rule over Mutal. You founded the dynasty from which my grandfather and father came. I hope nothing more than that the Eternal City will help me to preserve this legacy and to manage it in the spirit of the Divine Ruler. I am not clear about the nature of those who some still call messengers of the gods – but they are normal people in exceptional circumstances, I cannot describe them better. And they have plans, especially this Inugami who wants to forge an empire and is more successful than I ever thought possible. I want to stop him."

The Teotihuacán man felt that the question had to be asked that ultimately mattered when it came to the future role of his city and the whole alliance.

"Would that mean Mutal would stop conquering once Inugami is beaten?"

Inocoyotl did not miss the imperceptible hesitation with which Chitam replied. That was all too understandable. When a great gift fell into your hands that so wonderfully corresponded to your own secret desires and hopes, you didn't spontaneously tend to give it away, just because you disagreed with how you got there. But Chitam was a realist, and if not when he took office, then certainly now.

"I will reinstate the families of those places in their rightful offices and will not ask more than the usual tribute. Mutal will not strive for direct and lasting rule, not an empire, as Inugami intends to do."

Inocoyotl nodded. That was a clever answer, within the framework of the previous thinking of the Mayan rulers and thus acceptable for the other kings as well as for Teotihuacán. It made no difference whether Chitam would silently mourn no getting a new kind of realm – Inocoyotl was almost certain that he would –, it was all about the fact that Chitam did what had to be done not to replace the threat by the holy messengers with a new one, of which he was the author.

Because the spear that would be directed against Inugami could also pierce Chitam's chest when it was time. That the young king was clearly aware of this fact was shown by his well-chosen words.

"I'm going to do the following now," Inocoyotl said. "I will soon leave and travel home. It is time to report directly to my Lord and seek his advice. After that I will come back here if I am still welcome. If not, you'll find me among Inugami's enemies."

"Unless your king refuses our supplication."

"That's true. But I don't expect it. My Lord is of great wisdom. He sees the danger as yours and will do anything to eliminate it. We'll meet again, Chitam of Mutal."

The king did not look convinced, but probably decided to continue to nurture hope.

"It would be a good thing, noble Chitam, if you would live a life pleasing Inugami until then. You are of little use to all of us if dead, and if you start too soon, it will only lead to a waste of valuable energy. As soon as I have told you about my Lord's decision, we plan the rest. And if, in the meantime, you succeed in getting inclined members of the messengers on your side, then this should serve us in due course. Maybe you can put the balls of one or the other in the hands of the right woman. The tactic appears promising."

Chitam was seen to have conflicting feelings fighting in him. The young king's impatience was certainly hard to curb, his urge to retaliate for injustice suffered, especially his wife's death, was his greatest problem. But then reason prevailed, at least for the moment. He agreed.

"Noble Chitam, you must hold out now," said the ambassador. "I know what moves you, and your feelings ennoble you. Still, it would be fatal to take the wrong action too early. If my overlord accepts the leadership of the alliance against the messengers, he will want to consult with the other Mayan kings. All of this will take time."

"During this time, Inugami not only conquers Yaxchilan, but other cities too," Chitam grumbled.

"That might be true. I never said it would be an easy fight. But we can only strike effectively when we are ready. If we let the events push us, we miss our target, and the catastrophe is even bigger. If we fail, Chitam, nobody will stand in the way of Inugami, and he will achieve his goal of changing the world according to his will. Who knows if the glorious Teotihuacán will still be able to resist him? And imagine that: What limits do people or gods want to impose on a man who can then call himself the King of the Maya and the great Teotihuacán? We're playing a very daring game!"

He saw that his words had effect on the young king.

"I bow to your wise advice, ambassador," Chitam said softly. "I don't want to make mistakes. I've already made too many."

"What would you have done differently?"

"The messengers of the gods should have been caught and killed immediately."

"Would it have been so easy? Or is the power of their weapons just a rumor?"

Chitam laughed.

"No rumor, noble Inocoyotl. Not a rumor. No, it would not have been easy to do. But we should have tried. Mutal has sold his soul to Inugami and his dreams. Everyone is only talking about the great empire that we are building. Priests see themselves as kings, nobles as governors of large areas. Everyone dreams of the wealth that we are given, the power, and not a few begin to look longingly at the other big cities. If no one intervenes against this madness, Inugami will have willing helpers who will do everything possible to fulfill this dream. That is not the way of our fathers. My father didn't sacrifice himself for that."

Inocoyotl nodded. The story of the old king's death had affected him more than he expected. It was hard enough to inherit a throne this way. To see it slip out of one's hands like Chitam now was a special burden.

"We will do what we can, King of Mutal."

Chitam said nothing. It was evident from his face that he was now embracing melancholy, and it was clear that their conversation had ended. Inocoyotl muttered a few polite words of farewell before moving away from the king's presence.

Queca was waiting for him when he returned to his quarters. The officer looked at him expectantly. Even before he went to Chitam, Inocoyotl had told him to prepare for their early departure.

"We're ready to leave Mutal at once," Queca greeted him. "All the men rested and ate. If we start walking right away, we will still be able to cover a fair distance today."

"It's good, my friend. In an hour. I will give the Mutalese an opportunity to say goodbye. It's not fitting for us to disappear from the city like unwanted supplicants who have been turned away."

"Have we been turned away?"

Inocoyotl smiled.

"No, I do not think so. So my job here is done. Now we return home, and I report to the ruler. He will decide whether I acted well or have been in error."

Queca bowed respectfully and left. What remained unspoken between them was that this decision could also be a life or death decision for the envoy. And that Inocoyotl had only spoken of himself only, meant protection from the King's anger for the officer.

As far as that was possible.

20

"Lord, what does that look like?"

Balkun stared at the builder. The older man behaved appropriately respectfully, and Balkun was ready to believe him that the question was serious, of real interest. It was one of many questions asked today, and he knew that many more would follow. The problem was that he didn't know many of the answers.

"Lord, how should the warriors be trained? We don't understand the new ways!"

Balkun was able to answer this question at least in part. He had been trained in these new ways and had acquired a certain level of competence. Inugami's command – "Make me an army!" – wasn't easy to implement, but he knew where to start. And the willingness of the men of Saclemacal to learn was there. They had noticed how to lose to a new, a modern army, and no matter what happened, they didn't want it to happen a second time.

"Lord, what should the walls look like?"

That's where the problems started. Balkun was a farmer, not a builder. He didn't build anything. The largest he had ever built was his own mud hut. He had no idea, but Inugami's command had been: "Fortify the city! Build walls!"

The fact that the builders from Saclemacal asked him for advice on such things was of course out of spitefulness. They were competent enough to build a city wall. But they didn't want to go forward so readily, think and plan for themselves. They wanted the Governor, who spoke in the name of the messengers of the gods, to have problems piling on his lap so that he would eventually sink under the burden of his tasks. And they wanted him to say silly things that they could enjoy and by which they proved the governor's unsuitability.

They were on the right track with that.

"Lord, what should the sacrificial rituals look like? It will soon be a full moon!"

One of the orders that Balkun was most likely to sign was Inugami's clear instruction that human sacrifice would be banned in the future. Instead, only ritual slaughter of animals was permitted, and the priests had been made absolutely clear that any violation would be punished with their own execution. This did not stop an eager representative of the gods – Balkun had already had to carry out this judgment before – and the priests, as the most powerful group in every city, persistently showed themselves to be inconsistent. He knew the rituals as well as any peasant. And now he should give the priests instructions on what exactly should be changed? He wasn't ready for it. As long as the basic command was carried out, he didn't care.

"Lord, how much tribute do we pay to Mutal?"

This was as difficult to understand for Balkun as it was for the governing elite of the conquered city. Inugami had introduced a two-tier tax system – on the one hand, Balkun was required to levy a tax to keep his administration running and to care for a standing army consisting of the Mutalese garrison and a Saclemacal regiment. He also had to pay a regular tax to Mutal, which consisted of obsidian blades and food. All the other common tributes – gifts for the kings, gorgeous clothing, and the like – had been done away with. Inugami had invented a word for it that Balkun had a hard time understanding: "War economy." The orientation of all production was toward one goal: to wage a war of conquest and enable the armies to operate every day of the year. The instruction had been clear, but the former masters of Saclemacal had difficulty understanding the concept behind it. Balkun felt with them. But it changed nothing.

"Lord, when will the great Inugami come back?"

Balkun had no illusions about the motivation for this question. There was no ardent need to see the Master of the messengers again in order to feast on his delicious personality and extensive wisdom. It was more of a fear of control from the new ruler and the question of how long you had to manipulate the stupid peasant son Balkun. Because that's exactly what it was all about – overwhelming him with problems, then apparently submissively offering their own solutions, gradually letting the city administration slip back into the hands of the old elite in order to relieve the poor governor and provide distractions at the same time. Balkun had never been such an attractive man before, so beautiful, the city's daughters gathered around him and vied for his favor. Never before had Balkun been offered so much exquisite food and drink. If he decided to do so, he could spend his waking hours with permanent lust and gluttony. He felt the temptation one time or another, he admitted it to himself.

But they didn't know the stupid peasant well enough.

Balkun knew what he really wanted. Secure his position so that one day he could be reunited with his family. Inugami would take his home, there was no doubt about it. The Lord of the messengers had previously ensured that unnecessary slaughter on the ordinary population was avoided. He saw every Maya as the material he needed for his plans, and killing women and children would unnecessarily reduce that material and its potential expansion. So there was a good chance that his wife and children would survive the attack, especially since the warrior slaves had little interest in killing their own families.

Balkun wasn't even sure if they would attack the city's defenders. That was the big uncertainty factor now. Could Inugami rely on this army? It had worked in Saclemacal and Tayasal, certainly because the majority of the slave army originally came from Yaxchilan and had no extraordinary sympathy for the two smaller cities. But now the warrior slaves were coming home. Would Inugami be careful in his approach? This was unlikely given that the bulk of the army consisted of Mutal's free fighters. The slaves would die if they turned against their new masters. And if the fight was fairly light ...

If. But.

Balkun looked at the petitioners and notables in front of him. For them, the new governor seemed to be distracted a bit. Some seemed to be pleased. A ruler who was not completely on the job could easily be manipulated, looked overwhelmed and could not grow on the job. Was he dreaming? One would neither disturb him nor burden him with unimportant details.

Balkun smiled and turned to one of them. He took a deep breath. "I will take over the training unit for the new warriors myself in an hour. I wish that the best of them are in the front row and pay particular attention to what I do. I have worked out a precise plan. Some of my garrison comrades will act as instructors and implement the plan. If there are problems with this, contact the instructor. You are responsible for the new warriors."

One bowed.

Balkun continued to smile and turned to another. "The sacrificial rituals are the prerogative of priests alone. I don't want to touch your sacred duties, and I do not want to interfere unduly. Inugami's order must be carried out so that no more human sacrifices may be made. The priests decide which alternative sacrifices are suitable, and I want to accept their judgment. They should ask the gods for guidance and inspiration, and I am sure they will have an answer."

One bowed.

Balkun, still smiling, turned to the third. "We pay the amount of tribute to Mutal that is possible after the next harvest. The great Inugami told me to send a tenth of all food to Mutal. However, we only pay tribute to equipment and weapons after our own troops are well equipped with everything. We send the obsidian alone, which we do not need, together with the food, and only when the harvest is complete. That is my order."

One bowed.

Balkun rose and turned to everyone. He wasn't smiling now. "Yaxchilan is falling soon. The big city will become a slave to Mutal, like we are all slaves to the new empire. On the way back to the capital, the great Inugami will also pass by and ask if everything has worked out as he ordered. I advise you to make sure that is the case, because the Lord of the messengers is not a gracious Lord. Where he punishes me, the punishment also falls on you. My pain will only be mine, but yours will be felt everywhere, in the whole city. If you wish not to be punished, do your best to carry out all the orders. I can be missing and replaced, as Inugami wishes. But his hand around your throat will never come loose, I assure you."

His words hadn't failed, he could see that. He looked around, as if inviting contradictions, but nobody spoke.

"The audience is over," he said then, raising both arms. "Go."

Everyone bowed.

Balkun smiled again.

The throne room emptied except for the servants and guards. Balkun sat on his throne and looked again into the void.

Now he was allowed to ponder and dream a little. There was so much to decide and prepare, not least the best plan how he could reunite with his family, and how he would, one day, betray Inugami and Mutal.

There was no doubt in his mind that he had to and wanted to do that.

Perhaps the defiant men of Saclemacal would help him.

21

"It's not the army we once had," Nachi Cocom said, looking down at the warriors that had gathered in the main square of Yaxchilan. "It's not the army we wanted to use to defeat Mutal."

It was a statement, and he tried to keep the melancholy out of his voice as much as possible. But it was difficult for him. When he thought of what was lost, completely irretrievably, he simply felt melancholy.

"It's more than we can expect," his wife replied, nodding to him. "The surrounding towns have sent us men, as far as they can, to help defend our homeland. We are not Tayasal, my lord. We are not cowards."

Nachi Cocom had become the ruler of Yaxchilan without having specifically applied for it. At the time of the old king's departure, when he embarked toward Mutal, so full of anticipation and certainty of victory, Cocom had been lying sick on his bed, shaken by the fever. It was as if the gods had made sure that he couldn't take part in this fateful attack. He had not become a slave to the messengers, and his blood did not flow down the streets of Mutal. Instead, he, one of the city's highest nobles, had been made the last representative of an elite, of which most remained on the battlefield. He had let himself be driven more by the events than to actively control them, and when he took on this position, he knew immediately that he was facing a gigantic task. The expectations that lay on him were enormous. The mere fact that he did not act timidly and desperately raised him above many others in the city.

However, it had become a more interesting job than he had initially imagined.

The emissary of the alliance, a hurried traveler from B'aakal, had stretched out his hand in friendship, and he had taken it like a drowning man grasping for a piece of driftwood. The envoy had come with 200 warriors who had traveled the distance in hard marches, dispatched as soon as Saclemacal's case had been reported in B'aakal, and then contingents of other, smaller towns from the area had been added. All of them had to pay tribute, and Nachi had done nothing more than claim his right.

Along with the returnees from Mutal, those who were neither fallen nor slaves, Nachi Cocom had an army with which he would have gone into battle with some confidence under normal circumstances. But these were not normal circumstances. The returnees' descriptions had startled him. At first he couldn't believe all of this. But if even the envoy from B'aakal said that the danger was not imaginary, then there had to be something wrong with the rumors.

The Mutalese army was large, one of the largest, and it was full of self-confidence, as one would expect. But not so long ago, the men of Yaxchilan had been able to find out how much that could be deceiving. The difference, however, was that Nachi did not own any miraculous godly weapons he could use against the enemy.

If the reports from Saclemacal and Tayasal were correct, the arsenal of miracle weapons was also rather limited among the attackers. There were some impressive constructions, like huge bows that could do considerable damage, and Mutal's soldiers, at least those warrior slaves, were equipped differently and fought in a new way, which seemed to be quite threatening, very organized, not following the known principles. The individual fighter was less important – it was the unit that counted –, and the way of fighting was the same as if everyone were just puppets that were pulled by invisible threads. No more space for individual fame, for outstanding deeds, for personal triumph, but possibly fewer deaths on your own and more on the side of your opponents.

Ultimately, however, it was the simple superiority that posed the greatest danger, and knocking out this important advantage for the enemy was Nachi's defense plan.

It was a daring game. It could end in a slaughter that the history of the Maya had never seen before. Maybe plan was based on a fatal mistake on his part.

But it was the only serious option, and it was the new king's duty to use it. He would not throw himself in the dust like the rulers of the two smaller cities in front or let himself be largely defenseless. If he did so, the conqueror would be left unchecked, no one would seriously stand in his way, and the newly formed alliance of B'aakal would be weakened before it really intervened.

Nachi Cocom had to try, even if it included the possibility of his own downfall.

And his people were with him. He saw fear, of course, the same one that filled him. But he also saw determination, the courage of despair and the grief over the victims, whose cruel fate had already shaken them.

He had talked to them for a long time. He had wanted to convince them, not just order something. Everyone was now familiar with his tactics. His men would now go into town and inform the population. They would go to any hut, to any family that had sent a warrior to Mutal who had not returned. When the messenger army approached, they would all come together and form their own force. They would not carry weapons, only women and children, at best boys just before they reached the age of majority. Mothers who carried babies in their arms and who should oppose the warrior slaves. Their husbands, brothers, sons and fathers.

A dumb, defenseless army. No, Nachi corrected himself in thought. Not defenseless. Their power was not that of the atlatl, the spear and the ax. Their power was the carefully painted faces of women and girls, the big eyes of children. Their powers were the enthusiastic calls when a daughter or son recognized the father. A power from which only the completely heartless, the fundamentally changed, the brutalized and stupid could shut themselves off.

Of course, this demonstration could fail completely. There were Mutal's soldiers, the real enemy. They could press ahead with the attack, they could even turn against the slaves, drive them forward, threaten them with death. But how far would they go? Did the first woman, the first child of a warrior slave, die from a hurled spear, provide the tipping point where this new, so well-disciplined army

150

would turn against its creator? Nachi calculated exactly with such a development, with this reaction. He wasn't comfortable with it but lacked military power to defend himself conventionally. Yaxchilan had no fortified walls yet, although the new king realized that a new era had also begun for future urban layouts. A lot would change if they survived this war. The city would change. Not all old ways had proven themselves. The Maya had looked very much into the inside.

It was time to look outside too.

Nachi tilted his head back and looked up at the sky.

Or upside, if the Mutalese stories were true.

He stood alone in the throne room at Yaxchilan. His wife had said goodbye when all words had been said. She would now ensure that their children together with some companions would go to B'aakal to receive protection there. Nachi claimed this privilege if his fate were otherwise sealed in the event of a defeat. Even if he surrendered, chances were he would find death. He was a living symbol, and that was more dangerous than a martyr. Inugami seemed to be like someone who knew how to weigh his alternatives, and Nachi knew what he would do in the case, as a conqueror, as someone who wanted to establish an empire, a ruler like the Maya lands had never seen before.

He understood what was attractive about this idea. It was just far more difficult not to be the conqueror, but to be conquered. It gave him ... perspective.

"Lord, the wife of Balkun, as requested."

Nachi jumped from his thoughts and nodded to the servant. He waved. Moments later a young woman entered the throne room, looking shy. She was strong, with calluses on her hands that showed hard work. She wore a simple robe, but it had been cleaned and patched up for the audience with the king, and looked as neat as a peasant woman could appear, whose husband had disappeared since the campaign and carried the burden to feed her family alone on her shoulders.

She bowed deeply, obviously not quite knowing how to behave properly in the presence of the high lord.

"Get up," he said softly. "We'll sit down there."

He pointed to the two stone stools. In front of it was a low table on which the servants had served food, enough to satisfy them. The woman sat as ordered and hardly dared to look at him openly. Nachi sighed inwardly. That made this conversation neither easier for him nor for her.

"I need to talk to you about your husband, Balkun, if I'm not mistaken," he said, and immediately noticed how the woman's body stiffened and a fearful expression shaded her face.

"That's his name. Do you have any news? Is he alive?"

Nachi nodded.

"As far as I know, he's fine. Actually very fine. Yesterday a refugee from Tayasal told me what kind of fate befell him."

The fear did not want to disappear from the woman's eyes.

"Your name is Bulu, right?"

She smiled.

"Your husband is alive. He has risen. The messenger of the gods made him king of Saclemacal, by his grace. He rules the city in the name of the new conqueror."

Bulu stared at Nachi in disbelief, which made him smile.

"At first I couldn't really believe it. Tell me about Balkun."

The woman seemed to be awakened by this question. Perhaps it was also the realization that she was now the wife of a king that made her lose a little of her shyness. "My husband ... he's a simple man."

"I heard that he increased his family's wealth in his life."

Bulu nodded. "He was the fourth son of a farming family, without any inheritance or land rights of any kind. He married me and built our house. He works hard. Our store is filled with corn, the children wear clothes. My eldest son is very intelligent. A master builder took him on as an apprentice. Balkun worked very hard for this. He is a good man."

The last sentence came out a little weak, an indication that the woman was telling the king not simply a story but the truth. A good man who was now working for the enemy. After all, he would not be part of the army, and Bulu and her children would not be part of the human wall the king sought to build.

152

It was significant that Bulu's question took up precisely this thought. "Will he come to Yaxchilan, my lord? Will he be among the attackers?"

Nachi shook his head. "It is unlikely. Balkun manages the past conquest of the messengers. His task is not to expand the realm, but to secure it. He's in Saclemacal, as far as I know."

Bulu's face clouded. "What should happen now?"

Nachi nodded. A legitimate question and the reason why he asked her to come to him.

"Balkun is simple, you say, and yet it seems to have certain qualities. He is hardworking, I understand, and he has fought bravely on several campaigns, as I have been told. So he's not a man without courage."

"That's right, sir. But now he's a slave to the messengers."

"There are slaves of different kinds. Status doesn't say much about a man and his influence."

"I can't judge that, sir. We have no slaves. We're glad we're free."

"So the status must weigh on Balkun."

Bulu nodded without hesitation, and Nachi had the impression of openness and honesty again. "He loves his freedom and that of his family. We never got into debt or got into blood feuds. Balkun has wisely kept us away from all of this. I lack his protection."

The last sentence sounded weak again, a little shaky, and Nachi decided he was doing the right thing. "The enemy will attack soon. I'll defend the city as best I can, but I don't know how the battle will end."

"Yes, my lord," Bulu said worriedly.

"How big is your family?"

"Two daughters and a son, sir."

"The daughters still live with you?"

"They're too young to get married."

Nachi nodded. "I want you to collect your family and pack supplies. I will give you one of my men who will accompany you. You are traveling to Saclemacal, and as quickly as possible. To not meet the soldiers of the enemy, you will make a detour, so the journey will take a little longer. You should collect sufficient food and new sandals. Go to Saclemacal and return to your husband. You will be safe there, and you and your children will be fine."

Bulu looked at her king in amazement ... and with suspicion.

Nachi smiled inwardly. He liked it when people reacted that way. It was a sign of intelligence to suspect a ruse behind a ruler's blessing. Nachi's respect for this peasant woman grew.

"Should I deliver a message to him?" she asked.

"No."

"Should I ... advise him on something specific?"

"No."

"What should I do?"

"Leave and live with your husband in peace."

Bulu still had that searching look, but it was obvious that she couldn't think of another question. She hesitated, glanced at the dishes that none of them had touched. Nachi because he wasn't hungry, and the woman hadn't dared to eat in the presence of the king without being asked to do so.

Which Nachi had, of course, missed. He sighed. "Eat, Bulu, eat. I'll have something to eat too."

To emphasize his words, he picked up a flatbread and bit into it. As always, the food was excellent. The woman also took a heart and started nibbling on something. She looked very thoughtful. She was probably wondering what kind of fate would await her in Saclemacal and whether the difficult journey would be without incident.

"A clever plan, high lord," Bulu said then, without being asked. "You send me to my husband as a sign. You remind him of his king's loyalty and generosity. He should have a guilty conscience that he is now serving the enemies of Yaxchilan and should be prepared for when you or your allies ask for his help."

Nachi put the flatbread aside and looked at Bulu with a mixture of wonder and respect. He knew that simple people should not be considered stupid simply because they were not noble or had no education. "Good, you can read my mind," he said softly. "A bad plan in your eyes? Will you advise him not to go this way?"

"I'll advise him not to have a guilty conscience," the woman replied in a brave voice. "He went to battle and was caught and enslaved. If anyone is supposed to feel bad, it's Tatb'u, the old king."

"As far as I heard, he felt the consequences of his arrogance. But what will you advise your husband to do?"

"That he should do what he thinks is right. That has helped us all in the past, why shouldn't it continue to do so in the future? Balkun is not a fool, as you have rightly noticed. No fool is made a slave-king of a whole city. Balkun knows what he's doing, he always knew." She looked at him and paused for a moment as if to consider her next words carefully. "I know my husband. When the day comes when you want to send him a message to get him to rebel against the messengers of the gods, he will read that message and consider its content. But I tell you right away, it is not the question of the legitimacy of a king that drives him, but the question of what kind of world his children should grow up in. If he takes pleasure in obeying this Inugami, only extortion will keep him from following his heart. And here you are doing one thing, if you allow me this judgment: With sending me, you give away the instrument with which he could be blackmailed. That is exactly what will increase the weight of your words – or those of your friends – when one day they are spoken."

Nachi nodded slowly. A long speech for a peasant woman whom he had little confidence in and which contained wisdom, the right conclusions, and the desired perspective. Nachi felt strengthened in his decision. He would use the families of the other warrior slaves as a leverage, as he had decided, and this act might diminish his good impression on Bulu. But on the other hand, she was smart enough to know why he was doing everything he was.

Nachi looked at the flatbread he had picked up again. For a moment he wondered why he suddenly valued this woman's opinion. It may have had its own guilty conscience to carry.

No, most definitely, he did.

He sighed, now clearly audible, and smiled at Bulu.

"Eat in peace, wife of Balkun, and then leave in peace."

"Thank you, noble sir."

22

The sandstone shattered under the steady chisel of the artisan. Aritomo saw him skillfully use the obsidian tool and drive it into the stone from above with a flat mallet. He worked in a way that had two effects at the same time – the sandstone only lost as much of its consistency as was necessary to fit seamlessly into the wall, and the chisel was used as little as possible. However, it was common for such a chisel to have to be recut after one day and often to be no longer usable after a second. There was a whole chain of artisans who stood invisibly behind this man and who had to provide the tools he needed for his work. The lack of metal tools was a difficult handicap in the eyes of the Japanese. Iron ore was certainly found in Central America, and they would look for it, begin with simple mining and smelting, and not only revolutionize Mayan construction but certainly weapon technology as well. But until then, the locals mainly used the softer precious metals to which they had access but which were rather unsuitable for tools.

Aritomo shaded his eyes. The section of the wall here, directly on the street to the west, was the first to be built. They had already planned the wide opening for the gate, and the two parts of the wall that joined to the right and left of the street were each a good four meters long. The height should be three meters, with a wooden walkway behind it. The thickness, decided based on security and urgency, was no more than one meter, enough for the time being, in order to withstand an attack of enemies unfamiliar in the art of a proper siege. The building of the wall was necessary because everyone, including Inugami, knew exactly that any new military technology would spread like wildfire. The kind of onagers and catapults they built today would be part of the arsenal of those who resisted the Mutalese expansion tomorrow. The sooner and the better they prepared for that day, the longer Mutal would survive. It was in everyone's interest.

Building a city wall was not a particular challenge for the city's builders. Anyone who was able to build gigantic palaces and pyramids, understood the concept of a fortification with ease. It was surprising that the Mayan cities were largely unprotected, despite the fact that their external relations were often warlike. It had to have something to do with the tradition that Inugami had now started to break – to renounce the permanent conquest and occupation of an inferior city and, after a sufficient symbolic submission, to deploy at most one new dynasty and be satisfied with a tribute.

"A wall," Chitam said, looking at the work of the builders, who were concentrating on what they were doing and were not put off by the presence of the high visitors. "We're building a wall around us. This shows very well how we now act and think. I am not sure if this the will of the gods."

Aritomo did not know whether the last sentence really had to do with a newly awakened spirituality on the part of the king. Chitam had never seemed particularly pious to him.

"The wall protects the city," he said simply.

"From enemies that we wouldn't have had without your intervention."

Aritomo had not missed the sarcastic undertone. "You had enough enemies, too, and Mutal would have been attacked. The difference now lies in the nature of the struggle. I disagree with many things my commander does. You should have noticed that by now, noble majesty. But I think there's nothing wrong with protecting your own home as well as possible, and this wall protects the valuable life of warriors and residents alike."

Chitam wiped his forehead. "Ha! 'Majesty' no more. I think my title has lost a lot of shine in the past few weeks. My priests, the clan chiefs, are all raving about the new age that is now dawning. The wall is only a tiny aspect. They are all blinded by the prospect of power and glory. They see this structure more as a symbol of military rise and strength. Am I the only one who sees a fence that hugs us like animals?"

158

"Certainly not. But Inugami's vision is contagious, that's true."

"So you don't share this vision?"

Aritomo didn't hesitate to answer. He had prepared for this conversation, and knew what to say. "I want to do everything possible to ensure the safety and well-being of my crew, their survival in a strange world. But I don't think I have to forcefully submit this world to my will and dreams. Inugami disagrees."

"How far will you follow him?"

Aritomo smiled and nodded. "That is the central question, isn't it? But you consider me to be more than I am. What will happen if I openly oppose my leader? How many of my crew are ready to join me? What consequences can I expect?"

Chitam looked at Aritomo inquiringly, he seemed to understand what the man was getting at. "You are not alone, but by no means in the majority."

"That's the way it is. If I stand against Inugami, I am a dead man or at least a prisoner. And if I have allies, the same fate will happen to them."

Chitam seemed to understand but still didn't want to see it. "Your commander set my palace on fire."

Aritomo said nothing. He was listening.

Chitam spoke softly, but with strong emotion in his words, insistently, almost conjuring. He described the conversation again in detail that he had had with Balkun as if the constant repetition had to provoke a guilty conscience. "Your horror was limited when we first had this conversation, and I can see that little has changed," the king said dryly – and possibly a little hurt if one listened carefully.

"I've been thinking about it for a long time."

"What conclusions did you come to about my wife's death?"

"I'm afraid my commander ordered this assassination too."

Chitam grimaced, as if complaining that Aritomo was only now beginning to think of this. "You were not informed."

"I have not been informed until today. I've drawn my own conclusions."

Chitam looked at Aritomo as if by looking at the sweaty moon-like face he could find out if he was telling the truth. He gave it up after a few moments and stared at the construction again. "So what do you think, Aritomo?"

"I already said that. To openly oppose Inugami would not stop the catastrophe and would do little. But if I remain his deputy and if he continues to entrust me with important tasks, I will be able to ... limit the bad effects of his actions."

Chitam uttered a sound that Aritomo did not know whether it was a word or not. "My wife's death was not bad enough?"

There was bitterness again, an accusation and hurt in Chitam's voice. But the Japanese did not let himself be disturbed. "It was a tragedy. Had I known about these plans, I would have done anything to stop Inugami from doing so. And my commander knew that too – that's why he didn't let me in on it."

Chitam nodded. "I suppose so. So you will remain to work as his right hand."

"I don't see any alternative at the moment. Do you have one?"

"Yes."

Aritomo fell silent, waited, but it didn't look like Chitam wanted to reveal much more. In fact, the Japanese already suspected that this was the case. The king's long and intensive discussions with the envoy from Teotihuacán had by no means escaped him. Sawada had also told him about his encounter with Inocoyotl. Neither of them could assess the importance of the city the emissary represented. But if he believed what was heard, it was the regional superpower. It would not surprise him if Chitam, who traced his line back to conquerors from that metropolis, asked them for help. And if Chitam came up with this idea, then maybe other Mayan kings would as well. Aritomo had been intensively introduced to the political landscape. He still didn't understand all of the relationships, but the likelihood that Mutal's opponents would stand by and watch Inugami's expansion for much longer was extremely slim. With Chitam they would have a valuable ally, with Teotihuacán the leading military power at their side, and with him, Aritomo, a very important insider.

"I have to emphasize one thing again," Aritomo said softly. "I'm concerned with the safety of my people, whether they're blinded by Inugami or not. I will always stand up for any alternative that promises more security."

"You are indulging in a dangerous illusion," Chitam said now. "As the best-protected personality of the powerful Mutal, I was able to experience for myself that security is an idea that we like to calm down ourselves with but which can prove to be a very fleeting blessing."

Aritomo couldn't argue with him.

"But you have to weigh alternatives, just like me. Nevertheless, the day will come when I will remind you of this conversation, Aritomo Hara. Then you may have to make a decision that you're currently afraid of. I don't see a way to please everyone. This war is not a game. Everyone will have to choose one side one time."

Chitam leaned over to Aritomo's ear and began to whisper. "If you choose the side that fights Inugami, I can do nothing more than promise to do everything I can for the life and well-being of your people, regardless of how each individual decides. I swear on it with my blood. I have the impression that this is more than Inugami himself would be prepared to swear by."

Then the king took one last look at the construction site, beckoned to his guards and servants who had been waiting at a respectful distance, and started to move with them. Aritomo stayed behind, deep in thought.

The king's last sentence aroused doubts that had previously been hidden deep within. He had become less and less certain of his loyalty to the captain, sure, and that had caused him problems because it contradicted his oath and upbringing. But Chitam had pointed out a question he had not yet asked himself: what was Inugami's loyalty to his own people? What or who was he willing to sacrifice for his plans?

The fact that he did not know a clear and unambiguous answer worried Aritomo Hara more than he wanted to admit.

Much more.

23

"Land, without a doubt!"

Langenhagen lowered the telescope and nodded. He looked satisfied. As much as he loved the sea, it was a good thing to finally arrive. This is where his real work began.

"Our position is clear. If we interpret the nautical charts of the time-wanderers correctly, we have the northeastern tip of the Yucatan Peninsula in front of us. It is very likely that there are ports here at this time as well – we should see the first ones soon."

Langenhagen nodded to Köhler. It was obvious to him that he was happy. The long and exhausting crossing came to an end. As exhausting as the time had been so far, the sea voyage offered a certain monotony in its eternally identical procedures. But now the purpose of the expedition became tangible and the anticipation was palpable with all crew-members.

"We stay far out of the coastline. I want to avoid entering a port immediately. Our defense position must be secured. I want to go to one of the islands along the coast first so that we can build a supply base there. Maybe we can also find out from there what the political situation on the mainland looks like."

"If we can somehow talk to the locals," added Köhler. Indeed, that would be the biggest problem. To this end, they brought with them a master of the Ravenna Academy, who distinguished himself primarily by speaking and understanding seven languages fluently. He was even one of the few who still inherited the legacy of the time-wanderer-languages. There had been some effort to preserve both modern German and English, but everyone had to admit that ultimately this was reserved for only a few experts. The master belonged to this select group.

That would in no way enable the elderly gentleman, who had spent most of the journey below deck sick, to speak to the locals immediately. There was hope, however, that he would be able to learn the basics of the language quickly if they found someone who was willing to teach them. Above all, he should quickly create records, a dictionary, a grammar, a basis for many more people to learn the new language as quickly as possible. In any case, everyone had to learn and fast.

"What about Cozumel? The island is conveniently located." Langenhagen pointed to the folded map, the relevant section of which was visible.

"It is the area we are currently observing," Köhler said. "I think it will be inhabited because it is easy to reach from the mainland even with simple boats if the weather is fair. However, if we find a landing site on the side opposite the mainland, we should use it. We don't know anything about the inhabitants here, except that they were called Maya at the time of the time-wanderers. But they are probably not great sailors. If they only do coastal fishing and trading, there shouldn't be a major settlement on the sea side of the island, apart maybe from a fishing village."

The commander nodded slowly. "Well. A base here could help us. Even if the residents react aggressively, there cannot be that many, and military operations would certainly be very difficult for them, especially against our weapons. We'll take a closer look at the matter. I want four observers with telescopes on each ship. I want the cartographers to take action and compare the coastlines with the nautical charts. We start working immediately, including the measurements. There's no reason to put it off any longer."

"Yes, Navarch," Köhler confirmed the order.

"For now we're keeping our distance. I don't want to be noticed early by an adventurous paddler. As soon as we have identified a suitable landing site from afar, we will move closer – but not before."

"I'm sending the command to the other ships."

Since the shortwave transmitter was functioning again to some extent, communication between the units of the flotilla was restored, even if there was no direct visual contact. They had even received reports from Rome, though not always in full, and had sent their own short reports back, often repeated several times, in the hope that the fragments could be used to compile a complete text. The Morse code, which they had taken over from the time-wanderers, was well suited for this and Langenhagen knew that there were well-trained experts in the receiving station of the fleet, which had been set up especially for the three expeditions in all directions of the world. The long break, during which they had been unable to communicate due to the storm and its aftermath, had certainly been a great test of uncertainty for those who stayed at home. It was a relief to be able to report on the progress of the mission again.

A few minutes later, Köhler observed how the observers took up positions on the masts and on the bow, and the cartographer of the ship, loaded with paper and writing utensils, joined them. Everyone began to focus immediately on the distant coastline, and the artist himself used a telescope to search for distinctive formations that he could compare with the entries on his map. They had noticed long ago that the maps of the future needed to be corrected, because the coastlines had changed over the centuries, be it due to natural influences or human intervention. In the Mediterranean, where the construction of canals and harbors had had a visible impact, adapting the maps had been a major challenge that had lasted almost a decade. Köhler was excited to see how big the deviations were in the case of America.

And it was good that now, at that moment, they could start the serious work.

The ships turned. Your broadside now pointed to the distant coastline. The country's residents were unlikely to have optical instruments that enabled them to locate the arriving visitors. But there were always people with particularly sharp eyes, and caution would be required before the coastline was fully understood.

Köhler went below deck.

There, the crew members, who were trained as carpenters and builders, were already busy getting the tools of their work out of the boxes. They would be among the second group to go ashore after the soldiers, and if the general conditions turned out to be favorable, trees would be felled immediately and construction of the base started. There were pre-made plans to stick to, depending on the building materials available. The men would be ready, Köhler convinced himself after a short inspection. There was a sense of optimism everywhere, the great joy of the beginning adventure, the willingness to take the step into the unknown.

The marines had also gathered under the foredeck and began to subject their weapons to a final inspection. Centurion Angelicus was the commanding officer of the small force, not just the men of the *Gratianus*, but the whole expedition. Angelicus had served both on land and on water for many years, a veteran of the war against the Huns. At almost forty, he was one of the oldest men on board, apart from a few scientists. He was known for his courage and complete disregard for other people's lives and sufferings, and that was often helpful in a combat situation. Nevertheless, neither Langenhagen nor Köhler would send him alone without someone who was willing to ask first and fight second. Despite his beautiful name, Angelicus was not a man of diplomacy and leniency. Everyone was initially a potential threat and treated as such. He was someone who was ready at any time to go over dead bodies to achieve a goal, and had no problem in calculating the deaths of his own men. His tactical understanding and personal courage distinguished him, but there was a reason why he had never become more than a centurion.

Köhler nodded briefly to the massive man when he looked at him questioningly. He didn't want to disturb. Nobody voluntarily bothered Angelicus in his actions if one valued human dignity or front teeth.

Everyone was ready for the big day of landing. Köhler could feel it. There were no more arguments, no more frustrated faces. Everywhere the duties were fulfilled with tension and anticipation, even with dedication. Everyone whose tasks had to do with the landing doubled their efforts, so it wasn't up to him if there was to be a delay. For many, this was the reason why they went to sea – to get to places where no Roman had ever been before, to do a pioneering work, and, without a doubt, to achieve eternal glory. Köhler, who had a somewhat more prosaic view of things, could still not completely free himself from this feeling. He hid it behind the mask of professional serenity, but in his spare minutes, too, found himself reviewing his personal gear, making the first steps on strange shores in his mind's eye. A sandy beach, possibly, never-before-seen plants, animals whose shape was new, probably just as much as their taste, and then, of course, Terzia's calves as they waded through the shallow water …

At that point, Köhler generally ended his fantasies, because they seemed inappropriate to him. What this woman did with his imagination had long left the area of morally acceptable enthusiasm and was increasingly moving into areas where sweaty skin and rubbing it together played a prominent role.

That would only distract him now. And despite all the friendly flirting, he was by no means clear about his chances. In addition, he was not allowed to use his privileges as a member of the ship's command. There were only a few women on board. Everyone had been instructed to maintain the highest level of discipline.

Trierarch Köhler also fell under the category "everyone." He did well to remember this simple fact, as difficult as it was sometimes.

It took a few days to sail the coastline of the island from a reasonable distance until they found a suitable landing site. It was a wonderful sandy beach, as Köhler imagined, and the water was deep enough to get relatively close to it. Building a wooden pier would not be a big job, and the men on board were well trained for that, too. In addition, there was no settlement far and wide, no ship had been seen, no village, no soul on the beach. It was likely to be different inside the island, but once they set up their base, it wouldn't matter. The contact was inevitable. But if they did it on the basis of an established base, it might be easier.

Köhler himself entered the first of the three rowboats that would bring a group ashore. After a few maneuvers, the flotilla had anchored around 200 meters off the coastline, lined up like a string, the broad sides of the cannon rows facing both sea and land. The three large boats each held 20 people, and besides Köhler there were only soldiers under the command of Angelicus who would make the first step.

Security came first. They would go inland, not far, but far enough to identify any immediate danger.

No sooner had the sailors pushed the boat away from the *Gratianus* than the men lay down on their straps. Köhler sat next to the man holding the rudder and watched the beach getting closer. They were all fully equipped for a fight.

But there was no one to be seen.

The officer felt relief.

He wasn't here to fight. Angelicus might see it differently, but Köhler was fully aware of it. He might be a soldier, but here he was a researcher and felt that way.

Finally they reached the sandy beach. It was immaculate white. When the men pulled up the boat and piled ashore, they watched the nearby row of trees that marked the beginning of a relatively dense forest.

"Building materials," Angelicus said with satisfaction.

Köhler nodded. "Send a patrol a mile either way down the beach. Two patrols are to advance into the forest. If they encounter flowing water, the path must be marked immediately."

Water was one of the most important resources that the expedition needed. Their supplies on board the ships had run out. Even if this location ultimately turned out to be unsuitable for a base, a fresh water source had to be found before the journey could continue.

Angelicus nodded and gave his orders. Köhler himself trudged along the beach and examined the ground. A few meters inland it got a little rockier, which meant that a good foundation for the planned fort could be built here if they stayed at this point. The trees seemed suitable for the construction of the accommodation, one would not have to carry them far. It was necessary to reach far into the forest – they needed a free zone around the fort that could be defended by projectiles and easy access to fresh water, which they hoped would find. On the other hand, the fort had to kiss the beach, be connected directly to the pier, which was then also on the list of structures to be built. It was a work that required considerable effort, but which, if everyone tackled it, should result in a shell construction in a relatively short time. Further fortifications, such as the erection of a stone wall, could then be tackled with a somewhat reduced intensity.

Köhler saw the legionnaires set out in groups of three to take a closer look at the immediate area. Angelicus had apparently now decided that they would stay here longer, because he had ordered those who stayed behind to get out of the boats the tarpaulins they had brought. The fact that he nevertheless began to place guards in a wide area spoke in turn for his caution.

Köhler shaded his forehead. From here there was a hill about two kilometers away, which should actually allow a view of the interior of the island.

"Centurion!"

Angelicus stood next to him as quickly as if he had grown out of the sand. "Trierarch!"

"Give me three men. I want to go up there and survey the island with binoculars."

Angelicus roared something, and within a short time three strong legionnaires had started, one of them a decurio, who immediately saluted and took the order. Köhler grabbed another bottle of water and began to march toward the intended target.

24

"Of course that's the other alternative," Bahlam, King of B'aakal, admitted thoughtfully.

"It's a better option than getting her killed," his wife said, looking up from the work she was doing in the evening. It was relatively rare for Bahlam to find time to spend a few quiet hours with his wife, and she took the opportunity to provide her husband with advice in regard to his governance that he might otherwise have missed. Not that the massive man missed too much. He had an alert mind and was highly intelligent. But one couldn't think of everything, especially in times like this.

"It's dangerous," Bahlam said, looking at the empty mug in his hand.

"I suppose she is. I saw her training with the old warrior. She hurls the atlatl like a man. The spear rests lightly in her hand. Did you see the muscles on her arms? She got her own ax with the sharpest obsidian, which she maintains herself. She can split one of your soldiers' heads if you ever ordered her to be arrested. If you're not careful, she'll run past your guards like a cat and cut a big chunk of your bacon, and maybe more than you're willing to give."

Bahlam looked at his wife. K'abel was usually a reserved woman who knew her place. Every now and then, however, she showed a tendency to express her own opinion, and Bahlam had learned to react with attention, since she was amazingly correct. Fortunately, since these instances were rare, he did not blame her.

"It is very dangerous," he said. "A fire is burning in her."

"She wants revenge for her mother's death."

"She must never be Queen of Mutal. She will be powerful and strong."

"She'll remember her friends."

Bahlam sighed. "Or look for new enemies. She'll die, because I don't need any more enemies for my son."

"Or she'll be his wife and add her strength to the power of B'aakal, my husband."

Bahlam put the mug down. "That's your suggestion, yes. But she is quite young."

"Not so young anymore."

"Can we keep her in check for so long?"

K'abel smiled. "We have to, my husband. Do you seriously believe that the war against Mutal is over in such a short time? We need her as a symbol of our struggle. When Chitam sees that his daughter is alive and fighting for us, he will reconsider his loyalty to the messengers. To kill her too soon would be fatal."

Bahlam smiled back. "She scares me, K'abel. She is like a mountain of fire that is about to erupt. She is inspired by hatred and willingness to kill many warriors. I don't want her to put a knife in my chest one day – or my son's."

"I do not want that either. Marry her to him."

Bahlam nodded and pondered the fiery fire. It was dark outside, and the noises of the night came through the thick walls of the palace. The screaming of the animals from the jungle was hard to miss. It was a soothing background concert. The best time for the king to ponder the situation.

"My son may not like this."

K'abel let out a snort. "Your son is not asked. He has to do his duty. We taught him that, my lord, if anything."

"He's no longer a child."

"He is our son. He wants to be king. He'll pay the price."

"Ixchel as a wife … that will be a high price," Bahlam said with a laugh and shook his head. "I don't even know if he will ever really be king or just the one who will follow his wife's instructions."

"There are worse things."

Bahlam looked at K'abel inquiringly and forced himself to give an answer that would preserve domestic peace.

"The worse thing would probably be to establish her as Queen of Mutal," he murmured.

His wife had noticed that there was another answer on his lips and allowed herself a look of punishment.

"Or to have a young girl killed just for fear of who or what she might be," his wife added firmly. She had formed a clear opinion about this and was not ready to take her husband's perspective in this discussion. "The quick and easy way is not always the best, Bahlam. The gods thought of putting this girl in our hands. Remember that we have to implement their will and carefully consider every apparent coincidence. Have you spoken to the priests about all of this?"

"Should I?"

"You should."

His wife had always placed greater value on the priests' opinion than he himself. That may have been due to the fact that he knew some of these men from childhood and knew that their explanations and prophecies were often shaped by their personal views less of those of the gods, if one was willing to see the difference. On the other hand, it was always good to be on the safe side. And it was expected of him anyway, not just in the eyes of his wife.

"I will do it."

"Clever man."

"Are you talking to our son?"

K'abel raised her eyebrows. "If you wish."

"And who teaches the wild lady? She might respond by throwing a spear at me."

"Then you should make sure that you speak to her in an unarmed moment, my husband."

Bahlam noticed that his wife was not taking his fears seriously. On the other hand, he was now the young girl's guardian, and he had to make decisions. That he possibly saved her life was one of the aspects that he would better not mention in his attempt in persuasion. It would certainly not be a good thing to tell Ixchel that he thought she was a danger, nor that he tried to fight it by her premature death if she turned out to be unreasonable.

"I'll talk to the girl tomorrow. So it's decided."

K'abel nodded. "Your son will submit. He is not stupid. He knows what's necessary."

"He knows that."

"Ixchel will see it too."

"I don't care. She'll do what she is told." Bahlam tried to make a determined impression now that the decision had been made.

"When does the war start?"

The sudden change of subject only upset Bahlam for a moment. He bowed his head.

"I don't know. The alliance is growing, albeit in secret. Mutal has spies everywhere. We have to make sure that the messenger hears about the danger late. The central point is: can Inocoyotl make our cause understandable to the Divine Ruler? With Teotihuacán at our side, victory is certain. But I have to accept that Yaxchilan will fall first – and possibly one or two more cities. The realm that Inugami creates will already be relatively large if we are able to attack. It won't be an easy fight."

"When, Bahlam?"

K'abel had never had much time for long explanations.

"A year. Maybe a little earlier. I'll have to consult the priests in this matter too."

"It is wise. But you will go to battle and my son with you."

"That is to be expected. He will soon be old enough for the spear and the ax. I can't let him sit here. That would not do his fate justice."

K'abel nodded. "I will rule in your absence?"

"I'll take care of that. Every man who can carry a weapon comes with me. I need someone here I can absolutely trust."

"I will not disappoint you. Do the same and return, alive, whether victorious or not."

"A selfish view."

"The prerogative of a queen."

Bahlam smiled warmly and shook his head gently. "It's not a promise I can give you. We are both old enough to know that no one can do this unless the gods are inclined to do so. And their advice is too unfathomable for me to rely on."

The queen rose, her face suddenly showing deep marks of tiredness and worry. It could also be the shadows of fire flickering on her features, but Bahlam assumed that she was more concerned about all of these things than he noticed, and regretted that he had to put this burden on her shoulders. Ultimately, however, it was the messenger of the gods who confronted them all with this conflict, and it was now up to them to prevent the worst.

His own death, Bahlam realized, was by no means one of the worst things that could have happened. The subjection of B'aakal to the yoke of a strange, inconsiderate ruler who was apparently ready to break with good traditions and old ways was the worst.

And at least in one thing the king could be sure: His wife agreed with him in every respect.

However, that didn't make it easier for him.

25

"Lord, we won't be reaching Yaxchilan in two days, but the scouts' reports have arrived."

The man was some nobleman from Chitam's entourage who had not returned to Mutal with the king. Inugami had forgotten his name, if he had ever known it. These Mayan names were a terrible mess, and somehow all sounded the same. He didn't enjoy memorizing each one, and usually it wasn't necessary. He remembered individual men in terms of their functions, and that was the only reason why they were important. He knew Achak, the general who was to be found somewhere in the front, probably in the hope that a cheeky opponent would try something and could be cut to pieces. But the rest ...

They had left Tayasal after cleaning up and straightening everything out. Inugami had appointed another of his slave warrior officers as governor, a man who had shown himself eager to round up the extended family of the treacherous ex-king and at least publicly execute the male representatives. The city had been very quiet since then. This time Inugami had left only a small contingent of occupation troops. He promised to come back after the conquest of Yaxchilan to "make sure" a statement that caused the more rebellious elements in the population to think twice about doing something stupid.

"What do the scouts report?"

"It doesn't look like they want to surrender, my lord."

Inugami nodded. He hadn't expected that either. At some point, every streak of luck had come to an end, he had had no illusions about it.

"The new king wants to fight?"

"He is not alone, sir. The number of warriors can only be explained if one assumes that some of the surrounding smaller towns have dispatched men."

This was not a surprise either. Yaxchilan was a powerful city-state that claimed tribute from the surrounding towns, in this case in the form of soldiers.

"How many men will there be?"

"The scouts estimate about 2500, maybe a little less."

The force that the city could use to defend itself was slightly smaller than the remaining army of Inugami after having had to garrison two cities and Chitam had returned to Mutal with some warriors. The difference was that Inugami's people were better trained and equipped, and they all believed in divine providence. Still, this would be a real battle, with real deaths. Inugami felt a bit cold. Tayasal and Saclemacal were small fish. But now there was a test that was tough. Here his dream of the empire would come true or he would fail.

And since the incident that night, the thought of a possible failure hadn't left his mind. Whether he wanted to admit it or not, the attack had tarnished his self-confidence, and not only because he had been looking around for a threat ever since.

He resisted the impulse to check his pistol. Of course he would fight on the front line, and his miracle weapon had to make a good impression. The onagers and catapults that he had built would also be used, and he would mix the army of his warrior slaves with the most fanatical of Mutal's soldiers to ensure that no one dithered when he attacked his old homeland. Since everyone believed that the Yaxchilan criminals had the queen and her daughters on their conscience, there was nothing to complain about the angry determination of the Mutalese warriors.

"Then we should send more scouts to investigate the city's defense efforts. Do we have other reports? Are there refugees?"

"We didn't find anyone. The streets are clear. I suspect there are a few scouts from our opponents in the area, but everything else is free."

"Who rules in the city?"

"A nobleman named Nachi Cocom was crowned king, he seemed

to be the highest-ranking survivor to be found. We don't know him. He did not play a prominent role before the last ruler died, at least not to the outside world."

"But he seems capable enough – and determined – to organize his city's defense."

The man bowed his head. "A worthy opponent."

Inugami pressed his lips on each other. What did that remark mean? Was this Nachi suitable to test whether the messenger could actually do what he had promised all along? Were even his most loyal followers ready to bet on a sign of their silly gods to confirm his policy with a victory or show their rejection with a defeat? Inugami felt contempt and scorn for the ridiculous ideas of these savages boiling in him, along with anger at the lack of confidence expressed by these words.

He knew that if he gave in to his feelings now, it was a sign of weakness. He forced a smile.

"Worthy, no doubt," he said. "Tell me as soon as there are new insights."

"My lord."

The man turned and left. Inugami stared down the street. The march had been interrupted for a short pause. The sun was high in the sky, and the warriors were eating corn patties and drinking water. Everyone was exhausted, so the conversations were nothing more than a low murmur that was largely masked by the sounds of nature. Inugami took some water himself, then strolled along the line of resting warriors, accepted their greetings, watched everything with open eyes. Nobody would openly show him any doubts, but they were certainly there. The garrisons in the cities of Tayasal and Saclemacal consisted almost entirely of Yaxchilan prisoners, which Inugami had ensured. Nevertheless, the warriors from that city still made up the majority of his army, and he had to make friends with the prospect that one or the other loyal fighters would pinch the upcoming battle – even if this might mean his death. The attachment to their homeland was great among the natives; Inugami was willing to accept it, he even built on it and tried to manipulate this fact wherever possible. It would be stupid to assume that the new king of Yaxchilan did not consider this perspective. He appeared to be an active and determined man, and whether or not he was really a worthy opponent, he was the first to probably deserve this term.

Inugami realized that he was not looking forward to this battle. And when he thought about why that might be, he realized that it had nothing to do with the risks, the uncertain outcome or the like. He knew that after a victory he had to return to Mutal to consolidate his reign and find a solution once and for all for the actual king – whatever that might be. He would have to go back and start what was the least fun for him ... negotiate, seek allies, promise and redeem favors, make threats and carry them out, in short everything that was part of politics. That was not his way. He wanted to be the conqueror, the one who took historical steps, a man of determined action. The big gesture was his profession, the wide movement, the decisive step. He was the one who brought down the old order, who questioned everything that was before and who indelibly burned his name into the minds of his subjects. But all of this could not be achieved if he submitted to the intrigues, turmoil and imponderables of normal court policy, which all had the bad aftertaste of constant lies, denying everything and everyone, acting behind the back and pretending wrong facts. It was not his world.

He was Inugami, the bringer of the new order, the root of the new age. He did not want to decide on water pipes and where a new terrace for growing corn was created. There should be people for that. People who served him faithfully and kept all this everyday, annoying and boring stuff away from him.

He still had far too few of these people.

And that's why he didn't want to go back to Mutal.

He wanted to continue marching, to see cities fall before him.

He wanted to plant fear in the hearts of his enemies, crush their ranks, burn their temples. He wanted to break up their covenants, to show them the senselessness of their actions. He wanted respect, esteem, fear, myths that clung to his position, exalted above all and everything, a true messenger of the gods, but on his own strength and not because a priest said it. That was his way, that was his dream. In Mutal, however, the small mind, the limitations, and the terribly unbearable necessity would clasp him again. The very word "necessity" was like a slap in the face. The submission associated with this term created an almost physically palpable dislike in him. There shouldn't be anything like that for him. No rules, no constraints, no circumstances, no framework, but only the absolute and unrestricted freedom of his equally absolute will. Shaping the world the way he liked it. He was a creator.

Inugami stopped and nodded, imperceptibly.

A creator.

He was not an administrator of anything.

He created.

And he didn't want to stop until he took his last breath.

Because only for that, he was certain, he had come here.

26

Ik'Naah rose and bowed her head in front of the image of the goddess. Ever since she was ordained as the highest priestess of the fertility goddess, taking over the reign of the Isle of Swallows, she felt the burden of this task weighing more and more on her shoulders. It wasn't the numerous women who made the pilgrimage to be blessed, hoping that their wish for a child would finally come true. It was not the constant work of maintaining the temple without overburdening the island's resources. It was not the recurring question of which city the temple is now subordinate to and to whom Ik'Naah has to swear allegiance, when she wanted nothing more than to preserve the old neutrality of the Swallow Island and a place of pilgrimage, peace and the chance to enjoy contemplation.

It was the age that depressed her.

Without age, all of these problems would surely be easier to deal with, with more energy, perhaps a little carefree. Seen through the glasses of all the years, every challenge piled up mountains that found her old bones more and more difficult to climb.

It has been a long time since she came here. Many years since she found her calling as a servant to the great goddess. The earth and moon goddess Ixchel, after whom so many hopeful parents named their favorite daughters, was the goddess of protection for water, the rainbow and pregnant women, a powerful mistress and yet a being full of grace and wisdom, a force of kindness and not a deity who constantly asked for new wars. Perhaps that was why it was so difficult for her, as the mistress of the temple, to have to defend it against the desires of the neighboring cities. It had been easier for her to do when she was younger. Yes, she had a certain diplomatic skill, and for a long time she had been able to accomplish the task that the goddess had given her.

But now she felt tired and exhausted. The prayer brought her no clarity, no more certainty, but more tiredness. She felt the limbs of her body, how they began to protest with every movement and how she became almost as tired during the day as at night – and yet rarely found sleep that would restore her strength.

It was hard to admit that, but there was no doubt that it was time to choose a successor. There were many suitable candidates, but it was precisely in this situation that it was difficult for one of the youngsters to do the difficult task of keeping Swallow Island out of their neighbors' disputes. One would not be afraid, of course, but Ik'Naah felt guilty about the fact and the silent fear that it was not youthful energy that was the deciding factor, but rather the experience of old age.

The envoy from Zama who had arrived yesterday did not make things easier. Zama was the closest city to the mainland, and it was called the City of Sunrise not only because it was inclined to the east, but also because it was said that the blessing of the goddess would shine from the nearby island to the metropolis every day. For a long time she had gotten along well with the King of Zama, a city that owed a good part of its wealth to the numerous travelers who transited from there to Swallow Island, often daughters and wives of rich nobles, princesses, whose bodies did not want to take fruit and who came here to hope for healing from the goddess. But relations had deteriorated since the old king's death and his young son's coming to power. With the young one felt the need to step out of the shadow of the ancestor and to leave his own imprint in history. Wasn't there an island full of priestesses and priests with a city dedicated solely to prayer to Ixchel?

Ik'Naah found a good argument in not looking for a younger one to take her place. In any case, the big city of Zama hadn't done well so far.

Thus, Yo'nal Ahk, King of Zama, felt it was time to underpin the desires with deeds, and his envoy, though full of courtesy and awe, with a gentle voice and melodious words that were not intrusive, was quite willing to express his master's wishes with great emphasis.

Ik'Naah put her fingertips on the stone face of the goddess in front of her. The goddess looked to the side, she looked grim, determined, although she was a force of blessing, a guardian, a goddess of fertility and thus of life. She seemed to be looking past her highest priestess, into realms that only a goddess could see, and Ik'Naah's grief may have been too void for her to deal with.

No one knew better how moody the gods were in showing their favor than the priestess. Not everyone who prayed here got pregnant. And when the great storms came and the masses of water around the island lashed like walls, no amount of prayer could stop the destructive power of the element whose lord was the goddess. Ik'Naah could ask, and she would, again and again. But she had to take matters into her own hands and was not allowed to wait too long. Only those who acted gave the goddess the opportunity to influence something. Those who were passive couldn't do anything even with the Great Mistress's blessing.

She sighed.

She didn't want anything else than a little rest.

She realized that today she could not expect any further guidance or mercy from the goddess. Leaving the chamber deep in the heart of the temple, she climbed the carefully carved stone staircase into the large prayer room, which other priests were preparing for daily blessings at this time of day. The offerings were placed on the stone table, both as a grace for the goddess and for the maintenance of the temple. Many, especially wealthy supplicants, often brought whole loads of obsidian or gold jewelry to encourage priests to be particularly fervent in their intercession. Ik'Naah didn't think much of letting the goddess's favor be bought this way, though she would never admit it openly. She took what she could get, and maybe that was a mistake. Last but not least, Zama's interest in the island was related to the richly filled treasury of the temple. It was always more than just the favor of the gods which attracted the greedy, the priestess had realized a long time ago.

She went outside after checking that the preparations were proceeding properly. That morning two large rowboats had arrived from the mainland, each with twelve pilgrims on board. They would be received and then taken to the prayer room to undergo a fertility ritual that sought to fulfill their desire for children after the donation of their offerings.

Ik'Naah wished them all the best. She herself was without a husband and without children, and sometimes she wondered whether her decision to dedicate her own life entirely to service in the temple had been the right one. On the other hand, her personal asceticism raised her above other priests, and her reputation increased. She had to take every advantage she could, especially because after the ritual ended, she would no longer be able to escape the envoy. He had asked for another conversation after the morning prayer, and since the goddess had refused further inspiration to her servant, Ik'Naah would have to rely on her own abilities alone.

She went down the stairs to the temple entrance, let the early breeze run through her wide robe. Already, an hour after getting up and having a poor breakfast, she felt the weariness and the constant pain in her joints. It wouldn't be long before she had to use a stick to move around reasonably safely. From there, this was clear to her, the way was not far to the end. That wasn't a thought that made her bitter. What kept her busy was their inheritance that she would leave behind, not for children or families but for the temple, its status, and its masters. It was the last major challenge of her life, she knew, and she had to find the strength to face it.

"Mistress, the guest house is full," she heard the voice of a priest who had approached her respectfully. "The supplicants are ready."

"Have they been prepared?"

"We have instructed them."

"The prayer room is also ready. Send the procession as soon as I'm out of sight. I'm too tired today to lead the ritual myself."

"Two of the pilgrims brought a box of cocoa beans with the request that the high priestess will do the blessing personally."

Ik'Naah suppressed a sigh. Cocoa was one of the most valuable commodities, highly coveted, and an entire box was a significant asset. Someone wanted to invest heavily in her offspring. She smiled devotedly.

"Make sure the Zama emissary doesn't get wind of it. I don't want to arouse his desires unnecessarily."

"He's far away from the guest house, and we hear he hasn't woken up yet."

"Keep an eye on him. Don't hinder him, but he should be accompanied at all times."

"Mistress." The man bowed and left. Basically, there was no need to fear that the envoy would discover the temple's treasury. It had been wisely set up near the most sacred rooms, hidden deep in the foundation of the temple, where only consecrated persons to the goddess had access, and even of them just a select number. The ambassador would never dare to ask for access.

But if the king of Zama seized sovereignty, he might not be as reluctant to secure his share. The city priests would come up with a suitable cleaning ritual if it became necessary.

The old woman continued on her way until she came to one of the large stores where the temple's food supplies were kept. Due to the large number of pilgrims who flocked to the island, the temple had to provide more food than was consumed by the servants. Not all pilgrims were rich and could afford to make generous donations. Many poor women came for whom the trip was the greatest adventure of their life, and they too had an honest desire to ask the goddess for fertility. Just like everyone else, they were subjected to the ritual, and the priests made sure that the process itself made no difference as to the origin. Those who took the long and often arduous journey were not rejected, and those who had nothing to eat were catered for.

The administrator of this house was a man about the age of the high priestess and no less frail. Ik'Naah had known him for a long time. When they were both young, they had enjoyed the joys of their bodies together. Had these joys brought fruit back then, the man might have been her husband today. In this way, however, they had separated into friendship without ever losing sight of each other.

"High Priestess!" Yatzak greeted the woman and he bowed. Ik'Naah waved it off.

"Don't do that. Your back won't take it anymore."

"Honor to whom honor is due."

"Show me your respect by offering me some water."

Yatzak's chamber was large, and the stone shelves held inventory records, carefully kept and, she knew, always up to date. Yatzak's responsibilities were more manageable than hers, so she visited him regularly, a little time to reflect on her sorrows. The steward would continue to work, no matter who ruled the island, because there would always be pilgrims, and there would always be a need to eat and drink.

The crumpled old man did not miss the chance to serve her personally.

"How's it going?" she asked, holding the mug of water.

"We lack a number of fruits and ingredients for chi," said the old man. "Without chi there are no rituals, so we have to go into the woods. Cocoa is also lacking."

"I got some."

"We have to go to our own plantations, Mistress. Some of the plants will soon be ready."

Ik'Naah nodded. As a warehouse manager, Yatzak was also responsible for part of the temple's economy. He was assigned some of the corn fields, some of the sensitive and valuable cocoa plantations, parts of the forest with its numerous products. With ten men and women under him – beyond the farmers who regularly worked the fields –, he made sure that everything was there that was needed.

"When are you leaving?"

"Still today. I take eight men with me. I would also like to look for the rare medicinal plants when we are already on the road. It doesn't hurt to have enough of everything."

Ik'Naah nodded. Yatzak was always careful to have enough supplies, not a man who valued any risk. There was no better warehouse manager than him.

"It's good."

"What does the envoy from Zama do?" The realities of the world didn't ignore Yatzak. Or maybe it was his connection with the priestess that helped him develop interest in these things.

"He's sleeping."

"What will happen when he wakes up?"

"He'll have breakfast."

Yatzak sighed. "Ik'Naah, the wise, the impenetrable. I hope that our problem can be solved as easily as quenching the envoy's hunger."

The priestess laughed. "What answer do you expect, man? I don't know myself. It is clear what the Lord of Zama intends to do. The question is, do we go into it and risk an attack or not?"

Yatzak looked pensive. "Who are our allies?"

"Yes, that's the question, isn't it?"

"Have you sent messengers?"

"I sent messages."

"When does the answer come?"

"Maybe never."

Yatzak looked at her with incomprehension.

Ik'Naah sighed. "Strange things are happening on the mainland, my old friend. We are talking about gods that fell from the sky and a mighty war that has started. Something happened in Mutal, and not everyone is happy about it."

Yatzak clicked contemptuously. "Mutal is powerful. This naturally ensures that others are not happy."

Ik'Naah shook her head. "This is different."

"Tell me what you know."

"Too little. But if even half of the rumors are true, it can be that everything that happens here is only of secondary importance, and even those who would otherwise stick with us are busy with other things."

Yatzak's glance showed his concern. "That means we're at the mercy of Zama?"

"That means we have to represent our interests ourselves."

"I'm sorry for you."

"Thank you, but your sympathy doesn't help me."

Yatzak nodded slowly. "Yes, I'm no help." He looked seriously sad.

Ik'Naah felt the warmth of genuine sympathy fill her heart and placed a comforting hand on his shoulder. "Help me with your warehouse being full so we all have enough to eat. Having worries and being full is far more pleasant than having to worry about being hungry."

"That's true, but it's not very satisfactory for me," Yatzak murmured.

Ik'Naah rebuked an index finger. "You should have taken me as a wife. Then I would be in your ears every day."

Yatzak frowned and was apparently looking for an answer that should express both his relief at the missed opportunity and his continued regret for it. Ik'Naah gave him the opportunity to deal with this impossible task and enjoyed the silence of the chamber but then decided to redeem the old man who didn't deserve to be tortured by her any longer.

She rose and smiled at Yatzak. "My friend, I'm going. Rich ladies ask for my blessings, and unlike the goddess, I depend on their benevolence. Let me do my duty before I meet the envoy from Zama and try to put a stop to his desires."

Yatzak nodded and also got up, put a hand on her forearm, and tried to smile confidently, an effort that was obviously difficult for him. "You can come to me anytime and rest. But today I'm going to the woods and the plantations. Tomorrow too. But in the evening I drink from chi without conjuring up the goddess' visions. A mug will be ready for you."

The priestess returned the smile with genuine warmth and affection. It may be that she would soon bow to the king of the big neighboring town, but at least there was this old man who would comfort and accept her. It was a very nice prospect, and Ik'Naah felt great gratitude.

Then she turned and walked away. It didn't help to hide from the day's tasks, no matter how threatening they seemed. She was old but not yet old enough to pretend a weakness she didn't feel at all.

Her joints ached.

But her mind was still working properly.

27

"Well, Angelicus?" Köhler looked expectantly at the centurion. The beefy man had just received the last of the returning patrols and reported. The tents on the beach were set up, and three watch fires were burning.

"Everything calm in the area, Trierarch," said the soldier. "We don't have a settlement nearby, just the buildings you saw from the hill. It seems like a real city."

Köhler nodded. He didn't hide the fact that the sight he had enjoyed still impressed him. The buildings of the local residents were different from those he knew from Rome, but Köhler had been able to convince himself from afar that the Maya architects were outstanding experts in their field. Pyramids were popular basic forms, so the buildings reminded him of the ancient Egyptians. The construction was different, and the size of the buildings was not quite as impressive. Köhler had been able to observe the streets and fields from his viewpoint, laid out as if cut with a compass. He estimated that the city he had seen had a good 8,000 inhabitants and was therefore of an considerable size. The central buildings had given him the impression of serving sacred purposes, possibly temples, but perhaps also palaces of the local ruler. In any case, they had not arrived in the country of any primitive savages, but at a civilization whose achievements were clearly visible in the eyes of any observant visitor.

That made things easier on the one hand and more complicated on the other. A civilization of this level of development was certainly capable of engaging in convincing military activity if it thought it was right. However, Köhler found it remarkable that he hadn't seen any fortifications. The city was open, freely accessible from all sides. Sure, the mighty central buildings were good to defend, but there was no trace of a city wall or defensive tower. Did this mean that this was a peaceful people who knew no wars, no conquests?

It was all speculation, sure. Langenhagen would have to make a decision. So far, however, it was said only that they would keep themselves hidden and that the planned expansion of the fort would be refrained from. It was pointless to build a fortification so close to an impressive settlement center. This could quickly lead to misunderstandings.

After all, they had found a source of drinking water. Tomorrow the big barrels would be carried over from the flotilla to fill them. And an expedition of scientists was planned as far as they remained in sight of the rowboats. Köhler had successfully campaigned for Terzia. She would be grateful to him.

That was the point, apart from gaining scientific knowledge.

"Is there anything like military patrols or guards?"

The centurion grimaced.

"Not on this side of the island. The settlement gets denser the more we get to the west coast. But military? My people didn't identify an armed man. If there are soldiers anywhere, then only in the city itself, and even there I don't know anything that looked like a castle or fortress. It seems to me that this is a peaceful people."

Angelicus said that with a tone that just passed contempt. For the centurion, evident defensiveness seemed to be a central characteristic of a "real" civilization, an attitude that Köhler found not surprising in this man. As long as it did not determine his actions too much and the latter made no move to prove their neighbors' lack of "defensiveness" through provocation, Angelicus should think whatever he thought was right. Köhler felt that the centurion's special abilities – and preferences – would be used early enough. It was just a premonition, but if something started so well, something just had to go wrong.

They lay down to rest in the light of the guard fires. Köhler was pleased that his exalted status freed him from the night watch. The first shore leave after a long crossing had exhausted him more than he wanted to admit and show. No sooner had he closed his eyes than he fell into a deep sleep, from which he was awakened in the morning by the watchman at the agreed time. His first night ashore had been refreshing. Though his body had gotten used to the rocking oft he waves, the quiet and steady camp had been a blessing. Köhler felt more refreshed than in a long time.

It wasn't long before two more rowboats were seen to set sail from the flotilla. This time, along with a few other soldiers, the scientists and their material were on board. In addition, the empty water barrels were brought so that they could be filled immediately. When the boats landed, men were ready to deal with the barrels. Köhler expected many crossings today.

He himself greeted the researchers. The group was small at first: Beside Terzia there was a cartographer, a man named Phoebus, and an elderly gentleman named Domenicus, who introduced himself as a geologist, representative of a new science that was also introduced by the time-wanderers. Köhler had only heard about it in passing, but he knew that Domenicus would look at the landscape, take soil samples, and help with the search for raw materials.

"We will go on foot," Köhler informed them. "The forest is relatively dense, the horses are of no use to us here. We will not be far from the camp and will always be with an escort. I estimate a maximum of two hours for our first detour. First we boil fresh water. It will be necessary to drink a lot."

There was no opposition. When they had taken care of everything, three legionaries joined the group and stared with undisguised interest at Terzia's now sweaty robe. She wore pants, also a custom that the time walkers had made common. Before regarded as the clothing of barbarians, their practical use had become clear through the example of the men of the *Saarbrücken*. The fact that dressing like that was considered "chic" for a while certainly helped. This garment was also granted to women, and Terzia's legs filled it in an excellent way. Köhler abstained from comment. He couldn't forbid the staring from the men, for he would have to keep forcing himself to look away.

Shortly after they left the beach and entered the first forest, at least Terzia was unstoppable. Leaning over every other piece of greenery, chattering names in front of her, she began making drawings in quick and remarkably precise strokes. Köhler soon realized that her expedition would lead to disaster, because both Phoebus and Domenicus were visibly running out of patience. Finally he ordered two of the legionnaires to go on with the two men and climb the rock formations while he himself would play the watchdog for Terzia with the remaining soldier. The researcher herself hardly noticed anything about this development, because she had apparently completely lost her perception of her surroundings, being immersed in the island's flora. She knelt in the dirt, rummaged in the ground, scratched bark, plucked leaves, threw some quick drawings on the pad she carried, made of paper, another blessing that the time-wanderers had taught the Romans.

Köhler suppressed a sigh. That would take a while.

It was by no means uninteresting to watch Terzia at work. Although the conversation was rather limited – Köhler occasionally gave a grunt when the researcher called out "What is that?" Or "We have to look at it!" –, it was always a nice sight, someone watching enthusiastically at work. The fact that Terzia often had to crouch and bend forward or take comparable interesting positions for the purpose of her work added to the appeal of the observation for Köhler, and he was not ashamed to admit it. The legionnaire with him, who introduced himself as Adrianus and otherwise preferred to remain taciturn in the presence of the senior officer, threw interested looks at the woman's rear end, but then decided to use all his energy to sweat. The later the morning got, the hotter and more humid it became; the breeze blew from the land into the sea and brought little cooling. In the deep forest, more like a jungle, the air felt wet, and the insects that devoted themselves to the unexpected prey didn't make their life easier. Soon they had run out of water, and Adrianus had to leave twice to refill the hoses they had brought with them. Each time he reported on the progress of filling the barrels and subtly pointed out that a meal was being prepared over the fires on the beach. They had caught fresh fish and everything smelled very appetizing.

Köhler felt how his mouth watered at the description. Their food during the expedition had been rather meager – ship's biscuit and some bread, and hard cheese, which had not become more appetizing during the trip.

But Terzia was adamant. In the end, she had expanded the scope of her research beyond what was originally agreed. For a long time, there was no longer any question of visibility to the beach. In doing so, she showed a level of determination and assertiveness that Köhler never believed she would be capable of. The woman could be almost intimidating if she wanted to, and at least on Adrianus this did not fail to have an effect. Köhler maintained his stance but was also driven ever deeper into the jungle by Terzia's zeal for research. At least they would always find their way back easily, as they secured their path with markings that could not be missed. This, and the fact that no one got in their way except the tireless insects, prompted Köhler to be lenient.

When hunger became more pressing and he really did not feel the strength just to be satisfied with the ship's biscuit he brought with him, he decided to gather his authority as a man and officer, took a deep breath and ...

Terzia raised a hand. "Did you hear that?"

Köhler paused and listened. The sounds of the forest could still be heard, a background music he had grown used to. "I don't know ..."

"Footsteps!" Terzia whispered, looking at Köhler, who immediately felt alarmed. His hand went to the sword on his belt. Belted on his back, he also carried a musket with him. He listened again and ...

"And voices," he whispered back. "From the West."

"Yes. What are we doing?"

Terzia didn't look too scared, but sound caution had overcome her zeal for research. She might be a fanatical scientist, but she certainly wasn't tired of life.

"To the beach," Köhler signaled, relieved when the woman nodded in confirmation.

They turned, took a few steps toward the next mark, and stopped dead.

Instead of seeing the tree in front of them, on which they had drawn a strong arrow with thick chalk, there was an older man. He wore a tight loincloth and a skirt-like robe that left his torso free.

In his gnarled hands he held an ax with a shimmering black blade made of an unknown material. On his back he carried a tubular backpack in which he could place things without having to put it down.

He looked at them.

They looked at him.

Köhler remained motionless, holding out a hand in the direction of Terzia to warn her of sudden and thoughtless reactions. Needless to say. Terzia was prudent and even managed to put on such a charming smile that the tense stance of the old man, who had half raised the weapon, loosened a trace.

He said something. Köhler listened to the words with interest and patiently. He didn't understand a word. The language was completely foreign to him and he hadn't expected anything else.

It hadn't been planned that way.

But now he had to make the best of it.

He raised both hands, now without a weapon, to show his will for peace. Fortunately, Adrianus did nothing else. Köhler was glad that Centurion Angelicus was not with them. To be on the safe side, he would have chopped off the arm holding the ax.

Twigs cracked, and more men appeared, all loaded with tubular rucksacks and all with some kind of weapon, mostly knives, the blades of which shimmered as black as the ax. Still, they didn't look like armed men. It could be assumed that they only used the blades as tools to collect what they had entered the forest for.

Köhler relaxed a little.

Terzia stepped to his side and watched the arrivals carefully. Doing much more than looking at each other was impossible. Some of the younger men, fear and terror in their eyes, had raised their weapons menacingly. But they seemed to be listening to the old man, who addressed them in a few words, apparently preventing them from taking ill-considered actions.

Then the researcher spoke a few sentences, slowly, clearly, certainly just as incomprehensible to her interlocutors, but in a calm tone, friendly, anything but aggressive. Whether it was her way of expressing herself or the fact that she looked less threatening as a woman without armor and weapons, the old man lowered the weapon and smiled weakly. He replied something, also slowly and kindly, and spread his arms, pointing to his comrades. Köhler suspected that he was trying to explain why they roamed the forest and who they were. Terzia listened attentively, then pointed to herself and the two legionaries and did nothing but speak their names clearly. She repeated this process again, then the old man seemed to understand. He didn't waste any time introducing each member of his troop, just put both hands on his chest and said something that sounded like "Jatsack." He repeated it several times, and Köhler was reasonably certain that they had successfully completed the introductory round.

Terzia now made an inviting gesture toward the beach. She bowed a little, as if she were a housemaid leading a guest into the atrium. Köhler watched the old man's reaction, then took a small step in the direction indicated, bowed like Terzia to animate the Maya to follow them. They were visibly hesitant, which could hardly be resented. They met very strange-looking people who spoke an incomprehensible language, and although they didn't seem half as threatening as one might have feared, trusting them so much that they were marched somewhere was quite another matter.

The old man made the only sensible decision. He gave some commands, as one could quite clearly tell from his tone. Except for one, his companions turned and disappeared into the thicket before Köhler could make a sound. Where and with what order they were going, nobody had to ponder for a long time. The old man apparently wanted the remaining man to disappear, too, but the man resisted, and the leader finally gave in. A hierarchy was recognizable here, but it was not a very strict one, and although the old man was in charge, his authority was not absolute.

At first hesitantly, as if one wanted to reassure each other of the good intentions, then more resolutely, the newly formed group started to move. Delaying further contact did not make any sense, Köhler decided. It had happened, and now they had to make the best of it, and Langenhagen wouldn't contradict that either. As long as Angelicus hadn't come across locals and demonstratively informed them about the superiority of Roman weapons, everything was fine.

They reached the beach and immediately got the expected attention. It was Köhler's calm stance that immediately steered any excitement into more disciplined behavior. Angelicus also produced nothing more than a frown and a whispered command. The legionaries went, arms down, spread out across the beach, and apparently without a plan to attack. But if there was a threat from the nearby forest, they would be as ready as possible. In addition, Köhler always saw some men standing next to the rowboats, ready to push them into the water.

The old man and his companion only looked at the tents and the rowboats without much reaction, both of which were certainly products of human craft that they were already familiar with in one form or another. Even the half-filled water bins on the beach didn't seem to get their attention. Only when their gaze across the water met the clearly recognizable ships of the expedition did their eyes widen. They spoke softly, gesticulated, and kept staring at the line of powerful ships, which apparently impressed them very much. They got even more excited when a dinghy was dropped into the water by the *Gratianus* and headed for the beach. The little boat rocked in the waves, and apart from two oarsmen and Navarch Langenhagen, there was no one on board. The beach had been kept under surveillance with binoculars, and the arrival of the Maya must have been reported to the commander immediately.

Köhler relaxed a little. With the arrival of Langenhagen, responsibility would be somewhat removed from his shoulders. He was still able to pick up any shit at a later time.

When Langenhagen jumped ashore, the excitement of the two Maya had not yet subsided. But they seemed to suspect that Langenhagen was a leader. The Navarch had put on his breastplate, freshly polished, and the impressive officer's helmet. He reflected the light of the slowly setting sun, and Köhler had to admit that the sight even impressed him. The two Maya bowed deeply, and Köhler couldn't help but smile. No matter what these strange visitors were up to, the old man had come to the conclusion that a little reverence couldn't hurt.

Names were exchanged again, which took a few moments. Then Köhler briefly reported on what had happened.

"I don't know how to act now," Köhler admitted. "We can hardly communicate."

"Of course, but that was to be expected. In addition, we will soon be known in the city over there. We do the following ..." He waved Angelicus, and the centurion came up immediately. "Has the other expedition already returned?"

"Yes, Navarch, the geologist, and the cartographer are back."

Langenhagen nodded in satisfaction.

"We're going to break camp, except for a tent and a fire. All men back on the ships. A boat stays here. I don't want us to endanger ourselves unnecessarily. Köhler, you too are returning to the *Gratianus*. Send me our language genius tomorrow morning, he should prove himself now. I will stay here with him and two legionaries, and we are waiting for the visit that is sure to come. Then prepare the cannons and post the best musket shooters on the railing, as long as we have light."

"But –"

"No buts, Trierarch. Do as I say."

"And you?"

"I'll do what everyone always does when we don't know what to talk about." He stomped to the dinghy, reached inside and took out two objects – a tube of wine and a sack of food –, which he carried slowly to the next fire.

"We'll prepare dinner and invite our friends over there," Langenhagen announced, dropping the containers. "Centurion, which of your people is the best cook? I see that there is still some fish left."

"Diderius is not completely pitiful when it comes to preparation of food. He's got a knack for fish," Angelicus said.

"Then Diderius will be left with me."

"Sir, I –"

"Centurion, you take off as ordered. If something happens, I want an experienced officer to lead a landing operation that may be necessary. Is that clear?"

Angelicus saluted, although he could see that he would have preferred to follow a different instruction.

The two Maya attentively watched the conversation. Langenhagen's determined demeanor, Angelicus' reservations, then Köhler's approval. Terzia stuck to her smile, although at least the Trierarch noticed her disappointment at not being allowed to be present for the rest of the procedure. Köhler himself felt this too; he had hoped that Langenhagen would stay with the fleet and that this task would be entrusted to him here. But that was not why he would disagree with his superior. Langenhagen was the chief diplomat, along with the young senator, who, Köhler stated, would also remain on the ship.

He could only agree to this part of the decision.

It wasn't long before the efficient legionaries broke the camp, packed up their materials, and loaded the boats. Köhler was one of the last to leave the beach. Langenhagen had been with the Maya all along, and the two men had proven calm and prudent. When Diderius gestured to set up the cookware over the fire and began to prepare a simple meal, Köhler boarded and was set to sea. He looked back at the beach and watched the Navarch sit down next to the fire and invite the guests to join him. The fact that they did so after a slight hesitation indicated that they had gained a little trust.

Köhler sat and watched the men row. As soon as he arrived on the *Gratianus*, some orders had to be carried out. The cannons and riflemen ready, the ships in alarm, the beach under constant surveillance. He himself, he knew, would find little sleep.

It had been too good to be true.

28

Une looked at the sleeping figure of Lengsley, the outlines of which were indistinctly recognizable in the dark. He must have been exhausted from the accomplishments of the night, activities the king's sister had kept driving him to. She had to admit that the man had done his best and that she was quite satisfied. Of course, she had communicated this satisfaction in word and gesture, and the big man had fallen asleep with a smile that showed a bit of complacency. Une granted him that.

She straightened her torso and looked at the fireplace's fading flames. The night was cool for her but seemed to be still a very humid one for Lengsley, and she had taken that into account. In fact, she tried very hard to please him. She had listened to his description of local dishes and then started to work with her cook to find out to what extent the local ingredients could be approximated. That was not always possible, but the effort alone counted and had brought a pleased, even touched smile to the man's face. Otherwise she had been willing to do be pleasing even more, also when her own enthusiasm hadn't been too great. It was by no means uncomfortable sharing the camp with Lengsley and feeling his impressive masculinity deep inside. It was absolutely necessary to offer him this opportunity, because Chitam and Une had long talked about the role of messengers, the threat, the death of Tzutz, and the children …

The thought of her dead sister-in-law squeezed Une's neck again for a moment. She accused Lengsley of not returning often to the subject. She herself had been able to find out that the Brit, as he called himself, was not pleased with the events. So Chitam asked her to intensify her relationship with him. Good food and good sex have always been the means by which a woman could gain extensive control over a man. Men certainly had their advantages, and a few of the specimen were not entirely without intelligence. But once they had been sufficiently accustomed to the rewards they kept asking for out of creative urge, there was nothing they could deny. With Lengsley there was also the fact that he also had few friends among the messengers, most of whom saw him as a stranger, anything but equivalent. So the man sometimes felt a little lonely, misunderstood, and therefore opened himself to the caresses and consolations of the princess with special dedication and willingness.

Une knew that.

Une used it.

She enjoyed it with both her body and her mind, and calculated the prospects that would arise when Chitam was ready to openly turn against the messengers of the gods. Lengsley was a relatively safe bet among the messengers. That Aritomo, on the other hand, was a fickle fellow, a man torn between his conscience and his sense of duty, and it was difficult to predict how he would ultimately behave if he was faced with the only important decision. Of course, that could also be improved if there was only a young woman, allied with Chitam and Une, who cast a spell over Aritomo and who, with the same means, was ready to steer him into the pathways the Briton was already wandering into without knowing it.

Others who were critical of Inugami would ask Aritomo for guidance and follow him in both directions. The problem at the moment was: Lengsley did not have such a firm bond of loyalty, yes, he even experienced distance and dislike from the other messengers. And he knew so much. Une smiled. Lengsley would choose the right side, she was absolutely certain of that. As firm and determined as her fingers clasped his shaft and willingly lead it to where she could give him the greatest pleasure, the man belonging to it would also be willing to be guided in other things once she put her hands firmly around his soul. And this process, they judged, was nearing completion.

Une was still smiling. Lengsley would serve her and the city, and he would create himself a place where he was welcome. It served everyone. Everyone was happy. Une looked at her work and found that she had done well. She liked perfection in everything, carefully woven patterns, and here she had created one that was both aesthetically pleasing and served its purpose. That she also liked this man very much and found his style to be pleasant was her own little reward.

She looked down at her bare breasts, scratched in one place with dried sweat and dried sperm. She felt exhausted but not tired and decided to clean herself up. It was quite possible that Lengsley would wake up during the night – or be woken by her – to continue the conversation of her bodies. Then, if she was refreshed, with a pleasant scent, the experience would be much more enjoyable for him.

And that's what it was about.

"Can't you sleep?"

His voice pulled her out of her thoughts, and she turned to him, a smile on her lips. She read real concern in his eyes, and it was kind of touching. With all of his amazing knowledge and physical strength, Lengsley was sometimes like a child in her hands, even if his interest in her breasts was of a different nature.

"I woke up. I don't know why, either," she said softly.

The man also straightened up and put a hand on her knee. "You think a lot," he said softly.

"It's the times. They give you a lot to think about."

"I know."

Une just nodded. They looked into the almost extinguished fire for a few moments.

"Inugami will be back soon," Lengsley said then. "He'll conquer Yaxchilan and see if everything's in order here."

Une didn't turn her head away. Lengsley raised the issue on her own, she didn't want to interrupt the flow of his thoughts.

"Are you worried?"

"A little. We are not as far as we want with all the work we have been asked to do. The city wall is not yet two hundred meters long. We simply lack labor. We cannot at the same time ..."

"My beloved, you don't have to justify yourself to me. I am not Inugami."

Lengsley nodded and sighed. Then he shook his head. "Forgive me. I don't even know what I'm afraid of. Inugami is a man who often makes impulsive and arbitrary decisions. Too many blindly follow him. It is as if he has cast a spell over them. I am certainly valuable enough for him not to be punished excessively, but there is a high pressure of expectation on everyone, and not everyone can handle it like I do. I sometimes wonder what magic many people in this city have succumbed to."

"It is the prospect of power and fame, wealth and positions. It blinds a lot of people," she murmured. In her mind, she added that men succumbed to this temptation far more easily than women, but it was better not to say it out loud. Lengsley – to some extent Aritomo and a few others – were an exception, as were those who tried to kill Inugami's representative.

"He'll have to listen to your explanations and have to accept them. Who, if not Sarukazaki and you, should supervise the work and make sure that everything is of the right quality?" she added.

"The prince's disappearance will haunt him. He'll be looking for those responsible."

"You're not one of them."

"Is that so? I spoke to Isamu. Did I encourage him?"

"Who can predict the behavior of boys of this age?"

"I'm afraid something has happened to him."

Une drew a circle on his thigh with her index finger. "Nobody heard from him or saw him. The search teams sent out have returned home without results. We don't know anything, neither good nor bad. So why blame yourself unnecessarily? Maybe he's fine."

Lengsley shook his head again. "That's not the point. Inugami doesn't care whether he has been eaten by snakes or has been cared for somewhere. The prince opposed his will, thwarted his plans. This is something the captain can hardly cope with. The loss of the prince damages his reputation among his own men. It represents a loss for him that goes beyond the failure of his dynastic ideas."

Une rose imperceptibly. From that perspective, she had never looked at it. She concentrated and thought. Was the prince's disappearance an aspect that Chitam had previously neglected in his considerations? Could it be sensible, indeed necessary, to find the boy and use him?

Lengsley's discarded remark reminded her that she still didn't understand the messengers in everything, and this may have led to wrong assumptions or at least missed opportunities. She would have to talk to Chitam. And she had to listen to Lengsley more carefully. Some of the nuance in what he said may have given her insights that she had never been aware of.

"If you find the prince," she said carefully, "and he would continue to be rebellious, openly opposed to Inugami ..."

"That's a problem, I think," said Lengsley. "The prince is respected by the crew of the boat, he is a direct descendant of the highest authority in the country from which they come. Not only must Inugami be careful in his anger, the prince himself may also underestimate his ability to influence. So far, he has been very shy and reserved, almost fearful. That may have changed in the meantime."

"He ran away. I would say that has definitely changed."

"We don't know how he came to the decision. He didn't go alone. A friend accompanied him. Maybe he was persuaded."

Une sigh softly. "These are all thoughts that don't help. He will reappear or remain to stay away forever. Your brooding doesn't make things easier."

Lengsley nodded and stifled a yawn. He obviously felt much more tired than Une but probably wanted to keep her company.

"I'm going to sleep now," the king's sister lied, pretending she couldn't keep her eyes open. "The night was hard."

Lengsley smiled knowingly, again with complacency.

Une patted his shoulder. "Tomorrow we can worry about all these things again," she said. "You won't find a solution if you lack sleep."

"I won't find any solutions when I'm rested either," Lengsley murmured somberly, letting the woman pull him back into a lying position. "I feel very powerless. And I'm confused. It's hard to make decisions when you're constantly confused."

Une put a hand on his chest and laid her head next to his. She said nothing and waited for Lengsley's breath to show that he had found sleep again.

She looked at his profile.

"Don't worry, my dear husband," she whispered so softly that he probably wouldn't have heard her if he had stayed awake. "Your confusion shouldn't bother us, and it shouldn't hinder you."

She turned on her back and stared at the barely recognizable ceiling, listening to the sounds of the night and Lengsley's breath. She smiled again.

"I'll make the decisions."

And there could be no doubt about her determination to do just that.

29

Nachi Cocom watched the army approaching his city. Everything was clearly recognizable from his position. It was a formidable force, and the King of Yaxchilan would be the last one not to be impressed. He could not make out any details from here, but he was well informed by the reports of refugees and the descriptions of the scouts about many things, especially about the new armor, which made the warrior slaves into a uniform group, about the new training, who no longer attached importance to the function of the individual fighter but required everyone only act as part of the whole. Nachi had discussed this with his people for a long time and had received a lot of ridicule and rejection. He hadn't started a fight over it. The fact was that the news of this type of fighting would make the rounds. Even if Inugami came to an end here, it didn't mean that some of his ideas could not survive his work. In any case, Nachi did not believe that a victory over the messenger meant that everyone would then return to the good old days.

And that was true, above all, of the mighty apparatus that shot arrows, thick as arms, and bags full of pointed stones that caused pain and confusion, though mostly not sowing immediate death. Nachi had heard of all of this, and not one aspect of the narrative he had dismissed as lies. The biggest mistake he could make now was to underestimate the messengers. It wasn't a question of whether their way of fighting was good or not. It was about adjusting to it.

He let the army march on. He could have sent his soldiers to battle, but he knew that in an open meeting with no cover and no retreat, the new techniques of the enemy would have brought them misery. Should there be a fight, it would be out of the security of the buildings, with flanking advances, with constant pinpricks, using the city as a weapon. His generals were not pleased with this tactic, nor with the psycho-game being prepared in the city's main square, on which the great temples and his own palace looked down. An army of a special kind was rounded up there, and from the platform of the temple, which the king used to observe the scenery, one heard the crying of distraught children.

The king didn't close his heart to all of this. He didn't enjoy the game. It was not that he considered this a brave and honorable deed. But it was necessary, and his situation was desperate enough that no one had opposed it. Nobody was comfortable with it.

Nobody saw a real alternative that could possibly bring them victory.

And nobody was sure if it was one at all.

The warriors' leaders expressed confidence. Yaxchilan was not like the other cities. Yaxchilan was great. Glorious. Undefeated for a long time. No usurper would be able to subjugate a Mayan city a third time and take history away from it. Yaxchilan would not go down as a province of a new empire.

Nachi heard the words.

He looked at the square in front of him. Hundreds of women and children had been gathered there, all belonging to the men who had once been sent to Mutal. Nobody knew who died then and who would return today as a warrior slave. In some faces, there was even hope that the uncertainty would end and everything would have a positive outcome. Some of the women and children would find out for the first time whether her husband and father was still alive. Some would make do with the hope that they were left behind in one of the other conquered cities. Still others did not want to face their loved ones, as they might be forced to take up arms against them.

But to bring about exactly this situation was the idea of the plan.

Nachi understood all these hopes and fears, he even shared them. This special army was supposed to sow doubt in the ranks of the attackers, let the attack slow down, and undermine the opponent's morale. If this succeeded, the defenders had a real chance to win this battle. Their morale was good. It was about defending the homeland. Everyone would give his best for that.

In any case, the King of Yaxchilan swore, Inugami would have to wrest every reasonably fortified building from them. He would neither throw himself in the dust in front of the messenger of the gods nor run away fearfully, no matter how the battle should develop.

It was not a comforting thought, but it was this determination with which he managed to overcome his own very creaturely fear of what lay ahead.

He turned, went down the stairs, disappeared inside the building. The temple had been chosen as his headquarters; it was the best defended structure in the city. He would command from here and then switch between different buildings so that the warriors who no doubt were chasing him would not have it too easy.

Nachi reached a room where numerous sub-commanders were preparing to play their part in the battle and beckoned his servants to him. They had just been waiting for the signal, brought the weapons, the insignia of his power. Spear and shield, an ax, sharpened as much as you could grind obsidian, and then the feather headdress that he would wear on his head. A clearly visible target for the enemy, but also a symbol of orientation and leadership for his men. If nothing worked, Nachi would seek death with his own, and he had no illusions that this possibility was a very real one. But the silent determination he exuded when he picked up his weapons seemed to be spreading to the other warriors as well. There was no hesitation, no expression of fear, only tense expectation and the willingness to take as many enemies as possible with them to death and never to suffer the fate of having to serve as a warrior slave for the supposed messenger of the gods.

After all, they would have this chance. Inugami didn't make much of social status, one heard. Simple peasants became leaders, even governors. Nachi was no fool and knew that this prospect was attractive. It turned the well-known and God-given hierarchy upside down, it made possible an ascent only through bravery and loyalty, through proven intelligence in acting and thinking. The King of Yaxchilan was aware of the fact that this was a revolutionary concept that shook the foundations of the Mayan society, perhaps even more than the military march, which was only an appearance. Nachi knew that he was waging two wars here, one against the concrete enemy and the weapons he used in the field, and one against the new ideas that questioned tradition and, above all, the ancient connection between the Maya and their gods. It was a heavy burden on his shoulders. Even if he won the victory, he feared, the war would not be won until all evidence of these new ideas had been erased from the memory of the people. No stele in Mutal, no wall painting would sing about the messengers of the gods. No account of their actions would survive.

Nachi Cocom would personally ensure that any testimony would fall into oblivion. The seeds had to be wiped out of people's consciousness. Knowledge had to fade with the death of those who carried it. A generation, and everything would be forgotten. The symbol of the power of the messengers, their boat in Mutal, would be smashed and buried under stone, forever out of sight, forever out of mind.

It was an even bigger challenge than winning this victory today. Perhaps it would be necessary to destroy Mutal, not just to conquer it, but to erase it completely from the face of the earth, so that it no longer served as a provocation to the gods – and to remove any reference to the things that the messengers brought. Even then there was doubt that this would be enough.

Nachi Cocom sighed. What a big task. What a difficult act. He hoped that he would stay alive until it was completed, because who else could do it?

"Lord, the opposing army has taken a temporary position outside the city. The farmers fled here from the outskirts, unless they were already under arms. It seems the messenger is waiting to see if we want to face him."

Nachi Cocom accepted the report with a nod. Inugami was in charge of taking initiative. The King of Yaxchilan, however, would reject the offered battle.

Should he only come, Nachi thought with a smile. Should he just come.

His city was ready.

Its king was ready.

206

30

The bulk of warrior slaves was lined up in front of him in exactly the formation he had trained, in blocks of one hundred men each, disciplined, absolutely still, upright and attentive. Inugami stood on the hurriedly assembled platform and paused a moment to look at the weapon that had been forged by his hand. He enjoyed the moment, and pride he felt. And he knew that everything he said now would be particularly important in order to take the city in front of them, defeat the enemy, and at the same time not jeopardize the loyalty of these men. It was one thing to look at a formation that just stood there listening to its commander. It was completely different to set it on the march and to be able to trust that it was doing what it was told to do.

Especially now.

Nachi Cocom, king of Yaxchilan, was a cunning man, as Inugami had been allowed to learn.

He would have to play on the men in front of him like an instrument, subtle, virtuous, convincing. Inugami knew that he was not a gifted speaker. For a long time, he had been thinking about which language he would consider for his speech. English, which has been a compulsory subject for warrior slaves since their training began, or Maya, an idiom that Inugami reluctantly familiarized himself with, since he considered it inferior and difficult to pronounce, a burdensome duty.

But he had to talk.

So he chose English, with passages in Maya, carefully worked out with the generals and rehearsed in pronunciation, as an affirmation. He hoped that the parts would fit well together and make a whole that would have the desired effect. It was a risk, but life here had taught him that if he wanted to achieve his goals, he shouldn't shy from it.

Another look from one end of the formation to the other. There was attention, anticipation. The right sensations for this moment, and therefore he must not drag the moment out indefinitely.

He took a deep breath and spoke.

"Men! We are facing Yaxchilan, a city that has been home to many of you. I know what that means for you. You feel insecure. You are afraid to raise your hand against brothers, wives and children. You are afraid to break your oath to serve me, and thus to evoke the punishment that must inevitably follow."

Inugami took a well calculated break. The discipline of the slaves was good, but it was now hard to miss the fact that he had their attention. He immediately began to address their main concern and greatest fear, and he immediately caught them. Now it was important to use this correctly.

"Men! I tell you: don't be afraid! The King of Yaxchilan wants to abuse your old loyalty to your city! The scouts report he has gathered women and children, your relatives, and wants to send them to you so that you become fickle, lower your arms, and betray me. The new king is a smart man – and he is a man full of hate and without pity. He uses you for his war, but above all he uses those to whom your heart is attached to."

The silence was almost palpable. Of course, rumors of the defenders' tactics had already spread, but here was the open, honest confirmation, without any threat. Inugami felt that the men in front of him focused on him like a being, a common intelligence, united with their consciousness and their hopes. He suppressed a smile of triumph. He had to be serious, concerned, and determined. Any mistake could prove fatal for the rest of his life at those moments.

"Men! Listen to me! The King of Yaxchilan's plan won't work! Hear my orders: None of you will raise a weapon against a woman or a child, against a relative who is dear to you. You are warriors, not butchers! You are fighters with honor and as my slaves connected to my honor. And I say: No child should bleed, no woman should be hurt by the hands of my warriors."

208

A movement passed through the rigid mass of warriors like a wave through an otherwise still lake. Inugami felt the surprise, the sudden rise in emotions, the joyful confusion, the relief. Everyone remained silent, composed and disciplined, but the captain could read the faces of the warrior slaves. He played the instrument of manipulation, and he did it well. Better than expected. He learned. Inugami was not too proud to admit it, but he actually learned.

"Men! Be like the water and flow past this human wall that has been built to oppose to you. Whoever does not carry a weapon is not a threat. Run past them, slide through the alleys, through the corridors and rooms, do not stand in the way of this person. Where an opposing warrior uses your wife as a shield, hurry past. There are enough other enemies. Once they start killing their own people, they have lost all right to mercy. You will be careful not to make this mistake."

Inugami spoke loud and clear, and everyone understood him. There would be deaths. But there was no slaughter, and their leader did not ask them to kill whom they could not bring themselves to attack.

Inugami freed them.

He gave them absolution.

He gave pardon for avoiding an opponent, he gave them exemption and indulgence. He blessed their feelings and preserved their personal integrity as Yaxchilan men, fathers and husbands. He gave them a gift that would bind them to him even more than any training or brainwashing that has been associated with it.

And he made a promise to them.

"Men! Whoever takes the city for me should keep it. One of you will be the new master of Yaxchilan, and all those bravely fighting should be allowed to stay here, reunited with their families, and they should guard and administer the city for me. This should be your station, your base, from here you will march in the future and return here after every victory, loaded with fame, fortune, power, the respect of the world, and the admiration of your women and children. I give you this promise. Give me the power of your weapons, the swiftness of your legs, mercilessly kill every warrior who gets in my way, bring me the head of the new king so that I can make one of you king. Because this, men and companions, is my will and my will alone!"

There was no stopping now. There was a roar, a cheer, a fierce eruption of enthusiasm, and out of the chaos Inugami heard that his name was raised, again and again, like a rhythmic cry of war, and they all cheered him, warrior slaves, free men of Mutal, officers and nobles, leaders and led. The storm of emotions seemed to move the trees and shake the pedestal on which Inugami stood with both arms spread in a blessing gesture, recipient of all submission, transmitter of all promise. Nobody stopped them, and it was only minutes later that the shouting ended and Inugami knew that he was now their master.

He lowered his arms and bowed to his soldiers.

Cheers rose again. His name again, like an invocation, a prayer. Inugami stood there, a few more moments, then the captain climbed off the platform, his face a mask that showed neither his pride nor his triumph, and he walked to his subordinates with a measured step. They were ready now. There was nothing left to do, nothing left to say.

Yaxchilan would fall, there was no doubt about that. And if the defenders didn't come to them, they would get each one of them, and their messenger from the god would fight with them in the first row and lead them to victory.

"Good speech, sir," said one of his generals to him, and Inugami found the same enthusiasm in his eyes that he had seen among ordinary soldiers. He looked for Achak's gaze, which also nodded to him, an expectant beam in his whole posture, the battle ax in his gnarled hand.

"My orders apply. They all do. Nobody is punished who bypasses civilians and avoids raising their hand against them, and no hostage-taking by enemy soldiers is ended by attacking them. But anyone who turns away and joins Yaxchilan is put to death, instantly."

There was general approval and determination. Carrot and stick, the old principle. But Inugami was confident that the whip would not be used extensively in the upcoming battle. He had his people under control. He had given them the chance to be decent, and that was far more than they expected.

Inugami looked up at the sky. It was midday, and there was a scorching heat over the city. The speech had dried his mouth, and he felt that the words had left him with plenty of his energy. He resisted the urge to rest. He couldn't let the magic of the moment pass by. He felt the need for a drink of saké and pushed it aside.

"Distribute water to everyone," he ordered. "Everyone should drink a lot. Distribute the prepared tortillas, but not more than one per man. You don't fight very well on a full stomach. But they should all be refreshed and not thirsty. As soon as the water has made the round, we advance."

It began. Inugami watched as orders were given. Large calabashes and water hoses, already filled in the Yaxchilan cisterns outside, were passed around. They all drank greedily, knowing that they would soon be unable to quench their thirst. The tortillas were also distributed, baked smaller than usual, just enough to drive out the hunger, but not so powerful as to make them sluggish and limp. Inugami saw that the free warriors of Mutal also participated in the supply ritual and that the joy of being able to attack the old enemy was on every face. It was these men who would also kill retreating or fickle warrior slaves, and he could count on the Mutalese men to act relentlessly and effectively. They weren't their people. This was Inugami's advantage, and so far it has prevented overly strong comradeship. Inugami's intent was to turn the slave troops into an elite unit that was personally committed to him, free men and slaves alike. Separating them from the other soldiers was a clear tactic and would continue to be so in the future.

Those who otherwise had no friends, no allies, who had lost their old loyalties, turned their hopes to the only one who promised them security and prosperity. And that would be the Lord of the messengers of the gods.

Inugami stood in the shade of a tree, drank from a mug in small, methodical sips, rejected the offered tortilla, felt sufficiently refreshed by the liquid. Once the city was conquered, there would be a feast for everyone, and then there was enough opportunity to fill up one's stomach.

He checked his weapon, the pistol, and looked over at the one bodyguard of the unfaithful prince who did the same with his rifle. Two other Japanese, with no firearms, were entrusted with the task of maintaining the onagers and catapults and helping with repairs. Otherwise ... only Maya everywhere, among friends as well as among enemies.

No, he didn't feel threatened or lonely. No more.

These were his people, his tools. He decided that nothing better could have happened to him than traveling through time. It was a liberation and a development of all of his potential. Here he became the person he always wanted to be.

Inugami saw that everyone had drunk and eaten. He put his mug down.

Then he gave the sign.

31

It was a group of over a hundred Maya, some of them armed, who eventually showed up on the beach the following morning and did nothing but to stare devoutly, fearfully, and with fascination at the ships anchored on the coast. Köhler was able to make out the facial expressions of the men through the binoculars, especially the warriors, who clutched spears and axes, knowing that their weapons would not do anything against these sea monsters.

It spoke either for the culinary skills of Diderius or for the diplomatic skills of the Navarch that the night was calm and the morning remained peaceful despite the visible tension of everyone involved. The old man seemed to reassure the newcomers with a description that he performed with gestures, that much was clearly visible through the eyepiece. Arms were lowered, though suspicious looks remained over the water. What could the old man tell his friends? That they had eaten well and crouched around the campfire? Köhler did not know what Langenhagen had discussed with the old man, as far as one could assume a conversation, but when the signal came from the beach that he had been waiting for, he immediately let the boat out and ordered ten soldiers to row him over.

When he jumped curiously on land, the first thing that caught his eye was the map that Langenhagen had laid out. It showed where they came from, and it was apparently difficult for many of the Maya to understand what they were shown on paper. However, the old man – and a small group of more mature gentlemen, who were treated with a certain respect – looked at the cartographic image with keen interest, and if Köhler was not mistaking everything, one or the other seemed to understand what was said. In any case, a lively discussion broke out among the newcomers, and as far as Köhler correctly interpreted the gestures involved, it was about the ocean and themselves. The conversation was stimulating, but it lacked aggressiveness, and the Mayan warriors made a visibly relaxed impression over the course of the discussion.

Hands and feet and drawings painted in the sand were the basis of all communication. After another hour, Langenhagen had the old master from Ravenna summoned, who had already recovered well from the crossing and showed great interest in being able to prove his skills. By name of Andochos, he was extremely agile despite his age, although he was clearly not a friend of the water. But when he was safely landed by other legionaries, he approached the group like a young man. He was visibly delighted with the new task as well as the fact that the ground no longer moved under his feet. They got an idea of the geography of the island. It seemed that the city they had been watching was the only major settlement.

After a while they all agreed that the next phase of the contact should be started, and Langenhagen decided to go for it.

"We'll take Yatzak on board and some companions with him as he wishes," he told Köhler. "Then we set sail, circle the island and anchor on the other side of the city. I don't know if we can get it right, but in any case it is time to show people here that we are not a threat and do not want to hide. Andochos thinks that all these people here are just subalterns, and whoever rules over the island should be found in the city. We can't do much more here on the beach, I think."

"That is a risk," Köhler pointed out immediately. "If you have a lot of soldiers there – and a lot of boats –, they can try an attack."

Langenhagen did not contradict this assumption directly.

"We minimize the danger. Only the *Gratianus* comes close enough to the coast. The rest of the flotilla remains anchored outside and can intervene if something goes wrong. We can't avoid a certain risk – but we knew that before, didn't we?"

Köhler nodded. They had to take the next step, in this he agreed with his commanding officer. And he had apparently thought about it well. Köhler could not object to the proposed approach.

"How are we going to invite the old man?"

"Andochos and I will try to explain it to him."

Drawings and gestures were used again. Langenhagen drew the outline of the island on a piece of paper, which was acknowledged with eager approval. Then he painted in the position of the city and the six ships, also easy for the Maya to understand. He pointed to Yatzak and spread his arms to symbolically embrace other Maya, and then pointed to the *Gratianus*. Finally he painted a line from the current anchor point to the city.

The Maya began to discuss animatedly. The message had obviously been understood. Langenhagen and Köhler sat quietly, waiting. Although there were some high-ranking individuals, Yatzak seemed to be regarded as the one who found the strangers first and "talked" to them. When he spoke – usually not at all loudly, but carefully –, they all listened. That did not mean that they all agreed with him, that was quite evident on the faces of the discussants. But Yatzak's calm manner and his ultimately very determined demeanor made the difference. He spoke, he pointed at the man who had stayed with him overnight, then at the rowboats. It was a clear approval and thus a success of their difficult communication.

A decision had been made. Yatzak and his younger companion took a few symbolic steps toward the rowboats and gestured theatrically to the anchoring ships. They agreed. The rest of the group bowed to Langenhagen and the old man and headed for the city without haste to return. They would probably have reached the settlement well before the ships, but this was ultimately in the interest of the Romans. After all, this wasn't a surprise attack. If they carried home a message of peace, their reception would be friendlier; at least that assumption was not without reason.

Langenhagen nodded to Köhler.

"That would be it. We dismantle everything and raise anchor. The first contact went very well. People here seem to be reasonable enough. They are scared, but at least I was able to break the ice last night. A good sip of wine can be extremely relaxing. In any case, we have a basis for communication."

"Do we have that?" Köhler asked, looking at Andochos, who had joined them. "Magister, how is it going? Will we be able to learn the foreign language in the foreseeable future?"

"Or they ours," Andochos replied, shrugging his shoulders. "I've just picked up a few words. I cannot make a forecast based on this. There will be a grammar that I have to understand, and then the first thing we will have to do is develop a vocabulary. On the other hand, I do not shy away from teaching Latin or English to the willing here. I would like to say that our language is very logical and not hard to learn with diligence. There should also be talented people here who can easily tap into this knowledge. It all depends on whether we will have the opportunity and leisure to do so."

The teacher looked at Langenhagen with the last sentence.

"I can't offer a forecast either, Magister," he picked up the thread. "But it is my goal to build friendly relationships with the islanders. I don't mind staying here a little longer so that we can familiarize ourselves with the conditions here. The island location is even ideal for us, because it strengthens our defensive position. If someone disagrees with us, he must come over all by sea. Have you seen the looks of the people with whom you watched our ships? Awe, fear, sheer astonishment, even disbelief. I may be too hasty, but if islanders show this reaction, it indicates that the residents' ships here must be of a simple nature, enough to get people to the mainland in good weather … but obviously far from a threat to us."

"Many hunters are the rabbit's death," Köhler pointed out, picking up on the scenario he had already described. "A hundred small rowing boats full of determined warriors can be our undoing, as can a modern Roman-style frigate. Anyone who is willing to accept certain losses and is inspired by the necessary fanaticism will not be deterred by this awe if needed."

"Of course," Langenhagen admitted. "That is why we will exercise extreme caution and keep ourselves open to retreat. But if we build on what we have achieved so far, I am quite confident. Do you have any doubts, Köhler?"

"Navarch, I'm your deputy. It is my job to have doubts and to review your decisions."

Langenhagen nodded and smiled. "You are good at that. Keep it up. Andochos?"

The scholar raised his head. "Navarch?"

"I will do everything we can to get a teacher – first for you, but hopefully soon for larger groups as well. And I will do everything we can to get students ..."

"Children," the man said. "Ask for young students. Nobody learns a language faster and better."

"A mixed group. It's a question of time ..."

"No, Navarch. I am learning. Teaching is for others. I am not the only teacher on board the fleet. Well, no one specializes in languages like me, but teaching a student in Latin or even English – someone else can do that too. Almost all of the scholars we carry with us and some of the officers. I focus on learning. Teaching is not half as difficult."

"I bow to your judgment, Magister."

Andochos seemed to be confident that he thought it was the right decision.

It was less than half an hour before the rowboats were on their way back to the *Gratianus*. Yatzak and his companion looked excited, pleased, and without fear. Indeed, they couldn't see the future, Köhler pondered while he watched the two men.

But he wanted to admit that it had gone well for a start.

32

It wasn't that he was really a stranger here. The dialect was almost identical to his own. He looked like them and thought like them. But being a ruler meant distance, as Balkun found. You had no friends. You had no confidants. A normal king, a sprout of a long line who came to the throne after his father's death, could have friends – old counselors who had already brought you up and sons of other high-ranking personalities with whom you had grown into adulthood. A man like Balkun was a foreign body, he was not one of them. His children, maybe, one day, if the reign of the messenger of gods would last. But he himself was the one who was put into this place, the one who was upset, a symbol of the defeat of a once proud city that would never return to its former glory. No family, no high lineage, no glorious history.

A slave as ruler, a peasant, a man of the lowest rank. A shame for the city. A pain for anyone who still felt some pride and honor, and at the same time a constant reminder that eliminating this man would only lead to Inugami coming, punishing, and appointing a new governor – one who was probably not half as gracious and as understanding as Balkun was.

The warrior slave smiled. Graceful and understanding. Had it gotten so far that he saw himself like that? Didn't every ruler recognize himself as something special? Strong, brave, chosen by the gods, of the highest morality, of the highest intelligence, always victorious, always glorious? Mercy was not always one of the desirable qualities of a Mayan king, Balkun knew very well, who had spent the greatest part of his life serving one who really only claimed this attribute on a rhetorical level. But these qualities, which he now thought about, were they the first step toward the same reality-forgotten grandeur that well-born kings generally gave themselves in to?

It wasn't an idle question. It was not frantic self-doubt, not a quarrel with the way his new subordinates were devoted to him. There was a very concrete reason, as tangible as it could be, made of hard stone, cut directly from the nearby quarry and carried here by the strength of many men to the former royal workshop. Balkun stood in front of the stone, a cuboid, a good three meters high, one meter wide, an imposing piece, the surface of which had already been smoothed.

Good stone, durable, a monument to eternity.

A monument to him.

Next to the cuboid stood Hetza'k, the master stonemason, and behind him three of his men. The tools of their craft lay on the tables, the chisels and hammers with which they would attack the stone, force their will upon it.

No, corrected Balkun. It was only his will that was at stake here.

There were also the pots and pans with which the stonemasons mixed the colors. The stele would become colorful and splendid and would announce the inauguration of the great Inugami and his chosen governor, praising both and highlighting their deeds. It was the custom, and it was expected of every ruler, yes, everyone was very interested in it. The stele was then placed in the central square so that everyone could read it and put its message in their hearts. With this, they would also inform Balkun's posterity so that no one would ever forget him.

Before this could happen, the governor had to tell the stonemason what depictions the stele had to show. In regard to Inugami, he came up with many descriptions. Messenger of gods. Victorious conqueror. Descended from heaven. Enemies smashed, erased. Showing new ways, forging an empire. This made a wonderful and very impressive presentation. The more general question of Hetza'k, which news should spread their work, was less directed toward Inugami; Balkun had understood that well. It was a subtle point against him, the farmer's son, the appointed, the oppressed.

The slave.

What acts of glory had he accomplished? Which line did he refer to? What was his status, what gave rise to the respect that the stele demanded for good Lord Balkun? Hetza'k pretended that he only wanted to serve the new lord as he did his old king; to praise him the way he liked it. In reality, Balkun had realized that he wanted to show him off. Because what other than wild lies could the slave recite? What else than to commission a picture of himself that had to be an insult to every real king?

The face of Hetza'k could not tell what he was thinking. He was quite the respectful servant. His helpers all the more, submissive in the background, ready to start work immediately. He waited for instructions, and it was up to Balkun to give them and to make himself look ridiculous in front of everyone. This did not require a large audience. There were enough here that the word of his lies would quickly take to every corner of the city. And when the stele stood, when it was read, they all laughed at the hubris of the peasant-slave, who had been raised above his stand and now thought he was something he was not and never would be.

A smart move.

Balkun smiled and indicated a bow.

"Noble master," he said in a soft voice. "I am so honored to be immortalized by your capable hand that I lack the words to express my feelings correctly. You know, I am a man of simple origin, and I am not used to seeing my role and my person standing in the light of the gods. Do you have instructions and content enough for the great Inugami?"

"I think so, great ruler."

Hetza'k himself had made some good, thoughtful suggestions, and Balkun had approved them all with a dignified nod. Only somehow the stonemason hadn't thought much about the great Balkun, the one blessed by the messenger. Here he needed the instructions himself, in all modesty.

Not so quickly, Balkun thought.

"His appearance in the boat of the gods?" he asked. "His victory over the invaders? The blessing of new ideas and weapons? The submission of this city, without resistance, blinded by the greatness and wisdom of the mighty messenger of the gods?"

Balkun refrained from smiling. That little cut had to be, and it had hit. According to Hetza'k's expression, his mood darkened somewhat. The stonemason bowed low so the governor would not notice his annoyance, and Balkun accepted the gesture with silent acceptance.

"Everything as it happened, sir," Hetza'k forced out and straightened up again, his face a motionless mask. "But how should we glorify you now, great ruler?"

There was the tiniest undertone of irony in the man's voice, and if Balkun would have been an irascible and easily offended man, that would have been enough to punish him for it. But, he had cleared that up in the meantime, he was gracious and understanding, and apart from that a simple man who was used to insults from his wife, his masters and life in general.

"I am only a tool of the messengers. I stand by his side as a loyal servant. As the lord of the city, describe me as a builder, as someone who ensures peaceful order. Describe me as someone who has adjusted the rites and customs, all following orders. Let me be what I am, an executor of a stronger will. Give my name, but show modesty in it. Do not add a title other than *Servant of the Messenger of Gods*. Never put me over him. Let my feather helmet be humble. I don't fight, but I sit in court. I don't speak to the gods, but I don't act arbitrarily. I lack anger, I do not punish harshly and unfairly. But in everything I sit at the feet of Inugami, I am alone without power and without a family, an obedient man who pays respect to his master and demands the same from the inhabitants of the city."

Hetza'k stared at Balkun.

That was definitely not the answer he was expecting. It wasn't the silly overconfidence, it wasn't the cheap pathos he'd wanted to make fun of. It was a clear statement, a humble one, an honest one, and it did not speak of self-exaggeration. No honors for the little Balkun, no fame he never earned, no immortality he didn't deserve. He was only what everyone else was expected to be, an obedient subject, willing to carry out the commands of the Lord.

His helpers also looked somewhat disappointed. It would no longer be a joy to spread the words of the slave on the throne in all directions. There was so little in it that gave rise to laughter or contempt.

Balkun shook his head gently. No, there was something for contempt, but it was another kind of condescension that would now trigger his words. The point was not that he exalted himself, but that he turned out to be what everyone thought he was: the peasant, the dumb servant, the slave. A man without guts, not even capable of showing off, who just sat there and was tool in the hands of someone else without his own will.

This contempt, yes, Balkun would have to live with it. But to ridicule himself and lose the last bit of dignity, he wouldn't do that favor to anyone here.

He exchanged a few more words with those present, pretending that he did not notice their disappointment or even bitterness at his answer. All of them showed themselves to be in a hurry and tried to make suggestions to the ruler on how his – terrific – idea could be implemented. Balkun was reasonably certain that they would do as he had said and would not carve any hidden statements into the stele that did not honor him. Balkun might only have been a peasant, but he could read, and the stonemasons should have realized that he hadn't fallen completely on his head.

When he returned to his palace, he felt exhausted. Dealing with the city's small and large intrigues required a lot of strength, more than he had anticipated. The cool stone bench in the courtyard of the palace, which he had chosen as his favorite place, was more inviting than ever. He crouched, got water and some fruit, and was about to ask to be left alone for a few moments when a servant came up to him.

"Lord, this requires your attention."

He said that with a certainty that indeed piqued Balkun's interest. He put down the cup he had just emptied and nodded to the man.

"What is it?"

"A woman and children came to see you when you were at the stonemason's. The woman claims to be Bulu and your wife, straight from Yaxchilan."

Balkun jumped up, stared at the servant in amazement. His heart started pounding, and he grabbed the man's shoulder and pressed it so that his face grimaced painfully.

"Bring her in immediately."

"It could be –"

"Bring her! Immediately!"

The servant turned and hurriedly left the courtyard. It only took a few moments, then he came back and accompanied by ...

Balkun swayed. The storm of emotions was too strong, it could no longer maintain manly control. He didn't care who saw him and talked about it. There were no words to express what was going on anyway.

Bulu. It was her. His kids. There was no doubt about it.

For a few minutes, nothing followed but a silent hug. In terms of its intensity, it not only expressed the long period of separation but also all the fears and longings accumulated in it. It was like a liberating catharsis, concentrated on a few moments in which Balkun did not want to think and did not want to see, but only bathed in the relieved feeling of happiness.

When they broke apart, servants hurried over with seating. Food was brought in, sun protection put up. Someone at court had understood that the position of the ruler now included a wife and that it would be well-received to take appropriate measures. Whoever had arranged this, deserved Balkun's gratitude.

They sat in the shadows, and Bulu, her cheeks still wet from the tears of reunion, reported on her conversation with the new king of Yaxchilan, their trip here, which had been exhausting, and how other friends and relatives were doing. The conversation jumped back and forth, sometimes overwhelmed by her feelings, pausing for a moment, while the children, who were more relaxed and eager to eat, added something. Balkun listened in silence until it was his turn to tell the story of his very strange life since the attack on Mutal, and Bulu, though she must have heard some things, was wide-eyed at the changeable fate her husband was going through.

Finally, exhausted from the trip and the emotional storms, Balkun had the apartments prepared so that his family would find peace.

Here, too, the court officials had anticipated his orders, and everything was ready. For a tiny moment, Balkun felt almost joy in becoming the master of this city. After all, that was why the King of Yaxchilan had sent his family to him.

Of course, he had no illusions. It had nothing to do with philanthropy or pity. Nachi had undoubtedly been very calculating. This was a step to remind him, Balkun, of his old loyalties, his origins. The fact that there was neither a demand nor a request, that Nachi had almost made an advance payment without being assured of anything, fit into the picture. Balkun felt that he was grateful to the unknown king and that his critical attitude toward Inugami was confirmed. He may have conquered his old home by now, maybe Nachi was already a dead man. Balkun did not expect the defenders to be able to defend themselves against the disciplined force of the attackers for a long time.

But whatever seed the distant king had intended to sow in his heart, Balkun was certain that a fruit would sprout from it and thus the plan Nachi pursued was successful, regardless of whether he was still alive or not.

33

When they came to the first stone building, which consisted of more than one floor, an arrow hit the man next to him. The warrior gave an angry grunt and involuntarily grabbed the shaft that stuck out of his right shoulder and broke it off. He was smart enough not to want to pull the arrowhead out himself. Inugami saw that the man was now holding his battle ax in his left hand.

He smiled.

He liked that attitude.

"The House! Forward!" he cried, feeling an energy surge through him. The excitement of the battle, which triggered a unique concentration, could not be compared to any other feeling. It was as if the arrow hit had broken the dam. He felt that he was ready now and his warriors with him.

Two fighters in front of him, men of his bodyguard, kicked the barred door and pushed it back. Shadows became visible, a spear jerked forward, but the attackers skillfully evaded. Then they yelled something and stormed into the dark hole of the entrance, and Inugami followed them.

Hectic movements. There was a scream. A gargle, expression of pain. The call of triumph, fitting to it. Little was to be seen, much was in the shadow. The metallic smell of blood mixed with the dust on the floor, then a shadowy shape as it approached him, a damp ax gleaming in his hand. Inugami's right rose, he pulled the trigger. The pistol twitched. The shot echoed slightly, the attacker was hit, stopped dead, and then collapsed. Inugami took a step forward, sensed the presence of other warriors, saw a man guard his body guard trying to push past him.

Inugami went faster, climbed over the dead whose life he had just wiped out. The passage was narrow.

A room opened that led to a small courtyard. An atlatl was shot at him, safely from the roof, the javelin brushed his armor – as far as one could describe the plate woven of plants and fabric as such – and struck somewhere behind him. Inugami looked up, ducked involuntarily. He felt the draft of an ax above his head, then went on the attack himself. Inugami shot out of his crouched position. The enemy was still looking for cover, but it was too late. The blood-red dot on his chest announced the end, and he died quickly. Then the roof, a man who swung the atlatl again. Inugami used the time, targeted. No waste. Every shot counted. The pistol twitched, the *bang* echoed in the yard, piercing, then the scream, and a body went down, out of sight now.

His comrades, Yaxchilan's defenders, stared at him. They had never seen such a weapon, such a death. They exchanged glances, eyes widened, and their hesitation, their surprise, immediately fatalized them when Inugami's men invaded, took advantage of the moment, and immediately overran their weak resistance. It was crushed all around him, and for a moment the captain looked in vain for an enemy, calmed his violent breath, his pounding heart.

"Search all the rooms!" Inugami ordered. "Remember my orders. We don't kill anyone who doesn't have a gun. Women and children are to be spared!"

Confirmatory shouts signaled that his words had been heard. Many steps, people running, sounds from the house, screams. A cacophony of death, the music of blood. Inugami smiled. Achak would indulge in this tune, and probably did, somewhere else. But Inugami didn't enjoy it. He was just happy.

He looked around. The resistance here was broken. Battle noise continued to ring from the rest of the house, there was bitter struggle for every room. Inugami paid tribute to the king's tactics. Provoking a lengthy and bloody house fight was not a bad idea. Nachi suspected that Inugami wanted to conquer the city largely intact, had no time and little resources to rebuild a sea of rubble. No fires were started, at least not by the attackers, and nothing was willfully destroyed.

But the Lord of Yaxchilan may have been less scrupulous in his defensive situation.

Inugami hurried out onto the street. There was also fighting in the surrounding buildings. Screams and deaths everywhere, the sound of weapons, victory and defeat transcending every minute. He had no overview. He had to trust that the fight was going in his favor.

His bodyguard gathered around him as he proceeded up the main street to Palace Square, where the city's last and most important line of defense was, most of the soldiers and the new king of Yaxchilan himself.

Inugami wanted to go there. But carefully. He kept looking around, watching closely. It would be fatal to move away from the main body of his troop, to advance too quickly. That could seal its premature end, and thus the end of the battle. Inugami had no illusions. If he fell, his troops would disintegrate and run away like rabbits. There was no leader like him who could jump in the breach. That was the truth, and it was not bitter, because it was exactly what the captain wanted.

Everything with him. Nothing without him.

He kept marching. Every now and then one of his men came closer to him when a danger became apparent, for example a warrior screaming wildly on the street, blinded by the intoxication of killing and then struck by a targeted blow. Another atlatl archer appeared on a roof, the greatest danger to anyone using the road, and aimed at Inugami, but missed the captain and then had to fight back the attackers who had fought their way up through the building.

A blessing of luck was upon him. Inugami thought it was providence. He was destined to win and live here.

So he remained undeterred. Every now and then one of the sub-commanders ran up to him, reported on the progress in the streets next to them, dispelled the ignorance, painted a rough picture of the progress of the battle. The struggle was arduous. They cleaned every building of enemy warriors, and that turned out to be exactly as difficult and bloody as could have been predicted. There were setbacks. There were obstacles and defeats.

But there was fighting.

None of his warriors eased his efforts.

Inugami saw civilians driven out of their homes, frightened, some injured, but all able to run away from the attackers' weapons. He saw that no one was chasing them further, they were just being pushed out of the way, no blade was aimed at them. The greatest damage they did was to stand in the way, and the greatest damages they suffered were bruises and light wounds. It happened the way the captain had imagined it, but the greatest test was yet to come.

He reached the place. Stopped. Examined the army in front of him, and for a tiny moment a doubt crept over him.

Several hundred women and children stood there like a chain, close to each other, staring at the advancing warriors with a mixture of defiance and fatalism, which Inugami involuntarily admired. He knew that given a good time of teaching and development, the Maya would one day be able to develop a real culture that deserved the name of civilization. They certainly had this potential, although they had a long way to go, and the longer he stayed among them, the more he was moved to this concession. The determination with which the women stared at the warriors was a pointer to the emotional supplies that Inugami had tried so hard to tap into. At that moment, he felt confirmed in what he was doing – and in his decision not to let the slaughter happen.

He raised a hand. The warriors paused.

For a moment, the sweaty, heavily breathing men stood there, stained with the blood of their opponents, and the women and children opposite just stared at each other, looked for relatives. Everyone knew what was happening here, and many feared the worst. Eyes locked into each other. There were soft complaints. Children wailed. Warriors lowered their arms, their shoulders hung. Observation. Relief. Fear.

Some shouted something. Hands were stretched out. Someone was called by name, then another. Inugami still raised his hand, warning the slave warriors to discipline. He saw Yaxchilan's men line up behind the women, saw the atlatl archers on the steps of the temples hesitating to shoot, because they risked hitting their own people.

Nobody raised a weapon. Nobody stormed into the crowd of people waiting. The Mutalese warriors, too, remained calm and obeyed the command. It was a strange, tragic moment that decided so many things. And with every passing second, it became clear that there would be no attack.

And that the Lord of Yaxchilan had underestimated him.

Inugami hid his smile. He waited a moment longer for a runner to stand by his side and whisper something in his ear. The Mutalese men began to fill the streets around the square, still wrestling for every building and intersection, and were a lot more ruthless than the slaves, for this city was truly their enemy and every dead enemy a righteous victim to their Gods.

And they pushed on while everything was standing still here. Yet.

"Now!" Inugami called, dropping her arm.

His army started to move.

Screams of horror and fear rang out, women pressed their heads to the children, stared in horrified eyes at the warrior slaves, their husbands and brothers, and sons, as they took a few steps forward with their arms raised, apparently blind to the pleading requests, the tear-wet cheeks and the arms stretched forward.

Then another command, loud, barked in many voices by subordinates, rehearsed exactly like a dance.

The army flowed aside.

The men turned right and left and ran to the side, along the line of relieved and stunned civilians toward the surrounding buildings, fast, efficient, and so surprising that the opposing troops began to react too slowly.

The long line of women and children remained motionless. The storm slid by them and fought to disappear from the square, leaving them alone, unscathed, completely untouched and helpless.

Inugami also ran.

Now it was time to force the decision.

They stormed the temples and the palaces. The fighting spirit of his warriors had not diminished. They had spared theirs, saved their valuable lives, had not stained their hands with the blood of those who were dear to them, and did not die by the hand of those who wanted to force them to murder their own families. They were slaves, but they felt free, and the power of that freedom flooded them as they raised their weapons against the Yaxchilan men, and they did the act Inugami had asked them to do.

The fight started again. The captain himself marched toward the building, which was clearly identified as the king's palace. It was his job, part of his charisma, to personally kill this enemy, to face him in battle. He knew how important this kind of standing was, and he hurried up the stairs, ducked behind the shield of one of his bodyguards, then ran on. He raised the pistol, took aim, a shot was fired at one of the defenders who was about to sink his ax into one of the warrior slaves, and saved his life. Nimbus. Legend. Messenger of Gods Inugami, who saves the life of the lowest in battle with the miracle weapon, another story that would spread and that would lift him out of the crowd, more than pure violence and power could ever achieve.

Inugami had now understood that. He had to follow this path. Aritomo Hara was almost right when he called for measure and consideration. It was almost understood that there were different types of loyalty, and Inugami had to replace what he lacked in connection with the Mayan gods with a different charisma and legitimacy.

Hara had been correct without saying that.

When Inugami fired another shot that struck a powerfully dressed warrior like lightning right, he apologized to his first officer.

Then he had climbed more steps. Left and right of him men died, and it was horrible. But Inugami marched through the chaos as if nothing could happen to him. He ignored the desperate looks of his bodyguards, who struggled to keep up with him and provide adequate protection. The messenger of gods attracted attention. Courageous warriors who figured a chance jumped in his way and got the gun's attention. Inugami shot slowly and methodically, his arm safe. Every shot, every bullet, more precious than all obsidian and gold, hit its target. He took no chances. He still owned a few magazines, and he wanted no cartridges to be wasted. The invisible death, which was announced only by a sharp bang, was like a large arrow that hovered in the air. He drew resolute enemies to himself, as did loyal slaves, and so the battle culminated, with Inugami as the focus, and with every *bang* the men of the messenger realized that their prophet was walking among them and judging the enemy as they were.

The Yaxchilan defenders showed great bravery. Inugami paid them respect. It was the courage of despair, and this gave birth to acts of exceptional nature, a selfless intoxication of blood that, despite all the wounds, kept pushing some warriors until they found salvation in death. Inugami paid great attention to it, concentrated on details, only allowed himself to be carried as far as necessary so as not to lose touch with the front. He noted how the fighting was going on and the weaknesses of the enemy and friend. This battle was a school, and it produced lessons that Inugami intended to implement in the future training of his army. There would be more enemies, and they would be at least as determined as these men here. Only a small part of them would throw themselves in the dust in front of the messenger, and for the Captain, these were the most unworthy of them. Maybe useful, but without any dignity.

He reached the center of the palace. Every room was fought for. Screams of pain, expressions of anger and despair, everything echoed through the hallways. The stone floor had become slippery with blood and innards, some warriors lost their grip and stumbled into their opponent's weapon. Inugami did not have to move wildly or swing an ax, although he carried one with him. He stopped, sighted, pulled the trigger, all in cold calm, unmoving, the recoil easily intercepted with his arm, the next target already identified in the corner of his eye. It became tight as the corpses grew, the smell of the blood obtrusive, almost unbearable. When Inugami entered the throne room, seven opponents were standing around a man in a royal headdress, drenched in sweat, wounded, but upright, with arms raised, ready to sell their king and themselves as dearly as possible.

Inugami raised a hand.

The fighters paused. The warrior slaves and men obeying Mutal took a step back. While the noise of killing could still be heard in the rooms around them, silence fell on this room, and the group of defenders divided and let the king step forward. He was not an old man, perhaps the age of Inugami himself, slim and muscular, and he exuded a dignified defiance that did not suggest surrender. He stood in front of the Japanese, eyed his weapon, the sweaty uniform, both so strange, and then nodded slowly.

"You are Inugami, who is called the messenger of the gods."

"You are Nachi Cocom, formerly King of Yaxchilan," the captain replied bumpily and was only comparatively eloquent, because he had anticipated this meeting, longed for it, and could recite the sentence by heart. Inugami waved, and one of the bodyguards came to his side, a young man with a watchful expression on his face, who fought alongside the messenger mainly because he had proven to be particularly understanding and receptive in the English lessons. He would translate for him.

Nachi Cocom did not show whether he was angry because Inugami had already set him off rhetorically. It spoke for his adversary that he didn't bother with formalities, but rather got straight to the point. "It looks like you've won, messenger of gods."

"I have that impression too."

"What are you going to do with my city?"

"I make it mine, just like those before me and just like many afterwards."

The king looked closely at the Japanese. "I heard about your plans. You have great visions. Are you sure everything will fall in your lap if you just keep going?"

"No. Yaxchilan didn't fall in my lap. I count many dead among my warriors."

"That could have been avoided."

"You would have surrendered, king?"

"No. But you shouldn't have attacked."

Inugami smiled. "Yaxchilan attacked Mutal."

"What is it to you? You are not a Mutalese."

"But Mutal belongs to me now."

Nachi Cocom nodded slowly, as if this realization finally reached him, and he gradually accepted it.

Inugami thought that was theatrical. The King of Yaxchilan knew exactly what was going on, and that rhetorical games would sow no doubt about the legitimacy of the messenger of the gods. Nevertheless, Inugami enjoyed the exchange. That was something different from the murmur of the other deposed rulers and the acidic remarks made by Chitam.

"What is going to happen to my city?" the king asked with mild interest, as if none of this mattered to him anymore.

"I'll secure it, spend some time here, and then a governor will be appointed, an administrator who rules on my behalf and enforces my laws."

"What is your next goal?"

"Time will tell. Do you care?"

Nachi Cocom frowned as if irritated by the question. "What role do I play in your plans, messenger of gods – and the men here who are with me?"

"Your warriors, if they surrender, gain freedom. Whoever is caught with a weapon, I make him my slave. Whoever puts down the weapon and submits without further struggle should go."

The king looked surprised. Hadn't he expected such mildness?

He looked at his bodyguards and said something, briefly, quickly, so that the captain didn't really understand. But the explanation came from the actions of the men, who pretended to refuse their king's command, then gave way to his iron gaze. They put their weapons on the ground, fell on their knees, leaned their upper bodies forward, and pressed their foreheads to the floor in front of Inugami.

The captain looked down at them and left them in this position for a few moments to strengthen the impression and to show them that this was more than a formality.

"Rise," he said then. "Go."

The guardsmen exchanged glances with Nachi Cocom, who in turn made it clear to them to follow the instructions. Without further hindrance, the warriors left the room, accompanied by some of Inugami's men.

One could never be sure enough.

The palace had calmed down.

The fighting subsided. It could not be said whether this was also true for the rest of the city. The sounds from outside were swallowed up by the thick walls of the building.

The king continued to stand in front of Inugami and, unlike his men, he had neither put down his arms nor changed his dignified attitude. "What happens to me, messenger of gods?"

"I've had bad experiences letting people like you live," Inugami said. "It seems that this special form of grace is always badly paid back to me. So I think your death will be necessary."

"You say that in a tone that sounds like regret."

In fact, Inugami noticed that he must have spoken that way. He hesitated for a moment to see if he had any feelings, and found that the thought of killing Nachi displeased him.

Did he soften?

No, that was unlikely.

"I respect people who show bravery and determination," he said honestly, as the man deserved it. He spoke to a corpse and knowing that made it easier for him.

"Then I have to thank you for that."

"No, that's not necessary."

"Messenger of gods, I have a family. Wife and children. Will they share my fate?"

"No. As you may have noticed, former king, I have not ordered any of my men to kill the weak."

"That was smart. But does that also apply to my relatives? My son might think he should have the throne and plan to overthrow you."

Inugami laughed. "Many are making plans. He would only be one more. Should he become a danger, he will share his father's fate. And I don't mean to usurp this throne. If he is reasonable, he can have a peaceful life, grow old, and die unmolested, as your gods think it is right. Let's see what kind of upbringing he enjoyed."

Nachi Cocom didn't look like he was very sure about it. Neverthe-less, it was clear from his stance that he was relieved and believed the words of Inugami. This was all the more remarkable given that the captain absolutely intended to keep his promise. It only made

234

sense in exceptional situations to roam through conquered cities and show cruelty. And it didn't help to promise things and then not keep them. He was the word. The word was the truth. He couldn't contradict himself.

Inugami felt that the conversation was at an end. He raised his gun. Nachi Cocom fixed the strange thing in the hand of the messenger with a mixture of interest, fatalism, and a little fear on the face. He pressed his lips. No further communications to the world. That was fine; the audience was small anyway and now had other, more pressing things to do.

Inugami pulled the trigger, it *popped*, and the king's head was thrown back, the body slid to the ground, hit, and lay motionless. The bloody wound in the middle of his forehead stared upward, as did lifeless eyes of the shot man. Inugami made sure that the man was really dead – sometimes even people with skull wounds survived – and then turned to one of his warriors. "Take him out, tie his body to a stake. Everyone should see him. Don't disgrace the corpse, ensure it is not disgraced. Let him hang out for a day and give him to the family for a funeral."

The man nodded and waved to a comrade.

Inugami listened. No battle noise from the palace. A runner hurried into the throne room, paused briefly when he saw the dead king, then threw himself before Inugami. "Lord, the city is ours. There is still a little fighting, but many of the enemies have either fled or surrendered."

"Good, then it has be done."

Inugami watched Nachi Cocom being dragged out. He felt relieved and tired. His muscles trembled no matter how hard he tried to control himself. The sweat on his skin suddenly felt cold.

It would take some time before the next campaign. Now his way led him back to Mutal to see if everything was right. And Chitam ... the problem needed a final solution.

He stared at Nachi Cocom's feet dragging across the stone floor.

Inugami thought that Chitam would do just fine.

34

Ik'Naah stood where the mainland boats usually landed and said nothing. The large ship, lying on the calm water just a few hundred meters away, with the escort ships further away from the coast, caught her attention. No Mayan king had ever built such a vehicle. Every description of her people was surpassed by reality. First, she didn't believe any of this. As if the presence of the envoy from Zama wasn't enough, now something like that. Ik'Naah concluded that the goddess either hated her or wanted to ennoble her through a special trial.

The largest ships in the coastal cities, simple sailors, large rowboats, were nothing comparable to this could, as they could get a dozen people on board. Ik'Naah had also heard the stories about the arrival of the messengers of the gods in the distant Mutal and had given them no serious importance. They were rumors, nothing more, and she gave nothing to such murmurs. But this, this changed her perspective. Had the messengers come to her now? What message did they bring? What was expected of her?

How could she use her arrival for herself and the temple?

In any case, the envoy from Zama hadn't spoken to her since the news had been spread by the strangers. Instead, he had hurriedly sent a boat to his master with the message. The man stood next to her now, staring at the ship no less astonished, and she could literally feel how he calculated the power of the newcomers. Even if the young king of Zama had ambitions, as long as these floating monsters lay in front of the city, he would think twice about a possible attack.

Was that good?

Or would she exchange one yoke for another?

The thoughts whirled in Ik'Naah's head.

The rumors from Mutal were ambiguous, depending on who was on whose side. Ik'Naah felt that she had a thread of fate in her hand, the end of which remained hidden. Should she pull hard on it or let it go? And would it make a difference?

She saw a rowboat launch. She couldn't make out any details, the eyes were too weak for that. But the whispering of her companions informed her that Yatzak and his companion were safe and returned to her unscathed.

She felt a great burden falling from her heart. That she would have missed the old man so much, a strange idea. The folly of youth in the body of an old woman. She would have to think about these things if she ever had the chance.

Now she saw him return to her.

Ik'Naah had sent the warriors away. The other priests had insisted on them, but she had prevailed. She might have been wrong, but the large metal pipes that were beginning to protrude from the hull of the ships neatly lined up, didn't look as if they were elaborate decorations or just drained water that leaked into the interior of the ship. Any form of provocation was the wrong way, she felt that very clearly, and allowing warriors in sight would not send the right signal.

The rowboat landed, and the men climbed out. No, she had to correct herself: men and a woman, as she noted to her delight. In addition to the two Maya, there were five tall figures in uniformly cut clothing that covered the whole body. She had never seen anything like it before. She was able to classify some of the weapons these men carried. Other things – like the long, dark sticks tied behind their back – seemed strange to her. The men moved cautiously and slowly, as if they did not want to provoke carelessness either. Ik'Naah relaxed, as she watched Yatzak seem to be on good terms with the arrivals. The old fool, who volunteered for all of this and took a great risk, pointed to the high priestess and said something. She heard her name. Apparently communication was already beginning.

When the first of the men stood before her, he towered over her by more than a head. He smiled. It wasn't an forced smile, and Ik'Naah replied, maybe a little fearfully. Then she turned to Yatzak, who stood next to her and looked as relaxed as if he was just inviting her to one of her usual chats.

"This, noble lady, is a gentleman named Langenhagen. If I understand it correctly, he is the master of the big ship there. In fact, he may be the master of all ships, but I'm not sure. In any case, his orders are followed, and quite eagerly. He is a man of great power, Ik'Naah. But he appears to be of good will."

"Where does he comes from? What does he want here? How do you know if he has good intentions or not?"

Yatzak shook his head, a little too forgiving for the old woman's taste.

"I can't say exactly where he comes from. He showed me a map on parchment that I didn't understand. I think he thinks he has traveled across the ocean from a very, very distant country in the east."

"These ships are no doubt capable of long journeys," the priestess murmured. "And his intentions?"

"Well, he hasn't had anyone killed and has treated me well. What else he's up to, I don't know. We don't speak a common language."

Ik'Naah nodded. That was, without a doubt, the biggest problem they faced. Even so, the possibility of misunderstandings was big enough. But without the words ...

"I gave him your name. Everyone sees that you are leading here, Ik'Naah. These people are not stupid."

Her eyes fell again on the big ship. "I assume so," she said softly. Then she looked at the man named Langenhagen and watched him bow low in front of her, a sign of respect that he accompanied with sounds that, among other things, she was certain, contained his name. "I greet you at the Temple of Ixchel. My name is Ik'Naah; I'm the highest priest and mistress of the city."

She said it slowly, and the man's face brightened at the sound of her name. After all, the introduction was successful.

Ik'Naah made an inviting gesture. About a hundred meters away, still well in view of the large ship, she had a feast prepared. She was convinced that an invitation to eat would be a positive gesture for any people, and she had consciously taken this risk. She saw the joy on the faces of the visitors and was relieved that her guess was correct.

"You're smart, dear mother," Yatzak said confidentially, as they all slowly walked toward the low table with the heaped dishes. "I was also invited to dinner that was prepared in front of my eyes. Foreign dishes, but not without attraction. It seems we have something in common here."

They offered places to the guests and crouched on the floor. The strangers politely waited for Ik'Naah to reach for a meal, and first watched the other guests as they ate and what manners they showed. They showed great respect and tried to adapt as much as possible. But before everyone had given up their caution and the meal could begin properly, the man Langenhagen rose and bowed again to Ik'Naah, who had just settled down and felt little joy in having to get up again now. That was obviously not necessary, as the man had already kneeled next to her and handed her something with a smile.

A gift!

It was a leather case, as used by the Maya for the storage and transportation of documents. It could be opened at one end, and Langenhagen nodded to do just that. A rolled-up paper lay in the tube, which she now took out and spread out. It was a very beautiful, artistic and colored representation, which Ik'Naah only identified as a map after a few minutes. The man showed her an area of land and then tapped a certain place with his finger. It was another moment before she realized that he was referring to the island.

Then he pointed to another place, far away, on a land mass that was much larger. Ik'Naah took note of this enormity, apparently unmoved. She smiled gently and rolled the card back up to put it back in the container. She was unable to classify this information. Did the man point out his country of origin? And if not – what did that mean? How long did the journey take from that place? And what was the reason for such an elaborate voyage?

The high priestess suspected that answers to these questions would be a long time coming. One of the men, an older gentleman, almost as old as Yatzak, seemed to be listening to the conversations with

239

special attention. He also made notes on a wad of paper in a small, strangely simple font that was far from the symbolic wealth of the Mayan equivalent. Ik'Naah did not have to have prophetic gifts to understand that this was a scholar who tried to understand them better.

She beckoned to a man about the same age. "Daa'k, come to me."

The priest moved to her side. "Mistress?"

"You see that man, old and frail like you?"

"The priestess is very kind to me again today."

"He writes and writes. Take him aside. Show him the script, read the letters, slowly, like a child. Give him some of our words – simple texts that you use for learning, clear texts, written with large characters. Hurry up to your chamber and get everything. I have received a gift, and I want to return one."

"But I'm old and frail. Rushing is nothing ..."

Ik'Naah playfully slapped the man on the shoulder and laughed before he rose laboriously and, within his means, headed fast for the nearby buildings of the city.

The visitors had paid attention to the exchange and smiled when they caught the friendly atmosphere, the humor in the faces, and the way they dealt with each other. Everyone now seemed a little less cramped and they grabbed food, tried the dishes, and made appreciative sounds, either out of courtesy or out of genuine joy at the pleasure.

Ik'Naah also ate, because there was nothing else to do. She watched the woman who observed the area with open eyes and the old man who continued to write more than he ate.

"Mistress?"

"What is it?"

A servant had approached and crouched behind Ik'Naah.

"One of the pilgrims asks to be allowed to sit at the table."

The priestess frowned. "I'm really not happy about it. What does she want?"

"She just arrived yesterday, Mistress, from Mutal, and she says she wants to see if it is the same messengers of God who have visited her city."

Ik'Naah controlled himself. O the stupidity of old age! Naturally! Why hadn't she thought of it at once?

"She should come and sit down immediately. Make room for her!"

The strangers looked at the scene with rather casual interest, as there was constant coming and going at the table. When the young woman came up and sat next to Ik'Naah and across from Langenhagen, she said nothing. The priestess felt some regret for her. The pilgrim was almost a girl, maybe 16 years old, and the fact that she had been sent here to fight her supposed infertility through prayers and rituals said more about her husband than about herself. Her clothes, however, showed that she was a young lady from a high house, and there was no fault with her posture either. She just sat there, eating more to satisfy appearances than out of real appetite, and listened.

Then she looked at Ik'Naah and shook her head gently.

"They are very different men than those who visited Mutal from Heaven. Built bigger. Only one of them looks like them, a great builder named Lengsley."

Suddenly there was silence, and Ik'Naah looked around in surprise. Something had happened. The old man with the notes stared at the pilgrim and frowned, whispering something to Langenhagen. Then he asked the intimidated girl who had suddenly attracted the attention of all strangers. He spoke in his strange language, but the word "Lengsley" was also recognizable for Ik'Naah.

"Speak to them, child. It seems they know your messenger from the gods," she then encouraged the pilgrim, when she clearly hesitated to say anything else.

"What can I say?"

"Repeat the name you mentioned."

"I could do more. My brother received lessons in messenger language. It's called English. My mother allowed me to attend the class if I remained silent. I picked up some of it. I could say a sentence."

Ik'Naah saw the strangers waiting politely and smiling. Her whispering did not arouse any resentment. Well.

"Do that. It's worth the risk."

The girl nodded and turned to the old man.

"Lengsley came down from heaven," she said in awkward English. Ik'Naah didn't understand a word.

The man with the notes made a sound of surprise and began to talk to Langenhagen. Eyes widened. While all the strangers began to talk excitedly, only two of the visitors looked at the girl inquiringly, but by no means unkindly, namely that Langenhagen and one who had been introduced as Köhler and who was obviously also a man of some authority.

These exchanged meaningful looks.

The group's scholar turned to the pilgrim, asked something in the language the girl had startled her with. The latter shook her head.

"I don't know more," she said in English. "Unfortunately, I can't say more."

The man nodded soothingly and pleased, and the pilgrim looked relieved. Then there was a lively conversation among the visitors before turning back to the food, and Langenhagen bowed again to Ik'Naah and said something that sounded like an apology.

"No reason to regret it," said the priestess gently. "I wanted this. It also taught me a lot."

She turned and beckoned to one of her servants. It was important to use what she had learned, and to keep her own knowledge to herself might prove fatal.

"A messenger to Mutal, my dearest, as soon as possible. He should ask for someone there who can come here and speak the language of the messengers. I am writing a short letter. The man is to leave today. Prepare my seal and a gift for the King of Mutal. Who rules there? The good Siyaj?"

"Siyaj is dead," the pilgrim murmured. "Chitam, his son, is King of Mutal."

Ik'Naah nodded gratefully. "You have to tell me a lot more about everything that happened in your city. I want to give you the grace of a private ritual with the goddess for it."

The girl smiled a little shyly but seemed to be pleased and honored. "Thank you, great mother. I want to tell you everything I know."

The servant was already hurrying away.

When Ik'Naah returned to her guests, she saw that the man

named Köhler had got up and went to the bank. He signaled to the ship, and she watched a second, smaller rowboat launch. He apparently intended to return to the sea monster alone. Ik'Naah felt that this had to do with the conversation that had just ended. Was there someone on board the ship to report to?

It would take a while before she could correctly interpret the strange ways of the visitors, she was sure of that.

The table disintegrated into smaller groups than most had eaten their fill or at least did pretend so. The old man with the papers looked up when Daa'k came up to him with his writings and signaled that he wanted to show them to him. They sat to one side and stuck their heads together, excitedly engrossed in the characters, and soon the priestess could tell from the mouth movements of the visitor that he was already busy trying the sounds of those strange words. Langenhagen also observed this with visible satisfaction and nodded in the direction of Ik'Naah when their eyes met.

Yatzak came up to her and took her arm.

"Come on to the big ship and see for yourself the miracles. They'll definitely invite you."

"I'm not sure I should go on such an adventure at my age," she said doubtfully.

"It's calm weather. You won't fall into the water. And what does age mean? I was on board and really enjoyed it."

"You are a man and therefore easily a victim of recklessness. You are also easy to impress. And I'm older than you."

Yatzak smiled.

"Your high opinion of me is both a compliment and an inspiration, great mother."

Ik'Naah smiled back at him and pointed to the visitors who had gathered a little apart and whispered quietly together.

"What are we going to do with them now?"

"Learn from them. Above all, we have to be able to speak to each other. That is the basis of everything."

"Daa'k is already working on it. We want to give them time."

"Then I would suggest that we let things that can be seen speak for themselves. Show them the city. Guide them through the temples.

If anything will impress them, it's the way we pay homage to the gods. Our structures are our soul, Ik'Naah. Let us show them our achievements as they showed me theirs."

"A good idea."

She walked toward Langenhagen and gestured toward the city with a sweeping gesture, smiling invitingly. The man frowned briefly but then nodded, spoke to his companions, and they all immediately joined him.

Ik'Naah sighed. The day had been hard enough, almost exciting. Now there was still a hike ahead of her. She pulled herself together. The city was right in front of them, and there would be enough opportunities to take a break so that the facilities could properly affect their visitors. And who knew, maybe the goddess would give her an inspiration this time if she passed the temple. It could be that the presence of the strangers confronted her in their own way with the fact that things changed.

Ik'Naah looked at the men who were now beginning the march to the city next to her.

And there would be changes, she was absolutely certain of that.

35

Radio specialist Marcus Levius looked at the large mechanical clock on the wall. The central radio station of the Roman fleet was in possession of one of these rare examples, which had only been built by a manufacturer in Helvetia for a few years and which were in great demand everywhere. The admiralty had believed that radio operators should write down as precisely as possible when a message came in, especially with all those long-distance expeditions underway. Levius felt the presence of this gigantic wooden box as a threat, but despite the great knowledge of the artisans who created it, the watch did not seem to be working properly. No matter how many times he looked at it, the hands on the dial seemed to be stuck, and the end of each shift always seemed to be hours away.

Poor craftsmanship was certainly to blame for this. He couldn't imagine any other explanation.

The radio center was constantly manned by four radio operators on four receivers. Usually there wasn't much to do. The few ships in Rome that were already equipped with transmitters did not respond more than once a week unless there was anything special. There were also a few fixed stations, but these were connected by telegraph lines for domestic traffic, which enabled better transmission quality, were also open to private communication and mostly worked without problems. Despite all recourse to the technical knowledge of the time-wanderers, radio technology was still in its infancy and very fragile. Marcus Levius was more concerned with servicing and repairing the devices than receiving messages. After all, then he had something to do and wasn't just sitting around.

But now everything seemed to be working properly, and this was all the more regrettable because the hands of the big clock simply did not want to move again, although the clockwork ticked loudly and audibly.

Someone should fix the watch, he thought.

Marcus looked over at his comrades, who seemed just as bored as himself. Each of them took care of the news from certain broadcasting areas, although they all received the same signal. In the middle of the room sat Trierarch Titus Devinicus, a massive man. Marcus had never really understood why such a high-ranking officer was assigned to run the radio station. Devinicus and his night shift colleague did nothing more than sit more or less relaxed, eat food, and nod off the incoming messages before a runner brought them to the addressee. No officer would have been needed for that.

And for the only other case – that had never happened, although Marcus had been here for a good three years.

"Marcus, your people are coming in!"

His comrade's voice brought him out of his thoughts. He leaned forward and heard the call sign sent a third time. The expedition to America announced a message, and that unscheduled. Marcus's hand gripped the pen and dipped the tip in ink to cover the prepared paper with a Morse code transfer. He listened to the signals coming, short, long, in the order in which they formed letters, and his quill flew across the paper. He had learned the Morse code intensively until it chased him in his dreams or he found himself translating any uttered word into periods and dashes. It was like a second mother tongue, and he translated it with the instinctive certainty of a real expert.

This was exciting news, he noticed immediately. The expedition had met locals and a first contact had been made. That would not tear the ever-lazy Devinicus out of its lethargy, but Fleet Headquarters would take this news with great interest. It didn't take long – just one repetition –, and Marcus was reasonably certain that the message was complete. He looked at his handwriting – neat, as printed, as always – and rose to hand over the slip of paper to Devinicus, who took note of it with his eyes half open and did nothing more than wave to one of the runners present.

Marcus shrugged and returned to his seat.

246

Just in time to notice the second message.

He automatically converted the signals into letters. This automatism failed for a moment when he put down the call sign for the first time. He hadn't expected that. Nobody expected that in his position. It had never happened either. But when the same sign was transmitted for the second and third time, there was no doubt.

"Tr ... Trierarch!"

Devinicus looked up, eyes questioning, a sudden tension in the body that one would have sought in vain before.

"What is it?"

"The symbol ... the code ..."

It was amazing how quickly the officer took the steps to Levius. There was suddenly a disciplined silence in the radio center. Marcus felt the man's hand on his shoulder and understood the gesture, got up, and turned away.

"This is a secret for now," Devinicus said as he sat down. "Everyone leaves the room. Levius, you tell the navarch to come here immediately."

"It's late ..." the man protested, but the officer's stern gaze instantly silenced him. He hurriedly left the room with his comrades, behind him the familiar sound of an incoming message, which Devinicus personally accepted this time.

Levius hadn't known the trierarch could do that.

Some time passed before he managed to notify the navarch. As it turned out, he had been invited to a garden party at one of the city's senior officials, and when he passed the hastily standing guards in slightly deranged toga, Levius smelled that the officer had already consumed alcohol. Still, the older man was on his feet, and his eyes were far from cloudy, even more alert. Levius wanted to report, but the officer simply stormed past him to the trierarch, who had been waiting for him all the time in the radio center. The discussion that followed wasn't long before both men appeared and the navarch held a transcription of the strange message in his hand.

He stopped, looked around the waiting radio operators, and nodded to them.

"Men, there are interesting developments on our expedition to the west. I can't tell you anything yet, but something happened that the Admiralty expected – but much earlier than expected. You can imagine what it is about. We have already telegraphed to the court. In future, all reports from the *Gratianus* must be forwarded directly to Ravenna. The secrecy will be removed shortly so that you can all operate undisturbed. Until then, I need you to be patient. You all do a good job and have carried out your duties faithfully. Go back to your stations now."

The men moved.

"Levius!" The trierarch held the man by the arm.

"Sir?"

"Be careful. If there are new messages, immediate notification. An encrypted message may still arrive, but I don't think many come in this form. The Emperor will authorize us to record everything in plain text once he has decided what to do with the information."

Levius saluted and turned away. He sat down at his device, trying to fight the excitement. Of course, each of them, who now gave each other significant looks, knew what it was all about. Sure, the expeditions served many scientific purposes. Cartography, botany, geology, oceanography – all the new areas of knowledge that the time-wanderers had given them. New trade routes were also welcome, as were exotic goods and the search for the plant that the old-fashioned wanderers called with a certain longing "tobacco."

But the central trigger of these expensive and dangerous efforts was the search for more time-wanderers.

Everyone knew that there had been more than just the men from the *Saarbrücken.*

And the Emperor wanted to know it immediately, out of well-considered self-interest.

The radio message could only mean one thing: The men in the West had come across concrete information. And whether that would mean something good or bad, nobody could judge at that time.

Levius nodded. Exciting. It was very, very exciting.

And although he had to wait in front of the radio for some more hours, he felt the certainty that the boredom would not return so quickly.

He suddenly suppressed a yawn and looked at the clock.

Behold! Someone had fixed it.

36

"We're walking the coast from here," Ichik said, looking encouragingly at Isamu. "You are tired. The path is now easier for us. Once we're with my uncle, the worries are over."

"You say that all the time," the young Prince murmured, looking at his jagged hands. The long way through the jungle, always a little off the road, had left its mark on him. He felt muscles that until recently he had no knowledge of. Tree branches had whipped him, he had stumbled, scraped along trees, twisted his ankles – it was a miracle that he hadn't seriously injured himself. Each of these ailments was unimportant in itself, but all of them accumulated to a constant state of exhaustion and pain. Sleeping on the hard floor, in forks, or on rocks wasn't the biggest problem. Isamu was used to a frugal place to sleep and made no high demands on comfort. But sleep wasn't always easy. The noises of the night were varied and sometimes threatening, no matter how kindly Ichik spoke to him and tried to explain what was going on in his ears.

Isamu slept badly and everything hurt.

He had come a long way in a foreign country.

Still, he didn't regret his decision.

He looked out over the water of the Atlantic Ocean, which stretched calmly to the horizon. A flawless day, of perfect beauty, with the sound of the waves as a comforting background. Isamu had always loved the sea, and he was glad Ichik had led him this way. There was no ship to be seen, not even a small fishing boat, and no settlement far and wide. They still had a good way to go.

It was good that he had left.

He felt more free than ever in his life. Yes, he had lost weight in the weeks since he had fled, was almost skinny, and could count the ribs on his chest. But along with the upholstery, the prison had also given way, in the invisible bars behind which he had lived all his life. There was no Inugami here who wanted to make something of him that he was not, at least in this country and in this time. Ichik had been loyal to him, a true friend, and not because he was a prince, a king, a god, or whatever, but just himself. It was an experience that was new to Isamu, refreshing and making him crave for more of the same. If he could have a real friend, then maybe two. And if he deserved real friends, maybe one day a girl, who was not shown to him by courtiers, carefully selected, without will, a puppet in the game of power, without any choice and influence, and without any real sympathy for him.

Isamu found this prospect extremely promising.

Ichik crouched on the beach. The sun was at its zenith, it was oppressively hot, and it was good to move little at this time of the day and take it easy.

Ichik had also had reasons to leave Mutal. Isamu had only gotten this out of his friend over time, partly because they understood their languages too little, partly because Ichik was initially reluctant to reveal too much of his story. It had a lot to do with a father who gave the impeccable man of the highest nobility to the outside world, but whose fierce anger terrorized the family with brutality that even horrified a hard-nosed Japanese prince in this regard. It was not just Ichik who had been driven away by it, many years ago his father's younger brother had left Mutal for the same reasons and had to start a new life. Ichik knew about it fairly well, as letters from distant relatives occasionally arrived that were carefully hidden from his father's anger. They were on the way there, a clear goal and with it the hope of a different kind of life for both of them.

Isamu crouched next to his friend, and together they looked out over the sea, enjoyed the gentle, refreshing breeze and pondered their thoughts. They were not thirsty since they had only recently been able to fill the water hoses, but hunger was their constant companion, although Ichik had taught Isamu which fruits could be eaten. Unfortunately, the Mayan boy was a farmer and not a very good hunter, and the prince also had no special skills. Larger meals,

251

really filling your belly – they had had to do without this for a long time. They did not starve, but they were rarely satisfied.

And Isamu learned. He learned more than under the guidance of old Sawada, whom he regretted to leave a little more than he wanted to admit. He spoke Mayan and communicated with Ichik incessantly, and his friend proved to be a patient teacher. He learned about the country and nature, and he soaked up this knowledge. It was completely different from the useless ballast that he had had to buff all the years before. This knowledge served the world in which he lived and helped him to survive in it. He recognized the practical benefits and applied them immediately. It was a completely new experience for him to put knowledge into practice in his own way. He enjoyed it and was willing to put up with some hardship in exchange.

"When we're with your uncle ... what's going to happen to me?" he asked, and not for the first time. He was embarrassed by his own insecurity. The times were over when others had repeatedly told him what would happen to him. His first free decision had triggered a chain of events, and in that chain he was less of a game ball than a player, a development he may have been unconsciously longing for, but which sometimes overwhelmed him. Freedom without perspective, without any promise of security, turned out to be tricky, as he found more and more.

So he asked Ichik again, and as if the friend understood what was going on, he answered the question as if he was hearing it for the first time.

"My uncle will take us in, if only to annoy my father. He is just a farmer, but his farm is large, because he married well. He has two houses, and we will get a room in one. We'll have to work. You won't stand out if you hold back."

Isamu's great fear was that of discovery. Of course, the news of the messengers of the gods and their strange appearance, especially the peculiar cut of their eyes, had spread slowly. Isamu looked very much like a typical Mayan boy in many things, the tan of the skin he had adapted, the black hair was not unusual, and he was of a similar stature. But his eyes betrayed his origins more than anything else, and it would not be possible to hide where he came from in the long run. Ichik's uncle lived on the outskirts of the city, far from the hustle and bustle of the settlement, and so this fatal moment could possibly be delayed. But in the end it was inevitable, and what could happen then the prince could not anticipate.

He thought it likely that he would have to run again.

And then probably without Ichik, who would have found a new home with his relative.

Isamu frowned, moving a stone through the sand with his big toe. That was not a good prospect. It was the prospect of a restless existence without a real home. He felt almost ready to think longingly of his rigid life at court and in the cadet school, which he had hated, but now he maybe began to lack familiarity and security.

What did he want? Isamu scolded himself. First refuse the prison and seek freedom, now despair of freedom and longing for the prison? What kind of man did he want to be if he couldn't stand by his decisions and their consequences?

He took a deep breath, swallowed the emotions that came up, and tried not to think about what might happen at some point, but only about what was now and was right in front of him. That was challenging enough.

"Are we going?" Ichik asked.

Isamu nodded and got up, stretched his body, looked along the beach, sometimes rocky, sometimes sandy. "How far is it?"

"I do not know exactly. We'll be on the road for a while. If there is a fishing village nearby, maybe we can gather something to eat."

Ichik slapped his bag, which he had put on his shoulder. A central reason why he could no longer return was because he had stolen a handful of well-crafted obsidian tips for arrows and spears from his father when he was leaving. Isamu knew that this came very close to what he knew as cash. For quality of this kind, they would be given one or more meals and possibly even shelter.

Above all, the former was a good prospect.

They set out, each one with his own thoughts, and as sure as their steps were, they both felt insecure, and it wasn't just the grumbling in their stomachs.

37

"A great victory," Aritomo murmured when he heard the news the exhausted messenger had brought him directly. Only happy faces around him, triumphant smiles on lips, laughter, people patting each other on the shoulder. He nodded to the messenger, who bowed, and handed Lengsley the message that Inugami had written in Japanese. "A great victory."

The Brit glanced at the text. He spoke Japanese fairly well, but he couldn't read it very well. "No announcement of his return soon?"

"He'll have to stay a few weeks to sort it all out," Aritomo guessed, waving to his men, whose relaxed mood he didn't share but didn't want to spoil. What was a great adventure for them with the prospect of fame and power posed a problem for the first officer in the complex political network here in Mutal. But that was nothing new.

"When do we expect him?"

"We still have some time. He will announce when he leaves so we can prepare to receive him. He will also stop in Tayasal and Saclemacal to see if everything is right. The new empire is still a bit shaky. He won't let that take him off guard. He seems to be exercising great care."

"As long as he's victorious, no one will seriously stand in his way."

Aritomo shook his head. "As we know, a successful attack is enough. Armies are helpful but not sufficient."

Lengsley nodded and looked back at the paper as if it had the answers to their most important questions. In fact, it only increased the need to find an answer, which didn't make finding a solution any easier. "I think Chitam will now make his own preparations," Lengsley muttered, and one could see what that meant.

"He won't do anything rash. I have discussed it with him."

"How well do you know Chitam?"

Aritomo shrugged. "I cannot tell you."

"Then don't rely too much on the truth of his words and the reliability of his announcements."

"I would like to contradict you, but I admit that I find it difficult."

Lengsley sighed. "After all, a good part of the city wall will be ready when Inugami arrives. People work hard. We have already done more than two kilometers, and the work is going well. I guess the Captain will be happy with our progress."

"Everything else was prepared according to his taste. The returning men of Mutal were trained to fight and operate in a new way. New combat equipment was manufactured. If Inugami brings back enough people, we will have a pretty powerful army of warrior slaves and freemen, and it will get stronger every day. I want to see the Mayan troop successfully standing in the way of these legions."

Lengsley started to reply but was interrupted, because someone joined them. Daiki Sawada, Prince Isamu's old teacher, modestly drew attention to himself with frugal gestures. Aritomo nodded to him. Since the prince had disappeared, the teacher had plunged into language studies as if there was nothing else in the world for him. Among the Japanese, he was undoubtedly the one who knew the local language best, and he passed this knowledge on to the other crew members in tireless lessons. Although Aritomo did not attend every lesson, he benefited immensely from this zeal. In contrast to Lengsley, who had found a private tutor who paid him all her attention, he was even dependent on it.

"Master Sawada," the officer greeted the teacher. "What leads you to me? You must have heard of Inugami's imminent return."

"As a matter of fact, that is also the reason for my words. Lieutenant Hara, you know that Inugami will look for guilty parties who will be responsible for the Prince's disappearance. I'm afraid his punishing look will fall on me first."

The old man stood stiff, a prime example of discipline and self-control, but it was evident from his eyes that he preferred not to be the center of Inugami's attention, especially when it promised to be less benevolent.

"I'll talk to him," Aritomo promised. "It's not your fault alone. We all were not careful and should have recognized the signs earlier. As his deputy, I take full responsibility."

Sawada smiled and indicated a bow. It was clear from his expression that he hadn't come to him because of that assurance.

"Second lieutenant, you didn't quite understand me – although I thank you for your willingness to stand in front of me. I am quite ready to face the captain's wrath and justify my actions before him. It's more about solving the real problem. Isamu is gone. Our responsibility remains. My responsibility. We have to find him again."

Aritomo nodded.

"I am listening."

"I concentrated my inquiries about the Prince's whereabouts on his friend Ichik after we got stuck with other trails. That has proven to be smart. Ichik apparently had his own reasons to leave Mutal, and I'm not so sure anymore who is actually the driving force behind this adventure."

Aritomo raised his eyebrows and nodded to Sawada.

"Go on, that sounds interesting."

"Yes. In any case, Ichik obviously suffered from a ... bossy father, to put it politely. It took some time before someone was willing to let me in on the less appetizing details of the life of such an important family. But the man has his enemies, not just among his relatives. In any case, Ichik had already threatened several times before to leave the family's home and look for his luck outside the city. What is most interesting, however, is that he has a specific goal to choose from: his uncle was driven out under similar circumstances or fled from his brother, the eldest of the family and thus their head. I don't know the exact reasons, but it seems that no one is surprised that this clan is slowly breaking apart. Be that as it may, the uncle has settled in another city, and it is only natural that Ichik and Isamu steered their steps there – or rather, are still on the way, because the route is long and certainly not entirely without dangers."

Aritomo exchanged a meaningful look with Lengsley.

"What is your suggestion, Mr. Sawada? You have one."

The old man smiled. "An obvious one. We send an expedition to the uncle and either meet them on the way or can get hold of them at their destination. It should be worth the effort. I myself want to take part in this trip. It's time for me to learn about this country and get out of Mutal. There are now good teachers here who can take over my lessons. Itzunami speaks passable English and will continue to teach the Mayan language. I can gain valuable insights on the journey beyond catching Isamu."

Aritomo frowned. He was reluctant to send Sawada on such an expedition. On the other hand, he was not a member of the military but belonged to the imperial household. And it would be a sign informing Inugami that nothing was left unturned to pick up the renegade prince again.

"Of course you won't be traveling alone," he said.

"Itzunami wants to give me his own son and two of his servants as guards."

"It's good, but it's not good enough. I will also give you one of our men. I can't do without any of our few firearms ..."

"Ah, right. Lieutenant, you may have missed this."

The old man put a hand in his jacket pocket, and it came out with a Nambu A, an automatic pistol, as Aritomo and Inugami carried it. It was the first version of the handgun that all Japanese officers traditionally had to purchase from their own money. Lengsley grinned.

"I see our arsenal is larger than expected," murmured the Brit.

Sawada gave him a nod. "I am the Prince's personal teacher. It's my job to protect him if his bodyguards fail."

"I see," said Aritomo. "Do you have magazines?"

"One untouched in the gun, three in reserve."

Aritomo looked to the side, gestured for the teacher to put the Nambu back in. "I never saw that weapon."

"I understand, Lieutenant."

"Nevertheless one of our men will accompany you."

"Naturally."

Aritomo sighed. "When are you leaving? What is your goal exactly?"

Sawada carefully put the gun in the coat. Only now did Aritomo notice that a special bag had apparently been incorporated into it for this purpose. One should never underestimate an employee of the imperial household. "I want to start traveling in the coming days. There are only a few preparations left to be made."

"You call on me before you leave."

"For sure. And the question of where to go is easy to answer. It's going to a coastal town that seems to be of some importance. The name is Zama."

Aritomo nodded. Famous or not, he heard this name for the first time. "Good luck to your trip, Mr. Sawada."

And he said that very honestly for many reasons.

38

His feet burned, and he felt that he was no longer the youngest. Nevertheless, it was not appropriate to sit down without being asked to do so by the highest authority. Inocoyotl stood, his back pushed through and only slightly imperceptible against the cool stone wall behind him. An hour after his return to the city of the gods, he had been called to the palace. Meztli, the king of Teotihuacán, the lord of his life, well-being and future, really had his eyes and ears everywhere.

The ambassador didn't feel like a long conference with his eager king. The return trip had been unpleasant, extremely exhausting, with far too much rain and soft paths, with bad news about the Yaxchilan case – bad but not surprising – and an increasingly exhausted escort that he had been unable to push ahead at some point. Queca's departure from his service had been almost a relief, though the soldier was professional enough not to show it too much. He would certainly submit his own report at the appropriate time, hopefully confirming what the envoy was about to deliver. When he finally got there. If only he could finally sit down.

Just a little.

Inocoyotl had thrown on clean clothes and put on fresh sandals, had cleaned his hair and prepared himself so far that his appearance at court was not considered to be completely disrespectful. Nevertheless, the hardships of the trip could be seen, and even if not, his legs and feet cried out for rest, a massage, a hot bath – and just a good night's sleep in the familiar and comfortable surroundings of his own house.

That would have to wait.

"The Divine Lord is now receiving you!"

Inocoyotl pushed off the wall and nodded. The steward personally led him to the throne room, which was a good sign. Had he been picked up by a lowly servant, this would have been a subtle indication that Inocoyotl's reputation in the eyes of the Meztli was no longer entirely in a position conducive to further survival.

Inocoyotl immediately threw himself on the floor as he entered the chamber and saw out of the corner of his eye that apart from the Great Lord's closest bodyguards, there was no one present, no adviser, no minister, not even a personal servant. Was that good? He decided it was good.

"Rise and join me!"

The ambassador did as he was told and was able to find that a stool stood next to the throne, pointed to by the ringed hand of Meztli. Next to it was a table loaded with fruit, tortillas, and a jug of water. A great honor. He was still in grace, that much was clear.

"You just got home, so get some strength."

"The Divine Ruler is too kind."

"Maybe." Meztli smiled. "On the other hand, it doesn't help me if you suddenly fall over in my illustrious presence because you are too tired."

Inocoyotl bowed his head submissively. Meztli had always had a practical streak. He pretended to eat and drink and didn't have to wait long for the king to turn to him again.

"I received your letters, my friend. You told me about unpleasant things that worry me."

"My expedition didn't quite bring the success you expected," said Inocoyotl. "I have to ask for your mercy."

"You don't have to. If it hadn't been for you, important knowledge would have reached my ear late. Maybe too late. You did well. You are in my favor. Do not worry."

Inocoyotl couldn't hide a certain relief. He was almost so daring to bite a fruit seriously, but he still controlled himself.

"Now speak and tell me everything."

The ambassador hurried to immediately comply with the request. He spoke long, evenly, with precise words. He left no detail out but did not unnecessarily decorate his account with inventions that would emphasize his own role. He made his assessment again and again, but not too pointedly, and always neatly separated from the presentation of the facts. Meztli, that had to be held up to him, was silent all the time, made no comments whatsoever, and left it to his servant to depict the flow of events as he saw fit. Inocoyotl took his time, and when he finished, he felt his mouth was dry. He dared to take from the water without being asked to do so and only realized when he put the mug down again that Meztli was not watching him but seemed to be lost in thought.

"You saw the boat of the gods yourself, my friend? With your own eyes?" the ruler asked suddenly.

"Yes, my lord. With my own eyes. I've never seen anything like it before."

"Yes. I can understand. Let's try something, my friend."

Meztli snapped his fingers, and out of nowhere a servant appeared who brought him paper and writing tools. He disappeared as quickly as it had come. Meztli rose from his throne – a sight very unusual for Inocoyotl – and pulled out a second stool with which he sat down at the table. He pushed some of the dishes aside – Inocoyotl hurriedly helped him so that the high gentleman didn't have to do this low deed alone – and put the paper on it.

Meztli said nothing. He started drawing with amazingly sure movements. Inocoyotl controlled himself. The fact that someone was a supreme divine ruler did not mean that he had no everyday skills or preferences. Meztli was a good draftsman, maybe an artist. That's how it should be.

When the picture was finished, the King showed him the result.

"Did the god boat look like this?"

Inocoyotl was amazed at how precise and clear the drawing was. Either the great Meztli had listened carefully to his words and the ambassador had described the metal vehicle with great devotion – or ...

... he had seen something like this before.

Inocoyotl felt himself start breathing a little harder. His hand groped for the water pitcher to refill. No, these thoughts certainly misled him.

"So ... that's how it looked, my lord."

Meztli focused at him with narrowed eyes.

"Exactly or something like that?"

"It had ... that weapon ..."

"Ah yes, the weapon."

Meztli looked as if he knew exactly what his servant meant, and instead of painting the wonder weapon small on the god boat, he threw a second sketch on the paper, which showed it on a larger scale.

"Something like that?"

Inocoyotl just nodded and drank hastily. Pretty much the same.

It was very worrying.

"Describe to me the uniforms of the messengers of the gods. Their special clothes. You said they were very different from ours or those of the Maya."

The ambassador began his descriptions again and again tried to be extremely clear. It was fascinating what details came to mind when your life depended on it.

Meztli tried his drawing skills again. An image of a man appeared on paper, and every second he resembled the prototype of a messenger of gods more. Inocoyotl was even amazed to see that the narrow, strangely shaped eyes of the strangers had been captured inimitably by Meztli. When the ruler showed him the finished picture, the envoy found nothing to complain about except that it existed at all and that his ruler had been able to draw it with such accuracy.

Disturbing.

"They don't call themselves messengers of God, do they?"

"Some do, they like the name."

"But?"

"The correct term is 'Japanese,' I heard. I heard a few bits of their language. Very strange."

"Two languages, didn't you say?"

"Yes, my lord. One that they keep to themselves, another that they teach the Maya. They call it English."

"English."

Meztli rolled the word back and forth in his mouth as if it had a special meaning.

"You heard words from that English too?"

"No, sir."

"That is unfortunate."

The tone in which the King said this made Inocoyotl a little nervous. But Meztli did not give the impression that he wanted to punish him for this negligence. He returned to his throne with calm movements, again ignoring how his faithful servant drank the water. Today the air in the palace was really, really dry.

"So you negotiated an alliance, my friend?" the ruler asked.

"An alliance under your leadership – or none," Inocoyotl added. "Lord, if I was too cheeky and …"

Meztli raised a hand. "You were far away, and you had to act. I don't blame you. Do you hear?"

"Yes, gracious ruler."

"There will be this alliance, Inocoyotl. But there will be more than just eliminating a threat. My father told me that this would happen one day and that I had to be vigilant. I haven't believed it for a long time. Much of what my father told and taught me at that time sounded absurd. Over the years, I have even forgotten some things that I now need to refresh. I also have to apologize to him. I should have listened to him better."

Inocoyotl said nothing. He was hardly in a position to comment on the family relationship between the old king and his son. Whatever he said, it would be the wrong thing.

Meztli did not expect any reaction to this either. He asked his next question.

"And these wonderful weapons – have you seen them in action?"

"Not myself. But the descriptions of the people of Mutal sounded very convincing."

"The messengers of the gods themselves – were they surprised by their appearance in Mutal or did it appear planned?"

"Surprised should best describe it, my lord. The fact that their boat did not land in water but on a tomb … I spoke to their leader's deputy, and he frankly admitted that he did not know how and why he came here."

Meztli nodded thoughtfully. "That fits. Well. My father was right."

Inocoyotl blinked in confusion.

"What will we do now, my lord?"

"A good and well-justified question. I tell you: I confirm your alliance. I will mobilize the warriors of our empire and march into the Mayan territory. And I will lead this army personally. Whether you see it that way or not, my friend, a new era has begun. The great Teotihuacán will now give up his restraint and patience. We will do more than just protect our brothers, the Maya, from the messengers of the gods. We will submit their country to our gracious and just rule, to protect it from future dangers of this kind. These messengers of God are one threat. But there is more to come. There has to be more. The world is large ... much larger than you can imagine. A development has started that will change everything and all of us. But now the good news, Inocoyotl: I am prepared for it. Teotihuacán knew what was going to happen. My father told me, and he knew exactly what he was talking about."

Inocoyotl stared at Meztli and tried to find logic in his overlord's words. He was relieved that he was recognized for his actions. He was confused and afraid about the plans the lord of the city began to develop – or, if he understood correctly, that he had been preparing for a long time at his father's behest and would now put into practice.

Meztli rose from his throne again. "Follow me, I'll show you something. It is probably time, and it will no longer be possible to hide it anyway."

Inocoyotl obeyed. He trotted after the king, who strode out through the door behind his throne, down the aisle that was hiding there. Here lay the expansive rooms of the king, which normally no one was allowed to enter except the king himself, his family, and his closest servants. Inocoyotl occasionally saw a face peering out of one of the rooms and quickly disappearing. He found that the king led him downstairs, deeper and deeper into the foundations of the palace. No one was to be seen or heard here. He had no idea that the structure reached so deep below the surface of the earth. Soon they needed torches to find their way around, and the stairs looked unused, with dust in the air, whirled up by the surprising visitors.

They reached a chamber. Sunlight fell through a long shaft, a clearly delineated cone of light. The air was a little better too. The chamber was full of boxes, all made of material unknown to Inocoyotl. It wasn't wood, that much was certain. The surface was so smooth and seamless that he had never encountered a handicraft like this before. He touched it. Cool. A strange feeling. His fingers slid over it, and he didn't know what to do with the sensation.

Meztli stood in front of one of the boxes and opened it. He did so with a certain solemnity that Inocoyotl only considered appropriate. He looked past Meztli into the container. Inside was a black filling, as if cut from a single piece, and of an unknown nature. And there was an object that lay gray and dark in the sunlight and remotely reminded Meztli's servant of the miracle weapons of the Mutalese messengers.

It was really worrying now. Inocoyotl took a step back.

Meztli lifted the thing out with an almost devout motion.

"What do you think of it, my friend?"

Inocoyotl looked at the slender form, the function and origin of which was completely foreign to him and of which he only almost instinctively recognized that no hand in Teotihuacán or in Maya country could have built it. It was the weapon of a god ... whatever it was for.

"Lord, I don't know what to say."

Meztli nodded.

"Is that so?"

"Lord, if you allow me to be so cheeky, but it bears a very distant resemblance to one of the smaller miracle weapons of the messengers of the gods."

His ruler gave him an appreciative smile.

"I chose you for your job because of your keen observation skills, and you prove to me that my choice was right. What I have in my hands, dear friend, is an HK XM 29. This is the ballistic computer with the grenade launcher. The lower part is the kinetic weapon, a conventional gas pressure loader. A beautiful weapon, of a certain elegance and very effective and unerring. Do you want to touch it? Don't worry, the ammunition is in another box."

Inocoyotl raised both hands.

265

"Lord, I didn't understand a word."

"I believe you. It took my father a lot to teach me, and it took me a long time to understand everything correctly. I have a dozen weapons here with ammunition. I will choose eleven men to hold these miracles in my hands, and I will be the twelfth. Together we will defeat the messengers of God, subjugate the Maya, and then take a look at the world as my father predicted."

Meztli paused, looked at Inocoyotl, who was both confused and fascinated, and smiled at him. The ruler looked almost relaxed and did not seem to notice that he had plunged his wise and educated, experienced, and very clever servant into complete confusion.

Even though one could definitely see that.

"Be happy, my friend. You will witness the rise of a special epoch."

And with these words, the Divine Ruler put the weapon back in the crate's lining before gently closing it.

Inocoyotl was absolutely certain that Meztli was right. A special epoch, without a doubt. He did not understand anything and yet suspected so much – and no part of his hunch filled him with special joy.

But happy, he could already say that, he was certainly not.

List of characters

Achak: General of Chitam

Aedilius: Roman doctor

Agun: Agent of Mutal

Yo'nal Ahk: King of Zama

Aktul: Warrior from Mutal

Andochos: Roman scholar

Angelicus: Centurion

Aritomo Hara: First Officer of Submarine No. 8

K'uk' Bahlam: King of B'aakal

Une Balam: Chitam's sister, daughter of Siyaj, princess of Mutal

Balkun: Warrior from Yaxchilan and governor

Bulu: Wife of Balkun

K'an Chitam: Prince and King of Mutal

Nachi Cocom: King of Yaxchilan

Daa'k: Priest on Cozumel

Titus Devinicus: Head of a radio station

Domenicus: Geologist

Hetza'k: Mason

Ichik: Boy from Mutal

Ik'Naah: High Priestess on Cozumel

Inocoyotl: Envoy from Teotihuacán

Tako Inugami: Captain of Submarine No. 8

Isamu: Prince of Japan

Itzunami: Priest in Mutal

Ixchel: Daughter of Tzutz and Chitam, sister of Nicte

K'abel: Queen of B'aakal

Helmut Köhler: Trierarch of the Roman fleet

Langenhagen: Navarch of the Roman fleet

Robert Lengsley: British engineer

Marcus Levius: Radio specialist

Meztli: King of Teotihuacán

Nicte: Daughter of Tzutz and Chitam, sister of Ixchel

Phoebus: Cartographer

Queca: Soldier and officer from Teotihuacán

Yuto Sarukazaki: Mechanic of Submarine No. 8

Daiki Sawada: Tutor of Prince Isamu

Augusta Clara Terzia: Scholar

Yatzak: Warehouse manager on Cozumel

Made in the USA
Middletown, DE
07 November 2021

51820868R10149